Also by Mary Casanova
Published by the University of Minnesota
Press

Curse of a Winter Moon

Frozen

Moose Tracks

Riot

Stealing Thunder

When Eagles Fall

Wolf Shadows

ICE-OUT

MARY CASANOVA

UNIVERSITY OF MINNESOTA PRESS

MINNEAPOLIS

Published by the University of Minnesota Press
111 Third Avenue South, Suite 290
Minneapolis, MN 55401-2520
http://www.upress.umn.edu

ISBN 978-0-8166-9417-4 (hc)
ISBN 978-1-5179-0211-7 (pb)
A Cataloging-in-Publication record is available for this book from the Library of Congress.

Design and production by Mighty Media, Inc.
Interior and text design by Chris Long

Printed in the United States of America on acid-free paper

The University of Minnesota is an equal-opportunity educator and employer.

22 21 20 19 18 17 16   10 9 8 7 6 5 4 3 2 1

Dedicated to the memory of my father

This story is a work of fiction,
inspired by true events in northern Minnesota.

CONTENTS

PART I
Deep Winter   1

PART II
Slow Thaw   69

PART III
Dreams of Summer   163

Author's Note   249

For Further Reading   255

DEEP
WINTER

Folks try to predict ice-out—the day ice goes off the big lake—but it's always a guess. Sure, Rainy Lake may look solid—clear to the Canadian shore. That's when a guy makes mistakes. Some dumb cluck drives his Model T to his island cabin and goes through, losing the whole thing, front grill to back fender.

The change happens slowly, and the ice becomes unpredictable. Unknowable as your girlfriend. One day, you think you know exactly what she's thinking. You think you can tread safely, from one shore to the other. But you'd be wrong.

Nothing is what it seems.

There's a whole honeycomb quality about the ice. It changes from within. On the surface it goes from white to silver to slate gray to black.

Black ice.

That's your warning sign.

1

FEBRUARY 3, 1922

OUTSIDE THE WHITE TURTLE CLUB, OWEN JENSEN reached inside his mackinaw jacket. The check was still there, tucked safe inside his shirt pocket. He couldn't believe it. The loan had come with a few strings, but the check was his.

It could change everything.

Owen pulled on his leather mitts and filled his lungs with frigid air. Reluctant to go home, he walked around Ranier in temps well below zero. His breath formed small ice clouds. At the edges of his eyes, moisture froze his lashes together. Snow squeaked under his boots as he passed the bank, shops, and squat houses.

Lights flickered in the second story of the candy store, now closed. Outside taverns, horses with thick winter coats were tethered, heads low, waiting to be hitched up or ridden home. Model T cars and trucks waited, too. It wouldn't be too long before automobiles replaced horse-drawn wagons, sleighs, and carts. Owen had seen an opportunity, the chance to make something of himself, and he'd seized it.

Selling cars couldn't be much harder than selling rats, could it? Nine years back—a kid of only ten—he'd used his brains to bring in extra money. When his pet white rat, Salty, gave birth to a big litter, Mom said, "Find homes for them, or else." With the help of his best friend, Jerry, Owen toted Salty from bar stool to bar stool around town. Salty, with her pink eyes and pink tail, became a Hollywood starlet. "Ladies and gentlemen," Jerry began in a big voice—at least for a kid—and with a grand flourish of his cap. "Here, you will see the likes as you have never seen!" Then Salty emerged from Owen's sleeve. "Stand!" Salty stood on her back legs, her tiny front legs reaching upward and revealing puffy teats. Owen rewarded her with a peanut. "Kiss!" Salty raced up his arm and touched his cheek with her warm nose and whiskers. Customers applauded. When the grand finale came—"Hide!"—Salty scurried into Owen's sleeve, tunneled up, and peered out from his collar. Customers offered to buy her. Instead, the boys built interest, and when Salty's babies got bigger, the boys took them around town, sold them to the highest bidders, and made a kid-sized killing. Owen gave his earnings to his mother. She, in turn, put more food on the table.

He'd been resourceful then, same as now.

When he could no longer feel his toes, he headed across the railroad tracks back to a one-and-a-half-story house a block from the lake. A light glowed through the frosted kitchen window. Owen braced himself, turned the knob, and stepped in.

Dad—who rarely slept more than a few hours a night—sat at the table with his Bible open, his hair sleep-rumpled. "It's past two."

"I know," Owen said as he hung his cap and plaid wool jacket on pegs behind the door. In the small wall mirror, compliments of the local grocery, Owen's cheeks were wind-chapped, eyelashes frosted. His hair was cedar-colored, like Mom's—but as unruly as Dad's.

Tipper, a golden dog with one white paw, sat at Owen's feet, dusting the wood floor with his feathered tail. He pressed his wet nose into Owen's palm until Owen gave him what he wanted: a good scratch under the chin.

"Dad," Owen said. His heart banged around in his chest, but he kept his voice down. "I have something to tell you."

Dad nodded. "After enough booze, a fellow gets lots of ideas."

"I haven't been drinking," Owen said, standing tall, as if to prove it. "Not much anyway. I made a decision. A car dealership. It's the future and I want to get in on it. I'll start small, then eventually, if things go well, I'll expand."

Dad frowned, hands clenched on the faded floral table-cloth. "That's hogwash, Owen. You're nineteen. What with my heart giving out on me, you gotta be more responsible." He pushed up from the table and crossed his arms over his red union suit and barrel chest.

An inch short of Dad's six feet, Owen met his pale blue eyes. "I *am* being responsible. I can still help out at the creamery. Just not all the time."

"Shhh, you two," Mom whispered from the bedroom off the kitchen. "The boys are sleeping."

The past year had been a roller coaster. Dad's chest pains would come, then go. When Dad took to his bed, Owen covered for him at the family business. He hoped Dad would be around long enough for Erling and Knut to eventually run things.

"Why isn't *this* enough?" Dad stretched his arms wide, indicating the kitchen, the living room with a cast-iron woodstove. *This* included Jensen Creamery, the village of Ranier, International Falls, the paper mill three miles downriver, and the nearly hundred-mile expanse of Rainy Lake, which formed the border between Minnesota and Canada. *This* meant the lift bridge joining two countries and the Duluth, Winnipeg & Pacific Railroad that linked Ranier with the rest of the world.

The water kettle shrieked on the cookstove. Owen grabbed a hot pad, lifted the kettle by its wooden handle, and then filled two white ceramic mugs with steaming water. He pulled a small flask of brandy from his shirt pocket and added a splash to his mug. He handed the other to Dad. Plain hot water, the way he liked it.

Owen warmed his hands on the mug. He'd felt low for a few days after Sadie Rose returned last month to St. Peter, seventy-five miles southwest of St. Paul. He missed the way they talked about anything and everything; the way she felt in his arms, pressed against his flannel shirt, her head tucked under his chin. He'd always wanted to make something of himself—but now he knew *why*. Heck, she was the daughter of a state senator. But that only made Owen more determined to make a future worth sharing.

Silence stretched.

The new electric light flickered above the table. "She wasn't born upper crust," Dad said, as if reading his mind. "I'll bet the moon she'd be happy joining you here to help run things someday."

"Dad, she's getting an education. She wants to teach music, not get stuck—" He stopped himself. It was like talking to a cow. If Dad just once heard her play the piano, saw her shelves filled with books, maybe he'd understand she was meant for more. He exhaled in frustration and stared at the shelf above the drain board and hand pump. Grandma had painted six wooden plates in Norwegian rosemaling designs, one for each grandson. It's what she left behind. Well, he wanted to leave something behind, too. Something bigger than plates. So he'd started thinking up his own business.

Last year was up and down for the Ford Motor Company. On the heels of their five millionth Model T, Ford lost the guy with the brains behind their production to Chevrolet. Studebaker, on the other hand, had been strong for a decade. They made a range of vehicles and were priced right, too, from under $1,000 up to $2,500. Sure, they

weren't as cheap as Fords, but "Studeys" made up the difference in quality.

"I've done my research. I even asked Ennis for advice."

"E. W. Ennis?" Dad scoffed. "That's reaching mighty
high. When was that?"

Owen waved away Dad's question. "I couldn't get a
loan anywhere. I tried the two banks in the Falls. Then the
Ranier Bank." Owen pulled out his empty trouser pockets
as proof. "I wasn't about to ask you to put up the creamery
as collateral."

Regret played at the corners of Dad's eyes, as if he might
start crying. "Someday, things will turn around for us."

"I can't wait for someday," Owen said. "That's why I
talked to Mr. Pengler."

Dad stared at him. "Owen, no." He slowly wagged his
head and squarish chin. "You get tangled up with that
bootlegger, it'll come at a price, I'm telling you."

Owen swallowed past his Adam's apple and pushed
ahead. "He agrees the time is now. He likes my ambition.
In fact, he used to be the head chef at the Palmer House in
Chicago. He took a big leap, a big risk, coming here to start
the White Turtle."

"You don't think starting up the creamery was a leap?"
The bridge of splotchy skin across Dad's nose flushed deep
red. "Long as you didn't sign anything—"

"I signed an agreement." Owen pulled the check from
his shirt pocket. "Soon as I deposit this, I can order inventory, decide on location, how to advertise—all of that is still
to come." The more he talked, the more his dream took on
a life and energy of its own. "We could take Sunday drives.
Free advertising! Mom would love that and—"

"It's Prohibition, Owen. The country's changing damn
fast. It's getting crazy out there." Then his voice hit the
ceiling. "How could a smart guy like you be so blasted foolish? Don't you know Pengler has connections to Chicago?

They use submachine guns now! You want to bring that kind of trouble here?"

Owen groaned. "Jeez, Dad. It's a business deal. Nothing to do with Chicago or gangs or 'tommy guns.'"

"You think your girl wants you getting involved with—"

"Leave her out of this!" Owen flung his mug to the floor. It toppled, clunked, and then shattered against a leg of the cookstove. "I want to offer her a future, not one that *chains* her to me—especially here!"

"What's wrong with here?"

"Nothing. Nothing's wrong with it, Dad, if it's what I *choose*. I just don't want to feel stuck here, without options. Sadie's getting a college degree. Maybe she'll want to return, but maybe she'll want to live somewhere else, too. Maybe I'll want to live somewhere else someday, that's all."

Dad worked his mouth, like a horse evading a bit. Finally, he said, "Nothing's free, Owen. Everything—every damn thing comes at a price." Then Dad's voice softened. "I know I wasn't always the dad you wanted. I know you dreamed of college. But I did the best I could."

Owen bent down and picked up the pieces of the mug, avoiding Dad's sudden confession. What difference would it make now? Owen was doing the best he could, as well. What he wouldn't say was that before he could deposit Pengler's check, he'd agreed to help unload a truckload of sugar sometime soon. Everyone knew sugar was a key ingredient in making alcohol, but Owen couldn't see anything wrong with unloading it. Also, Owen agreed to sell Pengler a half dozen "Whiskey Sixes," specially rigged Studebakers designed to carry heavy cargo over rough roads. He couldn't say no. Those sales would help launch his dealership and help pay down his loan.

When Owen stood again, he met Dad's eyes.

"Think you know everything about everything, son. Don't say I didn't warn you." Then Dad turned away and closed the bedroom door behind him.

2

WITH THE CONVERSATION RINGING IN HIS EARS, OWEN bundled up and trudged back into the cold. Someday he'd get a place with indoor flush toilet plumbing, rather than freeze his ass off in the outhouse every time Nature called.

When he returned, the house was quiet, except for the fire crackling in the woodstove. Absorbing the warmth, Owen climbed the attic stairs. Tipper padded up behind him. Beneath the attic's slanted ceilings rose soft, deep breathing. Five cots and five brothers were packed in like sardines in a can, from seven-year-old Jake, curled in a fetal position, to fifteen-year-old Erling, whose feet hung well beyond the end of his bed. Being oldest came at a price, but Owen considered himself lucky to have a room of his own, no matter how small.

He turned on his lamp, undressed to his long johns, and climbed into bed. Tipper waited. Owen patted the edge of the bed and Tipper leapt up, circled at the end, and pawed at the wool blanket until it rippled.

"It's gotta be just so, doesn't it, boy?"

Tipper ignored him, pawed a few more times, then at last plopped down, off to the side from Owen's feet.

His mother had been off to the side for years. The first sixteen years of Owen's life, he'd watched her fret to feed a family on the pennies left after Dad's drinking sprees.

And Dad would have kept on drinking, too, had Owen not stopped him a few years back. Dad had stormed in, all whiskeyed up. It was hardly the first time, but that night he'd gone snaky. He had Mom up against the kitchen wall, those big hands around her little neck, yelling and accusing her of unspeakable things. Owen was too small to take him on, so he'd grabbed the shotgun. "Dad! Let her go or I'll shoot you!"

When Dad crawled home the next morning, he asked Mom, "Where'd you get those marks on your neck?"

Owen spoke up for her. "From you, Dad. You tried to kill her." Dad cried like a baby, head in his hands. After that, to Owen's astonishment—because drunks rarely give up their favorite pastime—Dad never took a drink again. He offered free buttermilk to drunks to help them sober up. He encouraged them to give up booze, too. Though Dad turned over a new leaf, Owen could never trust him. The family continued to pay a price. You don't recover from a financial disaster in three years, not with a family of hungry boys. Money was always in short supply.

Stirring up memories was like digging along the shore for arrowheads. Beneath top layers of sand were layers of dirt, clay, or granite. Once you started, you never knew what you'd find. Thinking of those early years never made him feel better. He rested his hand on Tipper's ribcage as it rose and fell. Morning rounds would come soon enough; Tipper always joined him, greeting everyone with a full body wag as Owen loaded the creamery truck with cans of fresh milk and wood crates of fresh eggs. He should try to get some sleep.

When Owen finally closed his eyes, all he saw was Sadie: dark waves cut boldly at her chin, eyes deep as the lake, her mouth wide open in disbelief the time she'd cast her lure and snagged the back of his upper arm. She burst into tears. It hurt, but he'd cracked up laughing. He found pliers in the tackle box. You had to push it through. You can't take a lure out backward or it'll tear the flesh. That's why they're barbed, to hook and to hold. He'd intended to be all steely and do it on his own, but the angle was bad. He needed her help. "I can't," she'd said, crying. "You can," he told her. And she did. Then, from the flask of brandy he kept on hand, she poured the alcohol straight into his wound. He yelped, but she wrapped her cotton scarf around his arm, then kissed him all over his face. The pain was worth every moment that followed.

His thoughts drifted to last summer with her at Melnyks' farm. Covered in dirt and grease, Jerry was bent over a tractor engine, stalled out with a wagon of fresh-cut hay. "Soon as I get it going for my old man and we finish putting up hay," he said with a wink and a sly smile, "I'm finding me a gal half as beautiful as you, Sadie."

Owen snugged his arm around Sadie's waist in mock ownership, and Sadie laughed, resting her head on Owen's shoulder. "You're a charmer, Jer. Hope you let the ladies down softly."

"Seriously, Sadie. I realize Owen wasn't born with my good looks or brains—just so you know, I'm waiting in line."

At that, Owen tackled Jerry at the knees and pinned him in the grass until Jerry sputtered out a half-joking apology.

He missed Sadie something terrible. He couldn't wait for late May and the day she'd hop off the train for the summer. He'd fold her in his arms, then steer her toward a lot of Studebakers. "Pick one to test drive," he'd say. Then he'd take the wheel, hit the gas, and she'd smile, her hair wind-tossed. But that was months away. Until then, he had a future to build, with or without Dad's blessing.

Before dawn, hushed voices rose from downstairs. Owen headed down the attic stairs.

As his feet touched the kitchen floor, Mom's voice rose in a tear-filled whisper. "They were arguing last night. He came to bed upset . . ." She was backing out of her bedroom, followed by Mary Austin, the county's first woman doctor.

"His heart's been bad for some time now, Esther," Dr. Austin replied in her level, no-nonsense voice. "This time, it simply gave out. All those years of drinking took a toll, I'm afraid."

"The Lord called him home then?" Mom whispered.

"Yes, Esther. I'm terribly sorry."

Then the doctor turned. "Owen, hello. I'm sorry, but your father—"

"I heard," he managed to say, and made his way past the doctor and his mother toward the familiar body angled across the bed, covered from head to feet with a bedsheet. Owen knelt. He rested his hands on Dad's unmoving chest. His fingertips brushed up against the Saint Christopher medal Mom gave Dad when he'd stopped drinking.

The clock ticked away seconds, minutes, a lifetime.

Inhale.

Exhale.

When Dr. Austin left, his mother hovered in the doorway.

"The medal," she whispered. "It's yours now, Owen. Take if off him. Please. Before the undertaker comes."

As if watching his hands move by someone else's will, Owen lifted the chain gently over Dad's lifeless head. He held it in his hand, unsure what to do with it.

"You wear it now," Mom said.

Owen hesitated.

"Please, Owen," she whispered.

Owen slipped it on. Saint Christopher, patron saint of protection. What kind of protection did Saint Christopher give, allowing a father of six to slip away? When Dad quit drinking, he encouraged Owen not to go down the same path. But Owen wasn't Dad. He could handle a little booze now and then. Yet here was his own father, reduced to a corpse.

Gathering the edge of the sheet into clenched hands, Owen determined—then and there—no more booze. He'd stop drinking.

He dropped his head to the edge of the sheet. "Dad," he whispered, crushed more by the loss of what might have been. Everything he'd wanted to escape—the creamery and the responsibility for his family—was all on him.

"You can't go!"

3

LATE MORNING, THE SUN HUNG LOW AND PALE. OWEN clapped his leather mitts together to keep his blood flowing. He wore his earflaps down and his wool scarf double-wrapped around his neck, yet a windless twenty-below seeped into unprotected gaps and stung his skin. Huddled into his coat, he passed Erickson's Fine Grocery, Lou's Trading Post, then the Ranier Depot and crossed the tracks.

A week had passed since Dad died. Everything had fallen on him like a steamship anchor. When you're nineteen— and suddenly responsible for keeping your mother and five younger brothers clothed and fed—every penny, nickel, and dime mattered.

The check in his pocket taunted him. If he deposited it at the bank, he could order inventory from Studebaker. He forced down his own wishes. He had to return the check.

Flashes of light caught his eye from the bank's large windows, topped in half-moon panels of stained glass. The morning sun illuminated leafy patterns of Tiffany glass—a reminder that there were fortunes to be made in this northern frontier. Fortunes made by the likes of E. W. Ennis, timber and paper mill baron, and Harvey Pengler, businessman and bootlegger.

Ordinary folks came north seeking fortune and gambled their lives—first on gold mines that went bust, then on logging, and lately on promises of fine farmland. However, after clear-cutting, removing stumps, and tilling deep clay, farmers quit working the land and returned to logging. The past week had changed everything; it was one thing to gamble with his own future. He wanted a car dealership, but not if it meant putting the family creamery at risk.

Under the green awning of a whitewashed, two-story building, Owen climbed the wooden steps to the White Turtle Club. He stepped in, setting off a metal chime on the door. He gazed around, feeling strangely disconnected, as if his brain lagged a few steps behind his body. Above the arched doorway to the hotel's restaurant, a stuffed moose head with a massive rack of antlers stared down with lifeless glass eyes. From pot roast dinners to all-you-can-eat walleye, to six-inch stacks of blueberry pancakes and the best breakfast sausage patties around, the White Turtle's restaurant was a town favorite that lived up to its banner: *Good cooking! Never leave hungry!*

"Hello there, Owen." From a door behind the lobby counter, Miss Izzy Larson, a woman ten years his elder, stepped out, ringlets falling alongside her rouge-dabbed cheeks.

He nodded.

"So sorry about your father," she continued, her voice thick as coffee that had been on the burner too long. "Used to come around here more, a few years back. A good egg, your dad. Used to buy rounds for his friends. Those were some swell times."

Swell times. He nodded and pulled a tourist brochure off the counter. His eyes glazed over the words as memories rose—like air bubbles long trapped in a pond's muddy layers—gave way and floated up. "Trail your dad," Mom had commanded, and by the time Owen was five, he shadowed

Dad at the local taverns, trying to slide Dad's change off the bar counter when he wasn't looking. Whatever he could sneak went back to Mom's coffee tin hidden under her bed.

"Owen, honey," Miss Larson said, nudging him back to the present. "You're a little outta sorts, huh?"

"Oh, sorry . . . Is Mr. Pengler here?"

She shook her head, setting her ringlets bouncing. "He's across the street at the bank, but he should be back any second." She reached below the counter, produced a cigarette, placed it in the end of a long cigarette holder, and lit it. As she inhaled, Owen followed her gaze out the window.

A man bundled tighter than a fish in newspaper, with only his eyes and nose showing, drove two shaggy black horses and a dray in the direction of the boat landing, likely heading out to cut ice. Every winter, folks cut huge blocks of ice, stacked and stored them in buildings under layers of wood shavings, keeping the ice available all summer for everything from packing commercially caught fish to ice for fancy cocktails.

Izzy exhaled, smoke swirling up around her head, and leaned on her elbows before taking another drag. "The restaurant opens in an hour for lunch, unless . . ." Her voice turned to coffee with sugar and cream. "Unless there's something else I can help you with this morning? Something to put a smile on your face?"

Owen shook his head. God no, he wanted to say. He had eyes and need for one girl, and one girl alone . . . and her name sure wasn't . . .

"Well, there's your answer now," Izzy replied and promptly turned away.

Mr. Pengler stepped in and removed his long, wolf-pelt coat. Made from pelts all charcoal gray, it almost seemed alive as he hung it on the coatrack. The top hairs caught the cold February light through the window.

"Mr. Pengler," Owen said, smoothing back his uncombed hair. It dawned on him what a fright he must look. For the past week, he'd barely slept. Only now, as he stood, did he measure time in the days behind him. There had been preparations for the funeral, people stopping to share their condolences, both at the house and the creamery. What mattered was that Owen had somehow managed to keep things going. Several local dairy farms supplied Jensen Creamery with fresh milk, which the creamery processed into dairy products that were sold from the creamery's front counter. He'd bought milk and eggs from local farmers, kept the creamery equipment operating, using the centrifugal separator to turn out the best butter you could buy. Everything was graded, repackaged, and sealed with the Jensen label, and he made sure the deliveries kept going to every restaurant, grocer, and logging camp in the county. With Dad gone, it was all on him. He couldn't possibly manage the creamery and take on the loan for starting a business.

He pulled the check from his pocket. "With my dad gone, things changed." Saying those words made the ache return to his chest and throat. God, he didn't want to cry now, not in front of Mr. Pengler, who removed his fedora and tossed it onto the top of the coatrack. It found its mark. Then he pushed back his prematurely white hair and with a few sprightly steps, closed the distance between them.

"Ah, Owen," he said, wrapping his thick arms and shoulders around him in a fierce bear hug. Then he stepped back, rested his hand on Owen's shoulder, and looked him in the eye. Only then did Owen see the well of sadness in Pengler's eyes. "Losing someone you love is the craps," he said. "C'mon, kid. Follow me."

Owen had been so absorbed that he'd completely forgotten Mr. Pengler's housekeeper—and sweetheart—had died not that many months earlier. "Oh, that's right, you . . . ," he said, ready to say more, but Pengler strode ahead, twisting his hand at Owen as if to say, "Leave it."

Owen followed Pengler into the restaurant. Under its

high tin ceiling, two chandeliers lit the room. White table-cloths topped a dozen wooden tables, each with matching chairs. "It's not the Palmer House," Pengler was known to say to new customers, "but everyone likes a nice place and a good meal." Though some customers turned their noses up when one of the ladies dined in the restaurant—"Can't they take their meals upstairs?" his mother had said—that didn't keep most locals away.

"You and I," Pengler said, walking behind the counter with its red and silver stools, "we're going to talk. Time for a soda."

"Okay."

Behind Pengler, a narrow chalkboard displayed sodas, from "Black and White" and "Strawberry" to "Brown Cow" and "Catawba Flip." Owen couldn't decide. But then Pengler turned, reached toward the floor, and opened a short door in the wall behind the chalkboard.

"Don't forget to duck," Pengler said, signaling Owen to follow.

On the other side of the wall a mahogany bar, lined with empty glasses and bottles filled with booze, stood ready for business. The scent of cigars hung above deep wooden booths and tables with cast-iron pedestals. Since Prohibition went into full swing two years back, many such counters claimed to be soda fountains. But Owen and Pengler were the only two in the "blind pig." It wasn't fancy enough to be called a "speakeasy," the upscale drinking establishments Owen read about in newspapers. This one didn't have crystal chandeliers, flappers in beaded dresses and headbands, and black musicians playing "smoky, brassy music," as one reporter put it. Speakeasies were more common in big cities; Sadie talked of a few in St. Paul off Summit Avenue, and a speakeasy on Wabasha Street built in a cave along the Mississippi.

Pengler grabbed a bottle of whiskey from the bar and poured two shot glasses full.

Owen put a palm out. He'd decided not to touch the stuff, but he didn't want to offend Pengler. "It's too early—"

"Nonsense," Pengler said, motioning to a booth. Owen sat down across from Pengler, leaving the shot glass untouched.

"You lost your father. I'm still reeling from losing my sweet Agnes. Thank God I have young Jimmy to care for, or I'd lose my mind. Or my heart would break to pieces. Or both."

Owen waited. He didn't know what Pengler expected from him.

"You are *not* returning that check," Pengler finally said.

"But I have to operate the creamery. And you've probably read the news, right there next to my dad's obituary. Henry Ford bought the Lincoln Motor Company for eight million. He isn't struggling; he's building an empire. I thought Studebakers, since they've been strong for a decade, were the way to go. Now I have my doubts."

"Sure, it'll be tough going for a while," Pengler said, "but there's no reason you can't start getting a few Studebakers from Detroit."

"South Bend, Indiana," Owen corrected him.

"Okay, so you remember what you told me? Thomas Edison was the second to buy one of their electric automobiles."

"Yeah, almost a decade ago," Owen said, "but they've gone to all gasoline since then." Owen pushed back from the table and sat taller. "Mr. Pengler, I can't get away to drive 'em up here. I won't have the time to keep a dealership going."

Leaning forward, Pengler clinked his empty shot glass against Owen's that sat untouched on the table. "That's why I'm going to help you. You really want to be in this dairy business forever? Your dad was a great guy, but did he really get ahead? Do you want to be slinging around milk bottles the rest of your life?"

Owen looked away. Of course it wasn't what he wanted. He felt like a northern pike on the end of a long line, being reeled in, crank by slow crank, as if someone greater than him was trying to take the fight out of him. He had to be responsible.

Pengler massaged his angular chin. He studied Owen with close-set eyes. "You got brothers, Owen. Not a one of 'em as smart as you. Bet they'll step up before you know it and be happy to run a little business. But you? *You* have more potential. I know it. And you know it, too."

Yeah, he knew it. He'd been the top of his class, a whiz at figures and dates; his last teacher, Mr. Chartridge, had insisted Owen apply to university. But when he'd returned from school with that notion, his mother disappeared to her room and Dad went for a long walk. There was never money. And besides, none of that mattered now.

"Next few months," Pengler said, "while everyone's waiting around for the lake to open up, I'll send some guys down there with jalopies—we're doing a pretty brisk business these days, so there'll be one-way cargo, not entirely legal cargo one way . . . Anyway, I'll have my boys drive back your new models at absolutely no extra cost to you. Before summer arrives, you'll have a small dealership, full and ready to go. They'll fly off the lot! Whaddya say?" Pengler beamed.

The check smoldered against Owen's heart.

"Owen," Pengler said, lowering his voice, "I'm disappointed if you change your mind. I thought we had a deal." He tilted his head, but didn't release Owen from his gaze. "I can order all the cars I need, but I wanted to give you a leg up."

"Why?" Owen asked.

"Good question." He rested his chin in his hand. "Maybe I see a little of myself in you. Thought you had gumption." He paused. "Was I wrong?"

A knock sounded on the other side of the blind pig's

door. Pengler turned away and rose, leaving his words hanging in the air. "Think on it," he added, as he walked to the door.

Owen stared at the amber shot of whiskey.

Returning the check meant a lifetime ahead at the creamery. Dad left nothing behind. Barely enough to cover the funeral. Owen conjured up himself at seven, ten, and thirteen years old, a kid tracing his father's unsteady footsteps from tavern to tavern. While Dad knocked back drinks, Owen had to reach up to gather loose change to bring home to his mother.

Dad had run the creamery every day like a hardworking father, but spent nights out drinking. More than once he'd come home late and let Owen have it with the belt for "not being responsible." Yeah. Dad taught him that everything comes at a price. The red steel truck that Owen loved more than anything . . . the birthday present when he turned six. He'd forgotten it outside; someone stole it; Dad found it by the railroad tracks, all busted up, and belt-whipped the snot out of him. Owen refused to cry. He would not give Dad that satisfaction. With each whack across his bare butt, he tucked his feelings deeper and deeper away.

He'd never walk out on his mother and his younger brothers, not until one of them could step in and take over. But the image of his own dealership, of a lot full of shiny, new automobiles, all waxed and polished, chrome bright as the sun, a lot filled with the most beautiful machines ever built on wheels . . . he couldn't let it go. If he went ahead with his dream, he'd have to be extra resourceful.

He'd find a way to make it work.

"So what do you think?" Pengler's voice floated from across the blind pig. Owen thought he was asking for his decision, then realized he was still talking to someone at the door. He heard enough to put the gist of the conversation together.

Ice conditions.

Whiskey.

". . . two feet thick all the way to Kettle Falls," the voice at the door said. "Darn near perfect."

Elbows propped on the table, Owen leaned his forehead into his folded hands. He thought of the pros and cons, the risks and rewards. Then a new surge of energy rushed through him, the same feeling he had whenever he laced up his skates, tottered on the steel blades for a moment, then pushed off onto a lake with fresh, promising, glassy ice. Heck, Owen told himself, he'd never gone through the ice yet.

When Pengler returned, he didn't sit. "That other favor I mentioned, I'll need help soon. Time to decide. Well, Owen?"

He stood up from the table and shook hands with Pengler. "I'm in."

Perfect ice is a rare find. The conditions have to be just right: deep cold, no wind, no snow, sleet, or drizzle. When it freezes just so—glassy and solid—there's nothing like it. On skates, a guy can get up a head of speed—almost like flying.

Air clean and bracing.

Intoxicating.

Breaths puffing white as you fly along the shore.

Steel blades carve and glide.

Arms pump, working in rhythm with your legs.

Sure, you could wipe out going too fast. You could run into a patch of weak ice. There's always some risk.

A guy just had to read the lake. Read the conditions. Keep his head about him. If something goes wrong, you better know how to stop: bend your knees, throw your weight sideways, and send up a spray of shaved ice from knife-sharp blades.

4

BEFORE LEAVING THE HOTEL LOBBY, PENGLER STOPPED Owen. "Oh, by the way. You any good at riding horses?"

Owen laughed. "Ah, no." He reached for his cap and jacket from the coatrack. He pictured himself, eleven years old, and the dare he'd taken to climb on a dappled mare without a speck of training. The mare reared, bucked, and twisted, and Owen ended up flat on his back, the wind knocked out of him. Jerry, however, who'd grown up with farm animals, climbed on and clung like a monkey, arms around the horse's neck and digging in his bare feet behind the horse's shoulders. Unable to toss Jerry, the dappled mare eventually yielded.

"Too bad," Pengler said. "I need a fella to ride Ace-in-the-Hole for the one-miler next month. Got a lot of money on another win this year. You sure?"

"Your horse has to cross the line with its rider, right?"

"That's the idea."

Next month's horse races on Rainy Lake were famous for bringing out onlookers and gamblers alike—and not only folks from around town, but some who came by train from Duluth, Minneapolis, St. Paul, and Chicago. There were races of horse-drawn sleighs, too. But the one-miler was the big draw, and Pengler's horse, Ace-in-the-Hole, always won.

Pengler continued. "I'm in a real bind. If you know any-body who can hang on for the ride of his life . . ."

"Wait, I know someone." Owen hadn't seen Jerry for a whole year, until he turned up last week at his father's funeral. Owen was surprised and pleased to see him home from the East Coast. Jerry had followed a girl out there and, no surprise, returned without her. All Owen knew was that Jerry had come back to do who-knows-what. He said to Pengler, "My friend, Jerry Melnyk."

"Melnyk? Really? I had no idea! Ha! And he's already on my payroll. I'll ask him myself then."

Owen wondered what kind of work Jerry was doing for Pengler, but he decided not to ask.

"In fact, you'll be working with him tomorrow night," Pengler added. "I'm counting on you boys."

Owen nodded, pushed open the door, and stepped out under the White Turtle's awning into the blinding sun-light. He'd agreed to help unload sacks of sugar. Over a hundred heavy bags. Working with Jerry made it all the better.

Owen strode across Main Street to the Ranier bank. He opened a business account, deposited the check, and used the bank phone to place an order with Studebaker Com-pany for twelve cars. Once he had the total, he made out a check, signed it with extra flourish—Mr. Owen Jensen—and asked for a bank envelope. Then he dropped it off at the post office, destined for the next train's mailbag.

Filling his nostrils with a sharp breath of morning air, Owen set off across the tracks. Making money was like drawing water. A guy couldn't get anywhere until he poured a little water in the spigot. *Primed the pump.* Then, when you work the handle, water rises up from the well, filling buckets to overflowing.

The sun warmed his neck. He felt lighter than he'd felt in days, and he let his mind drift like a boat on water. He remembered two years back, visiting Sadie at Trinity's cabin on Baird's Island. Those memories could carry him a lifetime. In darkness, he'd cut the motor, paddled his boat to the island's shore, and hid his boat under a low-hanging cedar. Water lapped, pine scent wafted, loons called back and forth on the water, their songs heartaching and haunting. He and Sadie talked for hours until they fell asleep in each other's arms. First crack of light, he slipped away, went back to the creamery, and made deliveries by boat across Rainy Lake. Those two weeks, he completely fell for her. She eventually returned home to the Worthingtons, but everything in his world had changed. There wasn't anything he wouldn't do to make her proud of him, to make her happy. Someday, he hoped to offer her a life together. A stable life. *Where* wasn't nearly as important as *how* to make it happen.

"Owen, did you hear the news?" Mom called as Owen entered the back room of the creamery.

He pulled his thoughts back to the present and hung up his jacket in his locker.

In the chilly air of the back room, Mom worked at a prep table with an apron over her plaid wool jacket, a scarf knotted beneath her chin. Her hands fluttered as she wrapped, sealed, and labeled small blocks of butter for sale.

"What news?"

"It's there in the paper." She motioned with a tilt of her head to the newspaper on the spindle-back chair. "Two bootleggers came across in a fishing boat—you know, where the water is open and the current is strong—and when they reached shore Sheriff Vandyke and his deputy were waiting for them. Shot one dead."

Owen's heart slid to his gut, then dropped another level to his knees. Pengler said Jerry was on his payroll. Had

Jerry gone off on some bootlegging business last night for Pengler? "Who got shot?"

"Didn't give a name."

What Owen had heard was that this new sheriff, Vandyke, was law abiding. Unlike the former sheriff, who was convicted of corruption and taking bribes, Vandyke was fighting bootlegging with a crusader's zeal.

Owen needed to phone the Melnyks' house. Make sure. He grabbed the newspaper and headed through the swinging doors to the service counter.

"Owen," Mom said, stopping him. He turned and met her eyes, which looked bigger than usual. Her pale skin sharply contrasted with strands of auburn hair; her cheekbones seemed more pronounced since Dad died. "Owen, I don't want to pry or ask questions. But things are getting dangerous. Better warn Pengler and anyone else you know . . . anyone who might be bootlegging. It's time to get out before things get worse."

"Mom, I'm *not* bootlegging, if that's what you're trying to say."

She nodded, then bowed her head and returned to packaging.

BOOTLEGGER FOUND FLOATING IN RIVER! SHERIFF CLAIMS SHOOTING AN ACCIDENT

Early Thursday morning, on his way to work at the paper mill, Mr. Adam Renschal reportedly spotted a body floating near the International Falls dam. He immediately alerted local law enforcement.

Shortly after, Sheriff Hugh Vandyke filed a report that he and Deputy Edgar Kranlin were aware of bootlegging activities between the U.S. and Canadian shores of Rainy River. "Last evening, in an attempt to enforce the Volstead Act," Sheriff Vandyke claimed, "our vigilance was rewarded when we spotted two men rowing from Canada to the American side. When they reached shore with crates of whiskey, we arrested one of the men, but the other managed to get back in his rowboat and flee toward Canada."

When asked about the bullet in the back of the discovered victim, Sheriff Vandyke responded that he would never shoot someone in the back. "I fired a warning shot across the water and it must have ricocheted against the water and struck the man in the back."

Mayor Danielson states that this incident "demonstrates how things are getting out of hand over alcohol in Koochiching County."

5

When Owen returned the next morning from his rounds at nearby farms, he parked the truck and then lugged milk cans into the creamery's back room.

At the counter, Mom chatted with Mrs. Brumbraaten, who was hidden somewhere under an ankle-length coat, scarves, and hat. She was a regular customer and big on lengthy one-sided conversations. "Well, after that cat drank the whole saucer of cream," Mrs. Brumbraaten said, "it went up the nearest tree and howled all night long . . . poor thing. And this morning, wouldn't you know it, he—"

"Excuse me," Mom said, raising her hand like a stop sign. From her apron pocket she produced a white envelope and held it out to Owen.

"Here, this came for you."

He immediately recognized the return address of Gustavus Adolphus College, St. Peter, Minnesota. His heart leapt. Three strides and a long reach, and the envelope was in his fingers. Each day since Dad had passed, Owen had intended to write Sadie and tell her the news. But each time he tried, he found it impossible to write it down. When he used the telephone on the wall behind the creamery counter, he hadn't been able to get through. Between the ever-busy party line, and only one telephone in the women's dormitory, he kept striking out. He'd wanted to be the one to tell her about his father. Owen walked through the swinging doors, met by the chilly air, the hum of refrigerators, and the icy cement floor in need of mopping.

He sat down on an empty milk crate and removed his gloves, eager to read her words, to feel her hand on his heart. Though unable to speak for so many years as a child, Sadie Rose now always seemed to know what to say to bring out the best in him. He slid a finger under the letter's flap and gently eased it open. Her stationery was a soft lilac paper that smelled faintly of perfume, and he pressed it to his nose. Then he held it out in front of him, admiring the page filled with her slanted and curved handwriting.

My dear, sweet Owen, he read, and smiled.

> *You cannot imagine the silliness that surrounds me sometimes here in Johnson Hall! At this very moment, there is a pillow fight erupting. You've never heard such giggling and screeching from these Gustavus girls, or "Gusties" as everyone calls us, and I'm not sure you would want to. I've locked my door to avoid being drawn into the battle, as I have a bit of a headache this evening, and I must study up before my Latin test tomorrow morning. Also, I've seen down pillows turn into clouds of feathers, as if a fox had invaded a hen house! I, however, would like to keep my pillow intact for its intended purpose: sleeping. But how does one sleep—or study for that matter—when at the other end of the hall, someone is practicing her operatic voice? Granted, she is a fine soprano, but these walls are thin.*

Owen looked up from the letter. Nothing about his father. She didn't know. She hadn't heard the news. Not only was she moving through her life knowing nothing about the hollow ache in his chest, the way he felt a foot underwater since he'd pulled back the sheet and looked at Dad's ashen face, but she knew nothing of his loan, his plans for his future—their future. In the space of a mere paragraph, the distance between them grew. With an exhale, he read on:

There's a Sweetheart Ball later this month. The 25th, to be exact. I rather dread telling you my news, because I don't want you to worry.

Worry? Of course he was going to worry.

. . . You know that at college a girl becomes friends with many students, both guys and gals. One of my friends, also a Music major, has taken pity on me knowing that my boy-friend is way up North. He plays the clarinet and his name is Samuel, but most everyone, except me, calls him Sam. Any-way, out of pity, he offered to escort me to the ball so I don't have to stay in the dorm all alone. That's thoughtful, isn't it?

Owen tightened his jaw against this oh-so-thoughtful clarinet-playing Sam.

. . . And so, I hope you don't mind and you don't get the wrong idea about any of this. It's nothing, really. Just a lit-tle dancing and music. A needed diversion from my studies!

Right. Just a little dancing and music. He knew how Sadie loved music, how in no time, she'd lose her shoes and dance in stocking feet—or barefoot. She inhaled music as if it were the very thing that kept her heart pumping and her blood moving through her veins. But in a way it made perfect sense. At five years old she was found in a snowbank and taken in by the Worthingtons. She'd suffered from acute ear infections and didn't speak for eleven years—until two summers ago. Over time, it was as if music had become her first language—voice her second. She played piano as effortlessly as breathing. And though she wasn't one to smile easily, once music started, she couldn't help herself.

A needed diversion from her studies. Of course she'd have a swell time! Irritated by the miles between them, Owen tapped his boot toe on the floor and continued reading.

. . . Spring seems so very far away right now. My advisor told me that since the need for teachers is great, I may be able to accelerate earning my degree. Though I would hope to solely teach Music, I realize that I may need to teach most

every subject when I return North. In fact, I have learned of
a possible tutoring position there this summer with a family.
Before you know it, I'll be riding the train back to Ranier.

Love,

Sadie Rose

Owen tilted his head back. He stared at the ceiling, at the
frosty line of condensation that formed along the crack.
There was something missing in the letter. *Before you know
it,* she'd written, *I'll be riding the train back to Ranier.* She
didn't say: *to you.* And Samuel? Why was she the only one
to call this "friend" by that formal name when everyone
else called him "Sam"? Did she think this fellow music student was too refined for as simple a name as "Sam"? And
what kind of diversion from studies did this Samuel have in
mind? This guy—no matter what name he went by—tipped
him off center.

He felt himself free-falling from a great height, his
stomach lurching up and out of his pounding chest. Like
the time he'd jumped off the forty-foot granite cliffs at
Anderson Bay. Flying in midair, he wished he could leap
back to the safety of solid ground. He'd screamed every
foot of falling, hit the surface feetfirst, and descended
down, down, down into dark and frigid layers of water,
until he pushed his arms against his sides and kicked hard
toward the light. When he surfaced, Sadie Rose met him
with applause and a smile.

It terrified him how much he suddenly needed her.
Here.
Beside him.
Living and breathing and in his arms.
He needed her warmth, her soft fragrance, her reassur-
ing kisses. She'd know what to say to calm him right now.
But she was some four hundred miles away. He had a mind
to get on the next train, ride down there, and take her to
the damn Sweetheart Ball himself.

He took off his cap. If he wanted to keep her, he was going to have to hold his own against better-educated guys.

He rubbed the back of his hand against his eyes, clenched his teeth, and noticed his unlaced boots. Mechanically, he drew the leather laces tighter and tighter, pulling his feet back where they needed to be. Underneath him and in motion. But one of the leather strips snapped in two.

"For cripes sake!"

He jumped to his feet and kicked out the bottom crate from a towering stack. The empty crates leaned, then tumbled over, clattering across the concrete floor, leaving numerous splinters and broken wooden slats behind.

He swore again, then kicked over a milk can, spilling a white stream as the metal can clanged to a stop on the concrete floor.

"Owen!" Mom pushed the door open. "Are you okay back here?"

"An accident, Mom. I'll clean it up." He waved her off and she left.

Owen looked around at the mess he'd created. Then he opened his locker and put the letter on the top shelf, along with his cap. He took off his jacket and hung it up. Heck with customers out front. He was going to try her again on the telephone.

He left the back room, stepped behind the service counter, and ignored Mrs. Brumbraaten's banter.

He picked up the receiver and dialed o.

"Operator," came the young woman's voice on the other end. Finally, he had a clear line. He gave her the number. On the other end, the phone rang twice, and then a groggy voice answered. "Hello? Johnson Hall."

Owen cleared his voice. "Hello. I'd like to speak to Sadie Rose."

"Most everyone's in class. I'm only here because I'm sick today." A pause, a deep hacking cough. "But I'll check her room." When she returned to the line, he knew what she was going to say. "No, sorry. She's not here. Bye."

Before he had a chance to leave a message, the phone went dead. When he lifted the receiver again, another caller was on the party line.

The creamery door opened, and the familiar customer—a small, scrawny man who had been coming by the past few months—removed his rabbit fur hat and held it against his jacket.

"Mr. Boshelink," Mom said, greeting him as if he were a regular paying customer. But this man was always short on funds, with a wife who was apparently anemic after their firstborn. Owen wasn't sure, but he had the feeling Dad always swept the man's debt under the table.

Dealing with Boshelink was the last thing Owen wanted to do. If it were up to him, he'd escort him to the door and tell him that this was no longer a charity. Dad was dead. Going forward, things had to be different. They had bills to pay, too.

The man smiled at Owen, then at Mom. He slicked his hand over strands of oily hair. He emitted an unwashed smell of sour and sweat. "I hear news. I so much sorrow." He thumped his misshapen fedora against his heart.

"Yes, thank you," Mom replied. "What may I help you with today?"

"Owen, dear," Mrs. Brumbraaten said, pulling her wool scarf back from her head of gray hair and tugging on Owen's sleeve. "Would you be so kind to help get the stray cat down from my tree? I don't dare get on a ladder. Your mother said you wouldn't mind, and it would be such a kindness, especially since I think I'm going to have to name it and make it my own. Will you then?"

For a second, Owen wished he could haul off and slug someone. But he closed his eyes and tamped down his frustration. He was glad for an excuse to step outside before he blew up at Boshelink.

He swallowed hard before answering. "Sure," he said.

If you can get through the long dark months of October, November, December, and January, you can survive winter. Come February, there's a shift in the air. The sun climbs high as a Ferris wheel and reflects off the snow, blindingly bright. It's enough to make a guy pause from his labors, close his eyes for a minute or two, and look skyward to feel the warmth on his skin.

He might start dreaming there's a sudden thaw around the corner or that marsh marigolds will start popping up soon in ditches.

But he'd be wrong to get his hopes up.

Winter isn't finished yet.

Not by a long shot.

6

SOMETIME WELL PAST MIDNIGHT—TRUE TO HIS PROM-
ise to Pengler—Owen climbed into the passenger seat of
Jerry's dented Model T behind the White Turtle.

"Good to see you, Jer," Owen said. "But if I have to miss
a night's sleep, I'd rather it be with Sadie Rose than with
you."

Jerry snugged down his bowler hat and shot Owen a lopsided grin. "Yeah, guess I would, too."

Owen punched Jerry's arm and they both laughed. They
fell back into their usual banter without missing a beat.

On a rutted, jarring road, they drove east of Ranier.
A whole year had passed without seeing Jerry, but now
that his friend was back from the East Coast, it felt as if
he'd never left. Owen thanked Jerry for showing up at the
funeral.

"You bet," Jerry said.

"Hey Jer," Owen pressed. "I didn't hear from you for a
whole year. You could have dropped a postcard in the mail.
Something."

"Yeah," Jerry said. "Probably should have, huh?"

"Ah, don't worry about it. So what were you up to?
Besides the girl you trailed out there? Did you find a job of
some sort?"

"Yeah, a few." Jerry didn't seem much interested in

talking about his past year, so Owen let it go. "So you're working for Pengler now?"

"Isn't everybody?" Jerry said with a laugh. "Apparently, you signed up, huh?"

Owen laughed. "No, not really. Just tonight. Part of our agreement to import specially rigged Studebakers." He told him about the dealership and the lot that would soon be filling up with new vehicles.

"Whiskey Sixes?" Jerry asked.

Owen nodded. "Yup. That's what they call 'em. After those arrive, I'm steering clear of bootlegging. Staying on the sidelines."

"That so?" Jerry kept one hand on the wheel. "Hey, how are things with your little lady, anyway? Did you score one for the team?"

First, Owen wasn't going to feed Jerry or anybody the details of his relationship. That was between him and Sadie Rose. Second, he wasn't even sure there *was* a relationship anymore. If Senator Worthington learned of Owen's foolish dealings with Pengler, he might try to ban Owen from seeing Sadie Rose, his newly adopted foster daughter. He didn't answer.

"Whoa. Things are that bad?" Jerry asked.

"Let's not talk about her right now," Owen replied.

"Life's one big risk, Owen. You jumped into your own business, assuming you'd be making money hand over fist. Am I right?"

It was true that Owen was optimistic, but he replied, "It'll take time to make a go of it."

"If you get stuck with expensive inventory, Pengler's still going to expect you to pay on your loan."

Owen mulled this over.

"My point is, Owen, that to be alive is to take risks every single second of every single day. You think those folks who'll buy your cars don't know that? They could get in a crash driving around; they could die. But is that going to keep them from getting themselves a set of shiny wheels? No, it's not. And that's why you're going to sell your stock, because there are lots of folks who just want to get behind the wheel of something fast and beautiful and see where it takes 'em."

Owen tilted his head at Jerry, as if seeing his friend for the first time. "You've actually thought about all this."

"Surprised? That I have brains?"

"I mean, you're a philosopher," Owen said. "You've given life some thought."

Jerry grinned.

"I don't know about that, but there's book smart, street smart, machinery smart, and even animal smart. Whatever you call it, everybody has brains. It's just a matter of whether they use 'em or not."

A snow-covered field turned silver beneath the hazy glow of a full moon. Between the towering barn, chicken coop, and newly built farmhouse, a lone white pine stood guard.

"So this is Pengler's place?" Owen said.

"Yup. He's a smart one. Before Prohibition went national, he was getting ready. He's got tunnels between the coop and the barn."

"Tunnels?"

"Sure. Crates of booze. Stills. And over there"—he nodded toward another shelter toward the water's edge—"a bunkhouse for workers. You wouldn't believe the network he has operating. Needs more guys all the time. We're lucky, y'know, to get in while we could." Then Jerry hopped out, leaving his Model T running. "It'll take me half a second. You take the wheel. All you do is follow 'til we unload."

As Jerry slipped into the barn, Owen opened the passenger door and stood under the expansive sky. The air was mild and damp, twenty-five degrees or so, he guessed.

To the north, somewhere on the frozen lake, or from the forest on the Canadian shore, a wolf howled. A single melancholy voice threaded through the air. Then another wolf joined in, deep as a cello, followed by another, its voice shrill and as high as a violin. And then another, and another joined in until a chorus rose up. The sound was so primal, so unnerving, that it penetrated Owen's skin, straight to his marrow. He shivered involuntarily. The wolves could be a mile away, or just beyond the barn, he couldn't tell.

A good time, he decided, to climb into the driver's seat.

When the barn doors swung wide, a dump truck appeared. The Packard was solid steel on heavy-duty wheels; its bed was mounded with hay to disguise the load of sugar destined for stills near Kettle Falls.

Another figure appeared. Pengler, tall and wide shouldered, walked from the barn toward Owen, sitting behind the wheel.

Owen rolled down the driver's window. "Mr. Pengler."

"Owen," he said. "You boys stay where the ice is thick. I've got a lot riding on this delivery."

"Got it." The last thing Owen wanted to do was go through the ice. He left his window rolled down, just to be on the safe side should he need a quick exit.

Jerry drove the truck alongside the Model T. With a big smile, he waved at Owen to follow.

They drove a few miles east, then veered off onto a boat landing and rolled down the embankment onto snow-covered ice. He assured himself, this time of year, the ice was two feet thick. Nothing to worry about.

Wheels crunched as they skirted between islands, following the "ice road" and hints of tire tracks heading east. At a half-football-field distance, Owen followed, glad that the heavy truck helped plow a path through new snow for the Model T. Owen's only job was simply to follow, just in case the sugar-loaded truck hit a bad patch of ice—and unload at their destination.

A thirty-plus-mile journey each way. It was a windless night and a faint ring wavered around the moon, casting enough light to illuminate their path, but not as bright as a spotlight. Owen thought about the fellow found by the dam with a bullet in his back. The last thing he and Jerry needed was to get caught by federal agents out to score a few career points.

As the miles of lake passed by, Owen yawned, forcing his eyes open and fixed on the dump truck's moving silhouette.

Out here, only two summers back, he'd had the crap kicked out of him by a couple of bootleggers. It was the year Prohibition went nationwide, and lots of folks were looking for opportunities to make a few extra bucks. Stills sprouted up everywhere. The day Owen found seven wooden crates of scotch whiskey in a caved-in root cellar, he wasn't surprised, but he didn't exactly know what to do either. His family was scraping by. On the other hand, booze was the very thing that had ruined his father for so many years. He walked away from the stash, but with each step, the old saying "Never look a gift horse in the mouth" clanged in his head. He thought about how a horse's teeth grow and crowd with age, making the front teeth protrude over time. Finding that stash was like getting a horse as a gift, and then peering into the animal's mouth to determine its age and whether it was up to your standards. In other words, a guy should be grateful when a gift comes his way. He decided if the stash had not been claimed, then he had no choice but to see it as an opportunity.

Eventually, on boat deliveries to summer island residents and tourists, he added bottles of Canadian whiskey with fresh milk, butter, and cheese that he kept on ice in a seat bench. But word got around, and after Owen made deliveries east of Brule Narrows, two guys jumped him. They said they'd let him live if he returned the rest of the whiskey—and the money he'd made from their inventory. When Dad asked, "Where'd you get the shiners?" Owen told him. True to their word, the bootleggers showed up at the creamery to collect their remaining hooch. Dad stood beside Owen, rifle cradled in his arms where the bootleg-gers could see it. They took the four remaining cases and the cash from Owen's outstretched hand.

"That's it, then?" Owen asked.

One of the men grunted, and they left. To his credit, Dad never mentioned the incident again. Thinking of that time, an ache suddenly filled Owen. He wished things between him and his father had ended differently. But there was nothing that could be done. Dad was gone. And whether he approved or not, those Studeys were rollin' in soon. Another gift horse he would be stupid to refuse. He'd keep the creamery going, but he'd find a way to build his own future, too.

He drove on, hitting an occasional ice ridge that rattled his teeth. They'd covered ten miles, at most, with another twenty to go. He kept his eyes on the phantom truck ahead.

Somewhere east of Diamond Island the dump truck turned sharply, heading closer and closer to a steep island.

"Cripes, Jerry! Where are you going?" Owen shouted. His friend must have fallen asleep at the wheel. Owen honked.

The truck kept moving and cut around the southeast side of the island.

"This is not the time for a shortcut!"

Owen had no choice but to follow. As he rounded the point, the truck was nowhere to be seen.

It had vanished.

"What the heck!" Owen scanned the expanse of ice toward Canada. He looked to the right and a cluster of islands. He hoped his eyes were playing a trick on him, but honest to God, there was no truck.

Then he spotted the dark patch ahead. Open water framed with jagged ice.

He put on his brakes. Go any closer and he'd be down, too.

"Nooo!" He pounded on the steering wheel and swore.

Owen clutched the medal at his neck. "Don't let Jerry go this way. Please . . ."

The patch of water quivered like molten silver.

Who knows how far the truck was down . . . still sinking . . . If Jerry had his window open, maybe he'd escape. Maybe climb out.

Time became a sharp-edged blade pressed under his throat.

He couldn't breathe.

Couldn't feel.

Couldn't think.

He couldn't dive down and save his friend in pitch-dark, deep, and freezing water.

In frustration, he pounded the steering wheel and swore again.

And then as he stared, a head bobbed up, a hand and another hand, swinging wildly toward the ice.

Owen leapt from Jerry's car. He took off his jacket and, holding it in one hand, lowered himself to his belly and crept across the ice to the open water. The ice beneath him protested, and he was certain he felt a crack run under him, from his head to his toes.

"Jerry!" he called, inching closer. "Hang on! Grab my jacket!"

Hand over hand, Jerry hit the surrounding ice with sharp cracking sounds. Ice picks! He had ice picks! Lots of folks carried them in their pockets when they went out on the ice, just in case. With handheld picks, Jerry slowly pulled himself forward onto the edge of ice, and then kept inching steadily closer and closer to where Owen stretched out. When he was in range, Owen tossed his jacket toward Jerry. It fell short. He tried again, and this time, Jerry latched on and held fast.

Owen began moving backward, pulling his friend's weight.

Jerry wheezed and coughed and moaned.

When they drew closer to the Model T—Owen felt certain they were far enough from where the truck had gone through—he rose to his feet, grabbed Jerry under his arms, and dragged him to the car. Jerry's hands were bare and icy. His hat was gone and water dripped from his head. Owen tossed him like a sack of potatoes onto the passenger seat.

"Jerry, you scared the living daylights out of me!"

"Gotcha," Jerry managed, as if he had just pulled off the biggest prank in the world, but then he fell silent.

Owen threw his jacket around Jerry's body. He removed his own hat and put it on his friend's wet head. He slammed Jerry's door, raced around to the driver's side, and climbed in.

With a roar of the engine, he sped back toward town, talking at Jerry, smacking his shoulder every now and then, trying to keep him awake. Engine heat spilled through the flow vents, barely warming the car's floorboards.

Not until his tires reached the mainland did Owen roll up his window.

Not until he passed the turnoff to Pengler's farm did the enormity of it all hit him.

Not only had he nearly lost his best friend, they'd lost Pengler's heavy-duty truck and all its costly cargo.

7

Tipper met him at the door, thumping his tail hard against the table leg. He licked Owen's hand, as if he understood the anguish Owen had gone through and had been waiting for him to make it safely home.

"It's okay," Owen whispered. When he'd dropped off Jerry, a light had gone on in the Melnyks' house. Owen helped Jerry—skin blue-gray and eyes half-mast—into his house.

"Too much drink?" Mr. Melnyk asked. "Rotgut no good."

"Not rotgut," Owen said. He said they'd been out walking on the lake when Jerry went through the ice. It was almost true.

With relief, Owen drove away, knowing Jerry's family would take care of him.

He yawned and shivered, suddenly aware he was chilled to the bone. He was glad for a warm home. "C'mon, Tipper. Let's get some sleep."

In moments, Tipper was snoring softly at the foot of his bed. Owen lit the small lamp, took paper and a pen from the bedside shelf, and began to write.

Dear Sadie,

Then he held his pen above the paper, unsure how to continue. He wanted to tell her how much he longed for her, how tonight, more than ever, he realized how in an instant, you and those you love can be pulled under. Just one bad decision. Just one simple error in judgment. And what you love—who you love—could be gone.

He closed his eyes, seeing the open water again, feeling sharp panic run through his body. What if Jerry hadn't surfaced? What then?

He stared at the two words and simple comma on the paper:

Dear Sadie,

No, he couldn't say all that. Finally, eyes heavy, he turned down the lamp and drifted off. His sleep was anything but peaceful. He woke often, reliving the sense of utter helplessness he felt when the truck disappeared. And when he slept, his dreams were nightmares. He dove underwater trying to rescue Jerry and bumped into his friend's lifeless body. Hold your breath! Hang on to his arm! He kicked upward, but as he reached the shaft of moonlight, he bumped into a ceiling of ice. The hole had iced over, and he slammed his fist against it. It wouldn't break. He tried again and lost his grip on Jerry, who slipped away, down again . . . He woke in a sweat, tangled in the sheets, his head crammed against the headboard.

At dawn he was relieved the night was over. Tipper stood up and shook himself before hopping off the bed. Quickly combing his fingers through his hair, Owen glanced in the small mirror above his narrow dresser. He looked terrible. Ashen pools formed under his eyes. His lips were chalky dry. Between his eyebrows, a line of worry. What a night—one he didn't want to relive.

His stomach grumbled and he headed downstairs.

"Mom, where's Erling?" Owen asked, taking a seat at the kitchen table with his brothers. Her back was to him, her ruffled apron tied in a bow as she fried eggs and turned sausage patties on the stove.

"He didn't want to wake you, Owen. He said you came in pretty late. So he headed off to do the morning run."

"Huh." Weirdly, Owen felt Erling had filled in for him, the way Owen used to cover for Dad. It struck him with a pang of guilt. He'd taken stupid risks, and for what? To help Pengler keep booze flowing. Speakeasys and blind pigs can't operate without importing booze from Canada or making their own with necessary ingredients. He'd agreed to unload sugar, but what of his responsibility to his brothers? He was as reckless as Dad had been in those early years. Just a different kind of reckless.

"Mom, Erling has school today," Owen said. "You let him cover for me when he needs to be at school?"

His mother turned. "Owen, he's fifteen. You think I can stop him? You were sound asleep."

He nodded and held back everything about last night. He needed to go see Jerry. See if he'd caught pneumonia. And they had to talk. They were in a fix. They had to tell Pengler what happened. And he wasn't going to be happy.

He walked across the street to the creamery just as Erling pulled in with the Jensen Creamery truck.

"Hey, Erling," Owen said with a nod. "I got the rest of this covered. Ride shotgun. I'll drop you off at school."

Erling seemed to study him, as if to assess if Owen was wallpapered or not.

"No," Erling said. "We'll unload together, then you can drop me off."

"Fair enough. I'm heading out that way anyway."

As they worked, Owen vowed to keep Erling in school. His brother wanted to play professional baseball someday. Well, why shouldn't he? If he could stay in school, finish high school, then he'd have a shot at a baseball scholarship. Play college ball for a few years . . . He laughed at himself. He was sounding just like Dad, thinking he knew what was best for someone else.

On the outskirts of Ranier, they rolled to a stop, and Erling lumbered off like a moose toward the square building and schoolhouse door. From the snow- and ice-covered grounds rose a flagpole and American flag, flapping in the breeze.

Behind the school were two outhouses. Girls and Boys. When Dad had informed him he was needed full-time at the creamery, Owen took out his frustration on the last day of school—with the help of Jerry and Netty Storm—to tip over the boys' three-holer. Miss Engerson made them upright it, replace the shingles, put on a new door, and give it two coats of fresh paint. When they were finished, the outhouse had never looked better. Only two years ago he'd been at school, but it seemed like ages.

With a shrug, he pulled back onto the road and began making his way toward the Melnyks' home. It pained him. He loved learning. He loved studying about ancient civilizations—Greek, Egyptian, Roman, Viking; about changes in society—feudalism, the Renaissance, and the Age of Enlightenment. He was fascinated by conflict and why social upheaval happened—the Napoleonic Wars, the War of 1812, the French Revolution, and the more recent Civil War. He loved learning how individuals changed the world, from Marco Polo to Ben Franklin to Abe Lincoln and Harriet Beecher Stowe. He loved debating recent events—how and why we got into the Great War and what was gained and lost; why Russia had undergone its own recent revolution. He even liked tests and competing against himself for high scores. He'd "borrowed" a few textbooks and novels from school, always intending to return them. He read before falling asleep. He knew he was reading late into the night whenever Tipper stopped snoring to lift his head, as if to ask, *You're still reading?*

At the "Blacksmith" sign, a few miles southwest of International Falls, Owen followed the snow-rutted road alongside the barbed wire fence. The pasture was devoid of cattle; no livestock huddled near spruce trees or hidden in thickets. Months would pass before cows would be out on pasture again. Until then, the Melnyks kept their live-stock in barns and paddocks—less tempting for wolves and coyotes. In a separate paddock, the two dappled drafts—

Daisy and Dot—stood side by side, dozing. With them, a new horse—a thick-coated sorrel with a white blaze and angular head raised high—paced a worn path beside the length of wood fence. He would have been a looker, but he was missing an ear.

The Melnyks' clapboard home towered, its roof peak nearly as high as the top of a nearby spruce. Most homes in the country were one-room cabins or shacks. But the Melnyks, who had immigrated from Ukraine, were an industrious lot. Mr. Melnyk eventually purchased land and now had eight kids.

Owen knocked on the door, and it opened instantly.

"Hello, Owen," Mrs. Melnyk said, her hair in two braids atop her head. "Come, come in."

He stepped into the kitchen, leaving his muddy boots behind.

"You want to see Jerry." A statement, not a question, that carried with it a bit of finger wagging. "Upstairs."

"How's he doing?"

"Last time he took to bed, he was breaking devil horse for Furstads. In bed two whole days."

Owen just nodded, then headed toward the staircase, glancing at the wall displaying a crucifix, an icon, and a photo of a soldier, Jerry's older brother, Joseph, who never returned from the trenches in Europe. For a moment, Owen thanked God—again—that Jerry survived last night. He wouldn't wish the loss of another son on the Melnyks. Losing a son to war was one thing, but losing one to bootlegging?

Beside the photo stood the glass-doored cabinet, filled, as always, with a changing assortment of Ukrainian Easter eggs. Displayed like candy in various glass bowls, the eggs were uniquely and intricately designed—reds and blacks, oranges and blues, deep greens and pale yellows—each painted in patterns that hinted at a foreign world left behind. Mrs. Melynk created them and sold them to shops.

"Owen," Mrs. Melnyk said. "When you go, you take one—for your mother. We are sorry about your father."

"Thank you, Mrs. Melnyk. That's very kind."

Jerry's bedroom door was ajar, and Owen peeked in before entering. Jerry was asleep.

"Hey, Jer."

Jerry murmured, his skin pale. His eyes flashed open, bloodshot. "Hey."

Owen walked to the window. A few dozen cows ambled around a towering pile of hay in the paddock. Ravens cawed on the leafless birch tree outside the window, then flapped off. It nearly killed him last night, those moments thinking Jerry was gone. He turned and said, "Just wanted to see if you're okay."

"A little fever." He pulled the blanket up to his chest, and the motion sent him into a coughing fit. "And," he began, then spat into a handkerchief. "I'm still getting a little lake water out of my lungs. I'm gonna be fine. But what are you gonna tell Pengler?"

"Me? You mean you. *You're* gonna tell him that you veered off the main ice road. I know you were trying to save time—"

"I'm not telling him that."

"You lost his truck, Jer," Owen said, keeping his voice down. "And the load of sugar. You think he's gonna just brush that off, like it doesn't matter?"

Jerry wagged his head, laughed, and started coughing again. "Hey, out East, the stakes of running booze were—" He marked an imaginary spot above his head with his hand. "But here, it's safe as a rabbit's den. Here you get a few feds; back there it's an army of 'em. Seriously, Owen. It's good work and good money. Pengler's gonna figure it's part of doing business, that's what I think. I'll bet he's making money hand over fist."

"You went through the ice, Jer. You could be dead by now."

"Yeah, well, that's this lake. She's a goddess. She demands something in return for all that beauty."

He was right. Every year, a few souls paid the price by breaking through and never surfacing.

"Jer, we're the ones who are gonna pay a price," Owen said. "And I'm not facing Pengler alone. So get outta bed. Better he hear it with you looking half-dead. He might show us some mercy. Besides, you gotta get your Model T. It's parked at my house. I told my mom you were too wall-papered to drive."

As Jerry climbed into the passenger side of the truck, the new horse snorted and whinnied, then charged back and forth along the fence, sending up a fountain of snow and dirt in his wake.

Owen lifted his chin in question. "Where'd you get that horse?"

In the light of morning, Jerry sported a light growth of stubble on his pale face. His eyes were bloodshot. "A guy claimed he was too flighty for draft work, so I got him for a song. Basically rescued him from a life of pulling logs. Rode him all the way home from Duluth."

"What happened to his ear?"

"Guess another horse bit it clear off."

By the time Owen pulled up to the White Turtle Club, Jerry had fallen asleep with his head against the passenger door. Owen shook his shoulder. "C'mon." Then they headed inside and asked for Mr. Pengler.

"I'll fetch him," Izzy said. "Just take a seat in the restaurant."

"Ah, this isn't a conversation for the public—"

Izzy peeked in the restaurant. "We're between break-fast and lunch. You can—" She pointed to the soda foun-tain. Owen and Jerry went through the hidden door and waited in the blind pig.

8

"YOU DID WHAT?" MR. PENGLER SHOT UP FROM HIS CHAIR the moment Owen told him what had happened. "You lost the Packard? The cargo? Everything?"

"We're alive," Jerry said, then coughed and spat into his handkerchief.

Pengler's eyes narrowed like a timberwolf's, assessing its prey. "That sugar was meant to go straight into production. You know how many stills are out there? You know how hard it is to keep up with demand?"

"Ten? Twenty?" Jerry guessed.

"It's not a question, Jerry!" Pengler swore. "You think folks south of here are gonna be happy? Think they're gonna say, 'Hey, Harvey, good ole boy, we don't care. It's just money'?"

Out of the corner of his eye, Owen noticed the bartender reach down under the counter, as if he might be going for a gun. He didn't know what Pengler was capable of when pushed into a corner. He sure didn't want to find out.

"Well?" Pengler pressed. "Think that's what they're gonna say?"

Jerry opened his mouth to speak, then must have thought better of it.

Owen piped up. "They're gonna want what they paid for."

A look of relief passed over Pengler's eyes, as if he was glad they'd come to some quick understanding. "Exactly, Owen. You're smart. You know how things work. So when I total up the costs of this loss, you boys are in pretty deep. The dump truck. The sugar. The loss of production." He closed his eyes, and his eyelids twitched as he calculated. Finally, he nodded to himself, opened his eyes and said, "Let's just make it an even three and a half grand."

"Thirty-five hundred dollars?" Owen choked, as if he'd just been slugged in the gut. He did the math. That was the same as ten Ford Model Ts.

"Afraid so."

"Where are we going to come up with that kind of money?" Jerry blurted.

"You're resourceful young men. You'll figure it out." Then Pengler stood and added, "I'll be generous. I'll give you two months from today. That's after the horse race. Jerry, I heard you're a good rider. You ride my horse and win, I'll cut you in on ten percent of the winnings. You could make up to six hundred—maybe as much as a thousand of what you boys owe me." He walked over to the bartender. "Pour these boys a shot of whiskey. I believe they're going to need it." And then he left.

When the bartender clunked two shots down in front of them, Owen was tempted. He needed something to calm the trembling in his gut and hands. But drinking at this hour of the day wasn't going to help his problems go away. Feeling as bad as he did, one shot might lead to two or three—and only make things worse.

"Thanks," Jerry said to the bartender, as if this was just any other day. "Hey, did ya catch all that?"

The bartender nodded. "I don't miss much."

"So, what will happen," Owen asked, "if we don't make Pengler's deadline?"

The bartender smiled. "If I was you, I wouldn't wanna find out. He's not a-running a creamery, if you know what I mean."

Jerry knocked back both shots. "Well, what's our next move?"

"Heck if I know. This isn't just another card game. Jerry, from what you were saying, you know more about this business than you've let on. You tell me, Jerry. Why didn't you think? Why didn't you think this might happen when you took a shortcut? You know the current's unpredictable around the islands!" He slammed the flat of his hand on the table. "You tell me how we're gonna come up with that kind of money!"

Jerry started coughing, pulled his handkerchief from his pants pocket, and spat.

Owen fell silent. Elbows on the table, he pressed his forehead into his open palm. He was disgusted at himself for thinking that anything related to bootlegging could be simple. How could he have been such a fool? Dad's words pounded over and over in his head. *Think you know everything about everything, son. Don't say I didn't warn you.*

"When your Studebakers get here soon, let's hope they sell like hotcakes," Jerry offered.

"If . . . maybe. You know what I think?"

"Shoot," Jerry said.

Owen motioned for them to leave. He didn't want the bartender listening in.

They climbed into the creamery truck parked outside. "We need to find a horse faster than Ace-in-the-Hole," Owen said. "You heard Pengler. If he'd cut his rider ten percent, then the winning purse must be at least ten thousand dollars. His horse wins every year. He's been unbeatable."

"One Ear," Jerry shot back, a smile spreading across his lips and reaching his eyes.

"Not just any horse," Owen said. "We need a horse that can win."

"I know. I'm serious. That horse is lightning on long legs."

Owen stared out the window, which was beginning to

fog on the inside. "I know he doesn't look like much," Jerry continued, "but if I can ride him and work him between now and the race, I'm telling you—there's a chance. I just know there have been moments. Never been on a horse with that gear. Part of me wonders if he was used once on racetracks. All I'm saying is that if I ask him for speed, he delivers."

Owen couldn't afford to take risks. Just because Jerry had an idea didn't mean it was a good one. "You're not being overly optimistic?"

Jerry crossed his arms. "He stands a chance. Honest. Besides, what have we got to lose? Maybe an entry fee? If he loses, we still have to come up with the money, right?" He laughed, but it wasn't convincing.

Owen started up the creamery truck and drove across the tracks to where Jerry's Model T waited. "So if you ride One Ear," Owen said as he parked, "Pengler will have to find someone else to ride Ace-in-the-Hole. He's not going to be happy with us, especially when you show up on a different horse."

"That's his problem," Jerry said, hopping out. He started hacking again and spat on the ground. "I'll tell him I have pneumonia and can't ride. I'll dust off a saddle, start working One Ear. I'll do what I can to get him ready for the race. You work on getting those Studeys here."

By the third week in February, clouds settle low and dark above the village.

Day after day, snow falls.

Sometimes it's just a light dusting. Other times it drops buckets of snow on every branch and limb, every car and rooftop. A quiet settles, punctuated by shovels clanging, the muffled voices of children, and the gargled call of ravens.

When the clouds move on, they take the warmer air with them, leaving everything deeper in snow. The skies clear, nighttime temperatures plummet to well below zero, and you brace for another cold snap.

9

AT THE KITCHEN TABLE, BEFORE THE REST OF THE HOUSE stirred, Owen added three lumps of sugar to his coffee, wondering how he'd blundered so badly. Two weeks had passed since they'd lost the truck. Since then, Jerry had started working One Ear in the pasture. Owen, for his part, had been on the phone with the inventory manager at Studebaker Company, who assured him they would have his vehicles ready to ship—any day now. If Owen could get them on the lot, he could start selling them. Each day meant waiting, and it was driving him crazy.

He wished he could make a train trip down and back to St. Paul. He drummed his spoon lightly on the table. He needed to see Sadie face-to-face to put his worries about her to rest. Besides, through her work with the Wilderness Society, she knew several attorneys. Maybe he could ask for advice on how to get out from under a bootlegger's thumb—where he could borrow a quick three and a half grand. Wasn't that what attorneys did? Help folks who found themselves in some sort of trouble? He stopped himself. More than a long shot, it was pure folly.

He exhaled a soft whistle.

Forget everything else, forget the debt, forget the creamery. It was Sadie he needed to see. He'd get down there and back quickly, but with so much snow the past few days, he was going to need help.

Getting to the outhouse had been an expedition. There was no going anywhere until someone started shoveling out.

With a huff, he set his spoon down and climbed the steep stairs to the stuffy attic. His brothers were all sawing logs. He felt bad for them. Dad hadn't been perfect, but at least Owen had grown up with a father around.

He leaned over the lanky shape on the end cot, surprised at how much Erling had grown into Dad's footsteps. Literally. Erling had grown into Dad's size 13 boots.

"Erling," Owen whispered, tapping his brother's shoulder. "Hey."

His brother groaned and rolled over.

"C'mon, get up. I'll wait downstairs for you."

After a shuffling of feet overhead, Erling appeared at the base of the stairs, tucking his red wool shirt over his long johns and into his trousers. "Got a lotta snow?"

"Yep." Owen pointed out the window at the brick creamery building across the street. High mounds crested over the street and right up to the entry door. "I need your help making the rounds."

"Can't you skip it for a day?"

Owen leveled an "are you kidding?" look at him. "You think cows and chickens are going to stop producing just because it snowed?"

Erling yawned and shook his head of hair like a yellow lab after a swim. "You're gonna get stuck."

Owen smiled. "Yep. That's why you're coming with me, so you can dig us out."

"School's probably closed today anyway," Erling said, lifting a dish towel off yesterday's fresh loaves of bread on the counter. He found a knife, cut himself a hunk, stuffed his mouth, and held out another one-inch-thick slice to Owen.

"Thanks."

Mom's door was still closed. "Hey, I'll make breakfast," Owen said. He fried eggs, sunny-side up, and thick strips of bacon, and it apparently didn't take much time for the scent to reach the attic and tickle the noses of the rest of his brothers.

In moments, they all plopped into chairs and Owen dished up their raised plates.

Erling smiled. "You know how to sling 'em!"

An hour later, under a brilliant sun, Owen and Erling were busy shoveling out around the house and creamery when the back door opened and the four younger brothers spilled out, bundled from head to toe, two carrying skates and two grabbing toboggans from the side of the house.

Mom leaned out the door, huddled in her plaid robe. "Keep those hats on!"

And then they were off, headed to the local sliding hill and ice rink.

Sweat formed under Owen's cap as he shoveled. Lately it was all he could do to stay on top of things. Along with the creamery work, he'd spent the past week and a half keeping a bonfire going at night behind Pengler's hotel. It wasn't a prime location, but the price was right, as Pengler reminded him: "You clean the junk piles outta there, you can use it until you can afford a location of your own." He'd burned old boards and debris. Next spring, Owen would have a small mountain of ash to clean up before the rains came and turned the lot into a muddy black mess. But for now, he had a rock-hard frozen lot that needed to be ready for a fleet of Studebaker six-cylinder models: the Light Six, Big Six, and Special Six. After he and Erling did rounds and finished up at the creamery, they'd have to clear the lot, too.

"I'm going heavy on Light Six models," Owen said to Erling. "More affordable, but still plenty solid."

"Yeah?" Erling replied, not losing a beat as he shoveled snow from around the creamery truck: bending, scooping, and tossing it aside.

"Come spring," Owen said, "I'm betting it'll be my home run model."

Erling stood tall, stretching out his low back, then took his shovel and mimicked swinging it at a baseball. "Only home run I'm hoping for," he said, taking a swing, "is the real thing. Did I tell ya? Babe Ruth's doing a national tour. Big cities, except for one stop in a little town. Know where?"

"I don't know. International Falls? Ranier?"

"Nope. Sleepy Eye, Minnesota."

"Where the heck is that?"

"Southern part of the state somewhere. And I'm going. I'm going to catch a train and see him."

"Is that right?"

Erling shrugged. "I just want to watch him and Bob Meusel play with a couple local teams."

"And what'll you do if you meet him?"

Erling shrugged. "Heck, I don't know. But you know you're looking at the next Babe Ruth, don'tcha?"

Owen reached down, packed together a snowball, and threw it. Erling was ready and smacked it into a zillion flakes of dazzling white.

They spent all day following horse-drawn plows and truck plows around the county as they cleared the main roads. Farms on side roads were going to have to wait until the next day. As Owen and Erling drove the half-filled creamery truck back into Ranier, the sun sank low in the West.

"Stuck seven times," Erling recounted, "with one smashed crate of eggs from your wipe-out." He laughed. "You were funnier than Charlie Chaplin!"

"Glad I could provide you with a little entertainment in your sorry life," Owen joked in return. His elbow still hurt from hitting a patch of ice as he'd carried stacked egg crates to the truck. He tried to save the eggs by taking the fall, but the top crate went flying up as his legs flew out—and just after he went down, the crate and some of its contents landed on top of him. He glanced in the side mirror. Egg was still clumped in his hair. If he'd just kept his cap on. He needed a bath. But that would have to wait.

As they drove down Main Street, the sun slipped below a gray and orange horizon. His heart sped up. There, parked just outside the White Turtle, and lined up as if at some beauty contest, were six, seven . . . more than *twelve* beautiful, snow-dusted Studeys. "Erling! Look at 'em! They're here!"

The driver's door of a yellow Light Six opened and out hopped Jerry. He took off his bowler hat and waved it high overhead. Owen honked back from the creamery truck and rolled down his window.

Jerry strutted over to the driver's door, his broad shoulders tucked into a heavy woolen jacket. "Special delivery! Rolled off the last train!" he exclaimed, peering in. "Pengler couldn't reach you, so he called me. Said they were here. So, Mr. Studebaker, where do you want 'em?"

"Behind the White Turtle," Owen said, motioning. "But I haven't had time to shovel it off yet. Gotta unload the creamery truck, and then we'll head right over."

Jerry tilted his head toward the Studeys and their drivers. "Me and the boys are still on duty. We'll get started."

"Thanks, Jer!" Owen called as he shifted the truck back into gear. Iwn double time, he and Erling had the truck unloaded and the separator operating at full tilt. They left Mom and the boys to disinfect milk cans. Then Owen and Erling hurried to the lot behind the hotel, just as Jerry and several guys finished shoveling it.

Under a darkening sky, drivers started up motors and turned on headlights, and then drove around to the lot. After Jerry parked a Studey, he jumped out and clapped Owen on the shoulder. "They're beauties, I tell you."

"I owe you, Jer," Owen said, shaking his head in amazement.

Jerry laughed. "Don't worry, I figure you're going to want an ace mechanic someday! Now, tell us how to park 'em."

"Face 'em this way!" Owen called, motioning to the drivers as if in a dream. One by one, the cars lined up, facing southwest, both for viewing and so the daytime sun might help keep the engines from freezing solid. But to his surprise, there were more cars coming—a half dozen more than he'd ordered. They were gorgeous, but this wasn't what he bargained for. He was already out on a pretty long and precarious limb.

One by one, drivers climbed out and headed inside the White Turtle.

Collar turned up, Owen huddled in his jacket alongside Jerry and Erling. He could barely believe it. He was glad to share this moment with Jerry, his childhood friend, and Erling, his closest brother. Wheels, grills, and running boards sparkled. Cars gleamed with fresh, perfect paint in an array of colors—pale yellow, navy blue, cream, burgundy, black—like jewels in a king's crown.

There was only one other person he wished could be there just then. He'd sweep her right off the floor of the Sweetheart Ball, right out of the arms of Sam-the-Damn-Thoughtful, and spin her around and around, right there under the emerging stars. "All of this is for you," he'd say. "For us!"

Jerry grabbed Owen's arm and tugged. "C'mon, Owen, let's go talk with Pengler." Then he lightly punched Owen's shoulder. "First one's on me—and don't argue. This is big! Time to celebrate!"

"But I don't get it," Owen said, still studying the lot and counting the Studeys again. "There's six more than I ordered."

"Oh, yeah. Pengler's special order." Jerry gave him his lopsided smile. "And lucky you. Heard he's buying a bundle of 'em."

"Really?" How could he have fifty percent more inventory—inventory already spoken for—without knowing anything about it? Whose business was this, anyway? He'd sent a check to Studebaker for the wholesale cost of twelve cars, not eighteen.

Jerry must have read his discontent, understood that he was forcing wide the jaws of this gift horse. "Owen, I tell you, things are heating up every day, with more and more hooch coming down from Canada, all the way from Saskatchewan. Pengler's no fool. It makes sense he's gotta have a bigger fleet to keep it flowing south." Then he tugged Owen's arm. "They're not going anywhere, at least for tonight. And hey, Erling, you coming?"

Erling shrugged. His towering frame seemed too large for his age, certainly too large for his jacket, the sleeves a few inches too short. "No," Erling said. "Go on without me. I'm headin' home."

As Erling turned and disappeared toward the tracks, Owen felt a twinge. He shouldn't have involved his brother in any of this. Erling had always looked up to Owen, and Owen promised himself he'd *never* let his kid brother down.

When Jerry pushed his shoulder, Owen turned away and headed into the White Turtle.

He needed to talk to Pengler.

10

DUCKING AFTER JERRY THROUGH THE SHORT DOOR INTO the White Turtle's blind pig, Owen was met by a wall of smoke and a woman's voice rising from the phonograph. He recognized the singer. It was Elsie Clark cooing, *"those Cry Baby Blues, You're gonna cry . . . baby . . ."*

Owen spotted Pengler at the far end of the room, where a round of applause rose from the group of men at a round table. Pengler pushed back his chair, stood up, and lifted his glass to Owen. "A toast to Ranier's newest businessman! To the beginnings of Owen Jensen's Studebaker business!" Clinking glasses, clapping, and cheering followed.

Owen recognized many of the guys from around Ranier. He'd gone to school with several, and yet there were more than a few new faces in the group, too. Izzy Larson was seated deep in a booth, leaning into the shoulder of Wayne Hopper, a councilman from International Falls.

Yeah, he'd like to celebrate, but how could he when the deal he'd agreed on was already looking skewed? He walked directly to Pengler and whispered in his ear. "There's more Studeys out there than I ordered. What's going on?"

Pengler pulled back a bit, yet beamed a smile, and then clamped his hand on Owen's shoulder, nearly forcing him to take a seat. "Sit. Celebrate. I'll tell you."

Owen complied, while the rest of the room went

back to their own business. Drinking. Smoking. Talking low enough that the lyrics floated above everyone's conversation.

> *Sugar o' mine, You're so refined . . .*
> *You won't do this! Won't do that! Now what's on your mind*
> *Cry Baby Blues, You're gonna die . . . baby . . .*

Then Pengler lit a Lucky Strike, inhaled, and turned away from Owen to one of the drivers on Pengler's other side. The men chatted quietly while Owen waited, as if he were at Pengler's beck and call. Heck, folks had nicknamed E. W. Ennis "King Ed" since he pretty much employed everyone, directly or indirectly, through the paper mill. Maybe it was time to add another king to the county. "King Harvey," Owen thought, King of the Underworld.

Jerry set down two glasses filled with ice cubes and light-amber liquid. "Cheers," he said with a nod, then lifted his own glass and took a drink. Owen didn't touch the whiskey. He needed answers.

Pengler turned. He leaned into Owen, his face inches away, and spoke low; this was between just the two of them. "I went ahead and ordered extra stock. The sooner we can get a dozen here and running, the better. I have inventory to move—"

"I didn't sign up for this. You ordered Studeys without talking to me? Whose business is this, anyway?"

Owen had agreed as part of the loan to convert vehicles for Pengler into "Whiskey Sixes," so coined after the first busts on cars stopped for illegally transporting whiskey from Canada into the United States. The vehicles were rigged to hold greater weight and to handle difficult terrain.

"Settle down. You're selling me extra stock, that's all." Pengler pulled a few folded sheets of paper out from his coat. "Here's the invoice." He laid three sheets out on the table, smoothing out the wrinkles with the palms of his hands. The fine print included wholesale figures and the model names and numbers. "Eighteen Studebakers. All bought wholesale, by you."

"By me?" Owen said. "I ordered twelve, not eighteen."

"Hold on," Pengler replied. He produced a check already written out and handed it to Owen. "I went ahead and made it out to 'Jensen Dealership.'"

Owen stared at the figure on the check. It was payment for a dozen automobiles, but far below full retail prices. He quickly calculated that the amount was enough to pay off a quarter of his dealership loan to Pengler. "Far from full price," Owen said.

"I hoped you'd be happy," Pengler replied. "The way I see it, I'm buying twice the volume from you, so a sizable discount seems only fair."

Though Pengler's smile seemed sincere, Owen nodded cautiously. He swallowed his frustration. He had the feeling that arguing with Pengler wasn't going to change his situation. At this point, the only way out was up. He would have to sell the remaining six cars at full price to make any headway.

Jerry stood off a few feet, then stepped closer. "I still say there's more money in bootlegging than in automobiles."

"Can't do one without the other," Pengler said. "And you gotta mix it up. Automobiles, trains, planes."

"Planes?" Owen asked.

Pengler nodded. "Sure, got a fellow flying my Curtiss Oriole. Gotta keep the feds guessing. Soon as you keep doing it the same way, you're going to get caught."

Owen crossed his arms. "I can't afford to go to jail or prison. My family depends on me."

"You're right," Pengler said. "And I admire that in you. That's exactly why I tell my employees if they get caught, if they're asked to testify about me and refuse, I promise to support their wives and children until they come home from serving time. It's only right. You can't run a business on the backs of your employees. We're either in it together or we're nothing at all."

Then he added, "Just so y'know, I called ahead and asked them to get 'em rigged before shipping. The way I see it, the risk is all on me, and you've just gained one very satisfied customer."

Someone had restarted the song. For a split second, Owen looked in the corner, just to see if Dad were there—a ghost playing the music again, just to haunt him.

> *Cry Baby Blues, you're gonna die . . . baby*
> *Kisses you'll lose as sweet as pie . . . baby*
> *I'm the bestest baby in our neighborhood.*
> *They say I'm not bad, but still I'm not so good.*
> *If I skidoos you're gonna cry . . . Baby,*
> *Those Cry Baby Blues.*

Then Pengler knocked back the last of his drink, pushed away from the table, and announced, "Time to load up! I want the automobiles outta here—long gone before sunrise."

Men in coats and jackets; fedoras, derbies, and bowler hats; coveralls and plaid shirts; gray hair and barely any chin hair, rose from tables like a small mismatched army. Jerry motioned for Owen to follow.

Owen tapped Jerry's shoulder. "Thought you said the Studeys weren't going anywhere tonight."

Jerry smiled. "I'm not the boss. Pengler's ready to load, we load. He says 'Go,' we go."

Instead of ducking back through the door to the restaurant, Jerry headed out another door, straight to the lot out back. In what had been a pine-board wall of photographs of fishermen and their prize catches, a door now swung wide. Owen followed Jerry through it, right out to the lot full of cars, where Pengler's men were already unloading crates of booze from the closest train car at the tracks.

Owen stood back, legs planted wide, arms crossed,

watching. The men formed a human chain and loaded the cargo into a dozen Whiskey Sixes—the ones Owen had apparently just sold. He wanted to feel proud, a sense of accomplishment. Here was an immediate payoff, the price he would pay to get ahead in the world. Going forward, he would stay clear of anything illegal. Everything would turn out in the end.

He lifted his chin and filled his chest with cool air. The temperature was dropping fast.

Yet, no matter how he tried to rally around this moment, all he felt was a dark, profound foreboding.

SLOW
THAW

Most folks say you need a four-inch thickness for walking, six for a horse, and eight for an automobile. But even in the coldest winter, wherever water is moving beneath the ice, a guy has to be careful.

Rainy Lake stretches north and east and south for nearly one hundred miles, and in all that vastness of inlets and island and bays, the water is always moving, some places more swiftly than others. It all flows west: Crane Lake to Kabetogama to Namakan to Rainy. It flows under the lift bridge in Ranier and down Rainy River, pausing at the dam in International Falls to power the paper mill, then dashes headlong to Lake of the Woods and up to Hudson Bay.

All that water.

Miles and miles of water.

11

When roses are red, bees hang around
When they are dead, bees can't be found
There'll be no bees around when your love grows cold.

HE MIGHT BE MILES AWAY, BUT HIS LOVE SURE HADN'T
gone cold.

After a long train ride, with a brief stop in St. Paul for
flowers, Owen reached St. Peter and headed straight to
Johnson Hall. Like a beacon on the Gustavus Adolphus
College campus, the massive brick building glittered with
lights. Owen tapped the brass door knocker, which produced a murmur of female voices within. With the bouquet
of roses in one hand, he finger-combed his hair back from
his eyes with the other, but the waves flopped down again,
nearly covering his right eye.

Sometimes, face-to-face is the only way. Too much had
happened since Dad died. Letters seemed inadequate to
tell Sadie Rose about his latest decision to start his own
business. There was all that. Plus the letter he'd received
just days ago from Sadie Rose, telling him she'd been asked
to the Sweetheart Ball. Not to worry. Right, Owen thought.

The door swung open, and a middle-aged woman with a
tight collar, buttoned to her chin, smiled cautiously. "May
I help you?"

Behind her, several female students clustered together, peering at Owen. All dressed in layers of lace and silky fabrics, they at first reminded him of angels, or a bouquet of faces, some pretty, others not as much. A sweet smell of perfumes and soaps wafted toward him, reminding him that his world of late had been filled with work and brothers and men. But he didn't want the company of just any female.

"Sadie Rose," he said. "I've come a long way to see her."

"It's after visiting hours," the woman replied.

"Oh, come on, Mrs. Dietzman, he's cute!" one of the college girls exclaimed.

"Let him in, please," said another.

At that, Mrs. Dietzman closed the door so that there was only a crack wide enough to reveal her taut face. "I'm sorry, she's not in."

"But you said it's after visiting hours. Where is she?"

"I'm not at liberty to say, exactly."

His heart dropped. "I took the train down from the border. I've come all this way, just to give her these." He held out the flowers as proof. "And to see her just for a little bit."

"I'm sorry," Mrs. Dietzman said again.

"Is she on a date?" he asked, bracing himself for the answer.

"Hey, I'm free tonight," one of the girls shouted, and an eruption of giggling followed.

"Girls," Mrs. Dietzman scolded, and then returned to the door. She must have taken pity on Owen, because she added, "If it helps, I'll tell you she's not on a date. Once a month, she takes the train to St. Paul for a meeting there. She'll be on the return train in the morning. She stays overnight with her family on Summit Avenue. It's a bit unusual, but she claims that these Wilderness Society meetings are educational in nature."

Wilderness Society.

From the start, she'd been interested in supporting Victor's cause to save Rainy Lake and the northern waterways from E. W. Ennis. Ennis, with his industrial ambition and unlimited money, allegedly had plans to turn the eighty-plus-mile-long lake and watershed into a series of sixteen hydropower dams. Owen knew Sadie cared about protecting the islands and inlets from high levels of flooding. If Ennis got his way, the grand lake would turn into a giant bathtub—a reservoir—all with the purpose of keeping his mills and expanding empire thriving. But Owen hadn't a clue that Sadie was staying overnight once a month to attend Victor's meetings.

He gripped the base of the bouquet as his hands dropped to his sides. "I know all about these meetings. I'm from Ranier."

"Washington State?"

"No, up north. Near International Falls. These meetings, they're about the wilderness there. Trying to protect it."

The woman nodded politely, but the door was now closing. Owen pushed the toe of his boot in the door. "The meeting. Do you know where they meet?" He glanced at his watch. "If I catch the last train north to St. Paul, maybe . . ."

"Young man, I have no idea," Mrs. Dietzman answered, this time glancing down at his boot with a frown. "And please remove your foot from this door, or I'll have to get security."

"The basement of the Yangley Building!" one of the students called from behind. Then she wedged her rosy face just under Mrs. Dietzman's. "They meet in the basement. She said meetings sometimes go half the night!"

"Thanks," Owen said and grinned back at her. Perfect! He could meet up with Sadie and bend the ear of one of the attorneys, all in one visit. He removed his foot from the door. It closed with a resounding thud. He spun away. Racing ran down the sloping campus toward the river and depot, he caught the last train heading north as it began to chug out of the station. He found an open seat, drew a deep breath, and dropped his head into the bouquet of roses.

An unmatchable fragrance. He just hoped she wasn't getting roses from other suitors at Gustavus. Or from the score of attorneys she met with each month. Or the handsome Harvard-educated Victor Guttenberg.

Vic Guttenberg.

From the first time Owen had met Victor on Falcon Island, they had always gotten along swell. Owen knew that Victor would rather be on his island than in St. Paul, yet he sacrificed his own wishes for the wilderness he was determined to protect. He was a decent fellow, but that didn't stop a spark of jealousy from igniting in Owen's gut. What if Sadie's interest in him had become something more? After all, Victor was a Harvard grad. He'd explored vast stretches of wilderness by canoe, all the way up to Hudson Bay, with muscles to prove it. He was articulate, a violinist, and a captivating storyteller. What did Owen have to offer in comparison?

The train swayed and clattered alongside the Minnesota River. Mile by mile, Owen clenched his jaw, willing the train to move faster. He had to try to find the meeting before it was over. It was as if he'd grown short of breath these past weeks. He needed to see her just to fill his lungs again.

When the train at last crossed the Mississippi River and slowed to a stop in downtown St. Paul, Owen gripped the handrail, ready to jump off. Under the cavernous ceiling of Union Depot, he hurried out a door and into the crisp night air.

He checked his pocket watch; the hands read 9:32. The girl at the dormitory said the meetings went "half the night," but that was all a matter of perspective. He had to hustle.

From the window of a horse-drawn cab, Owen peered at patrons as they flowed from the Shubert Theater. In the distance, gold gilt horses dotted the massive dome of the state capitol. Around another street, he spotted the St. Paul Cathedral topping another hill. Everything about the city was grand.

The cab pulled up to the Yangley; Owen paid the driver and stepped out onto the slushy street. In the upper stories of the towering brick building the windows were dark. He wondered if he had the right place. From what he could see, there was nothing going on. He stepped up to the entrance doors of heavy wood and glass, but they were locked. A white-haired doorman limped from a bellman's counter inside, where a small lamp burned softly.

The door cracked open.

"Young man," the doorman said, "this building is closed up tight for the night."

"I'm part of a meeting," Owen ventured in a whisper, hoping that if there was a password needed, he could come up with whatever it might be. "The name Victor Guttenberg? Does that mean anything to you?"

"Ah, perhaps," the elderly man replied. "And you are?"

"Owen Jensen."

"Wait here," the man said, locking the doors before turning away.

Owen waited as the man disappeared into the shadows. Growing impatient, he glanced up and down the street. With a clunk, the door was again unlocked.

"Come in," the doorman said. "And forgive me for making you wait in the cold."

"I—" Owen began, but stopped short.

Several feet beyond the door stood Sadie Rose. He absorbed her in one glance. She cut a sleek silhouette, with a tailored jacket and skirt that flared just below her knees.

Her legs curved at her calves and tapered to slim ankles in stylish heels. Her felt hat, with a tawny brown ribbon and single pheasant feather, dipped slightly over her right eye. At only eighteen years old, she wore a simple air of confidence the way some women wore diamonds.

"Owen?" she said, as if she was trying to figure out who he was, suddenly appearing out of nowhere. Her curls glistened, framing her face and dark eyes, wide with surprise. She stared at him, at a loss for words. "This is just so unexpected. What—what are you doing here? Is something wrong?"

He strode straight up to her, wrapped his arms around her waist and lifted her off the ground, and kissed her briefly. "I just had to see you."

She stepped back and looked up at him. "It's just so odd," she said quietly. "You took me by surprise. We're in the middle of an important meeting."

Her reaction stung. He'd taken a risk surprising her, but even with her plans to attend a dance with someone else, he'd expected she'd be happy. Not that she had to leap into his arms, but this? "Important," he repeated.

She nodded, her eyebrows drawn. "You know these meetings are quite secretive. I'm not sure how the others will feel about your knowing about them. I must have let it slip and mentioned this location, otherwise how—"

"The girls at your hall told me," he said.

"Oh."

Her face flushed. "I'm not great at keeping secrets, apparently."

"No, but I am. I won't tell another soul," he assured her, placing his hand briefly on his heart. Then he reached for her hand.

It was warm, soft, and delicate. And the familiarity of her skin made him feel that everything could go back to normal. "Sadie, how about if you and me, we just head out and find someplace where we can talk, be alone."

She glanced back toward the elevator door and then turned to him. "Owen, I am terribly sorry to put you off, but I committed to this meeting. You understand, don't you? I'm part of it. You must know I'm keen on you, but right now—" She leaned forward, kissed him, and then pulled her hand from his. "I'm needed downstairs."

He was taken aback. "And you think I don't need you?" His words carried a hint of bitterness.

Her lips tightened, as if to hold back what she really wanted to say. Maybe there was already more between her and this Sam fella than she'd let on in her letter.

"My dad died," he blurted.

"Oh no!" she said. "So that's why you came straight here, without notice. When?" She tilted her head at him, then stepped closer and hugged him.

"Nearly two weeks ago," he said, breathing in the sweet scent of her freshly shampooed hair. He rested the top of his chin on her head.

She shifted and looked at him. "Two weeks? But why didn't you tell me right away?"

"I tried, but I could never get through on the line. When I tried to write about it, I just couldn't."

She nodded. "What happened?"

"Heart attack. Died in his sleep."

"Owen, I'm so sorry. I truly am." She threw her arms around his waist. "How terrible for you," she murmured into his shoulder. "I know you weren't always close, but he was your father. You were lucky to have him beside you all those years."

For a few moments longer, Owen savored her closeness. He kissed the top of her forehead lightly. "I've missed you. I had to see you."

She nodded, then again glanced at the elevator, as if remembering her greater commitments. "Oh, I feel terrible, but I must get back. Or . . . join us if you promise to be a bystander. It's all young lawyers, and they are risking their jobs to meet like this. That's why downstairs . . . and with candles."

Owen rested his eyes on her. She had no idea how absolutely beautiful she was. And from head to stylish toe, she was dressed as smartly as any young woman in the Twin Cities. Of course she'd captivated the attention of that clarinetist. And she no doubt was winning the admiration of these young attorneys, as well as Victor Guttenberg.

His thoughts were like oxygen to low-burning embers. He seethed with frustration. If he went down to their secretive meeting, there was no telling what he might say or do. How could he watch her in the soft glow of candle-light without wanting to have her to himself? How could he bear to know that she met with these men, taking notes or whatever she did, every single month? He had thought she was his, that she'd promised her love to him. But maybe he'd been wrong to assume such a thing. Here he stood in his jacket and wool cap. While downstairs, those attorneys were likely sporting the latest suits and spouting the latest in political news and gossip. Even Victor, with his Harvard experience, probably left his wool shirt behind for something a bit dressier. He was always entertaining and artic-ulate, no matter the setting. No, if Owen showed up at that meeting, he'd be a damn fish out of water.

The fire in him burned hotter. Everything primal in him wanted to grab her, tell her to get her coat and boots, and tell her she was taking the train north with him. Tell her that "wilderness" was endless and it was never going to disappear. But what about him? He was standing there, right in front of her, his heart outstretched in his hands. He wouldn't wait around forever. He held his emotions on a tight leash.

"No, you go to your meeting," he said, his voice gruffer than he'd intended. "Don't worry, I didn't make this trip just for you. I had other business anyway." There was no point now in asking for help from her attorney friends. "I'm heading back," he said. "Just go back to your important meeting."

"Owen, please," she began, hurt flashing in her eyes.

Before she could walk away from him, he spun away and strode out the entrance door. Outside, he refused to look back and set off like a man on his way up. Head high. A purposeful stride. He filled his lungs with air, damp and chill, and exhaled puffs of white as he followed the city streets back to Union Depot.

And that's when he remembered. He'd completely forgotten the bouquet of roses on his seat in the horse cab. After all the effort he'd gone through to find her fresh flowers, and he'd blown that, too.

"Wouldn't have made any difference," he muttered, as he stepped inside the depot's vast emptiness. A policeman strolled the corridor, whistling as he twirled his nightstick. Owen found an empty bench. He didn't dare lie down, for fear of looking like a tramp or vagrant.

He let his mind drift.

He was only five or six years older than Owen, but Victor Guttenberg had accomplished so much in a short time. He'd come north from Iowa. Had his own island on Rainy Lake. An explorer. Heck, he'd paddled clear up to Hudson Bay with his Ojibwa friend, Billy Bright, and back; the first white man to make the journey. And now, Victor had gone from standing up locally against E. W. Ennis's plan to build dams that would change the natural pathways of a long chain of lakes—to taking his fight to St. Paul and beyond.

It was a long shot to think Victor could actually stop Ennis's industrial might—it was like Jack and the beanstalk and the all-powerful giant—but Owen admired Victor for trying.

In comparison, what was he doing with *his* life? Keeping a creamery going, a roof over the heads of his mother and brothers. Starting a business in the lot behind the White Turtle. And hanging over it all was a new debt—thirty-five hundred dollars—due in six weeks.

In contrast to the chilly, echoing train terminal, a memory surfaced of a sunny afternoon last summer on Falcon Island with Victor, Sadie, and Trinity Baird:

They swam off the island's eastern point, then pulled themselves up onto the warm rock, long and smooth as a whale's back, and dried off in the sun, laughing as Victor told about barely surviving the last leg of his expedition home. He told of stuffing straw in his boots and pants, of breaking ice as it formed around their canoe on rivers and lakes.

"November?" Owen had said, shaking his head. "That's winter up here. What were you thinking?"

Victor crossed his deeply tan arms over his swim tank. As if he were a Greek god and truly offended, he stared Owen down. But a half second later, he broke into a broad grin and laughed out loud. "Clearly, Owen, I was not thinking— that's what I was thinking back then!"

Trinity tilted her head back, her blonde hair glistening as it dried. "You have to be tough," she said, "if you're going to be wild."

"Wild," Sadie said. "Huh. Up until last summer, that word never existed in my vocabulary."

"That's why I'm your new best friend," Trinity said. Then she motioned to Owen and Victor as well. "We're your new best friends. Here to help, as needed. Isn't that right, Owen?" she teased.

Owen and Sadie shared a glance. By that point in the summer, they'd become more than friends.

He exhaled. He had no control over Sadie's decisions or her heart. He forced himself to sit tall on the depot bench, pulled his cap over his eyes, and waited for the next train north.

As March arrives, you feel a change in the air, a softening of winter's hard edges.

Sun warms the forests around Rainy Lake. It warms loggers as they fell virgin pine, strip them of branches, and roll them to the frozen shoreline. It warms the logs as they wait to be floated west across Rainy Lake and down Rainy River to the paper mill.

The sun warms rooftops around Ranier and train cars loaded with lumber. It warms the backs of mutts who amble in search of scraps from tavern to restaurant, garbage can to dump pile. It falls on the backs of old horses, warming their stiff bones and muscles sore from months of pulling wagons and sleighs through town and out onto the endless lake, still frozen like granite. Sun warms the roofs of your six shiny Studebakers, sitting in the cleared lot behind the White Turtle.

Everything waits.

12

A FULL KEY RING CLANKED ON HIS BELT LOOP AS OWEN swept snow from the tops of his inventory. Even if he hadn't yet sold a single car (other than the ones to Pengler), he was right to go with Studebakers. They'd been the strongest-selling automobiles nationwide for the past decade. The company had started building solid horse-drawn wagons and then horse-drawn automobiles. In 1904 they'd produced the first electric-operated Studey, and now gasoline-powered beauties. He folded his arms across his chest and admired his fleet, each one individually handcrafted, unlike Ford's mass-produced factory models. A Ford was cheaper, sure, but a Studebaker was built with genuine craftsmanship.

He hoped folks would be willing to pay more for quality.

He just had to get the word out. And when the ads he'd purchased in the *International Falls Journal* starting running, folks would start buying. Plus spring, technically, was around the corner. But who was he kidding? This far north, there wasn't spring. Winter gradually released its hold until one day, you looked again, and it was summer.

Snowbanks clung to the backside of the White Turtle and four-foot icicles dangled from its roof, but Owen imagined blue open water, the sound of motorboats and tourists hopping off passenger cars. Two months or so to go. When summer finally struck, who would resist taking one of these Studeys out for a spin? Who would resist driving with their sweetheart or parking by the pier when the sun set on Rainy Lake, the sky amber till ten thirty or eleven o'clock at night?

He sure wouldn't.

And there she was—her lovely face—framed again in his mind.

Owen removed his hat, ran his hand through his thick hair, as if to rid her from his head. Since returning from St. Paul, he'd intended to let go of Sadie Rose and let her live her life. She had other interests now. Between her life of music on campus and her meetings, they had less and less in common. It was time to loosen his grip on her.

Easier said than done.

He missed those times they didn't have to talk at all. Just watch the sun set over the water and slip down on the other side of the lake, as if Canada stole the sun every evening and America snuck it back each morning. If Sadie Rose were here, he'd be happy doing anything or nothing together. Without her, it was like he was trying to fill up hours and minutes and seconds.

As he turned from the lot and headed toward the creamery, he glanced past the empty pier at the frozen bay. It was last August, and they'd been fishing on Sand Bay. As he walked, the memory returned.

She'd sat on the middle seat, her line off one side. He sat in back, his line off the other side. They were fishing for walleye, jigging where the water ran deep, a hundred yards upstream of the lift bridge. A half dozen walleye were already on the stringer. The sun was setting, a regular fireball. In its light, Sadie's face glowed. All around her, the water flickered with tongues of orange and red. While he was admiring her, her rod suddenly bent sharply toward the water. "I have a big one!" she shouted.

In the same instant, he felt a solid tug on his own line. "Hey, me too!"

"Sadie," he coached, "if it's a northern pike, you gotta tire it out, give it some slack, then bring it in again. You gotta work it."

He gave a quick jerk of his line, hoping to set the hook, and when he did, Sadie's rod flew from her hands and out into the choppy water.

"He yanked it right out of my hands!" she said, standing in the boat. "I couldn't hang on to it!"

And then Owen reeled his line in, chuckling, until he produced her rod at the edge of the boat. "Looks like we caught each other."

She laughed out loud and then restrung her hook with a fresh silver minnow from the minnow bucket. But no sooner had she put her line back in the water than she burst suddenly into tears.

"What's wrong? Did you get hurt? The minnow? You know I'll bait your hook for you."

She pressed her hand across her mouth, placed her fishing pole in its holder, turned toward him, her knees touching his, and buried her face in her hands.

"Sadie, sweet Sadie. A bad memory?" he asked. He knew she had memories and nightmares sometimes, because she'd told him. Memories of being out in a snowstorm, terrified, searching for her mother. Nightmares of things she'd seen at the boardinghouse. Things no child, she'd said, should ever see.

But always, she'd told him her secrets in whispers.

And not once with tears.

"Sadie, Sadie," he whispered. "What's wrong?"

He dropped to his knees on the damp floor of the wooden boat. He wrapped his arms around her shoulders. He lightly kissed the top of her head. But she kept crying, her back heaving. He didn't know what to do, didn't know what to say, so he waited. When her breathing returned to normal and she sat up, wiping her eyes, he held her face in his hands and kissed her forehead, the tip of her nose, and then her mouth. Together they shut out the world, and the anchored boat cradled them, bobbing on the chop as the darkness enveloped them.

At last, Owen asked softly. "Can you tell me now?"

"In three days," she began, "I go back to school."

He nodded. She'd entered college the fall of her sixteenth year. Though Owen was a year older, he was already two years behind her in formal education. "You have to. You're starting your sophomore year."

She drew in a breath and held it. When she exhaled, she said, "I don't want to lose you!"

To that, he'd laughed lightly. "I'm not going anywhere," he replied. "I'll be right here when you return."

Only now as he approached the squat, brick building of Jensen's Creamery did Owen wonder. That night in the boat. Had Sadie seen a different future . . . and understood that things would change between them? Since that night, he'd always thought Sadie's outburst of tears had been sweet, an unnecessary worry about *his* finding someone else.

Maybe she'd feared—even known—she'd be the one to drift away.

It was after five when Jerry, without setting off the brass bell, entered the creamery.

Owen looked up from his ledger. "Sheesh, Jer. You're quiet as a cat burglar."

Jerry smiled impishly, and with the grace of a vaudeville actor, swept his bowler hat from his head and bowed. "Gentlemen."

"Hi, Jerry," Erling added, suspenders hanging loose on his trousers and standing beside Owen. They'd been going over the books and invoices since Mom went home with a headache. Truth was, Erling was a little slow with numbers, but Owen tried to be patient.

"Clear the counter for the day," Jerry said, pulling a

flask from his jacket. He held it out, offering it to Owen and Erling.

Owen shook his head. "We're still on the job."

Jerry took a drink. "Heck, I'm always on the job. Besides, that never kept your dad from drinking back when."

Erling's body tensed. "He stopped drinking years ago," he said defensively.

Owen walked out from behind the counter. "You're both right. No sense in arguing about what was."

Jerry nodded at Erling. "Hey, I didn't mean anything by it. I joke around. Sometimes say things . . . you know, go a little too far." He reached his hand out to Erling. "Sorry, buddy."

Erling's chin quivered, but he reached down and shook Jerry's hand.

Jerry capped his flask, put it squarely away in his jacket, and clapped his hands together. "So, the latest news. Hear about the photographer in the Falls? The latest rotgut casualty."

"Foxridge?" Owen said, surprised. "Yeah, I knew him. His business is on Main Street in the Falls. He's got a wife and kids."

"Had," Jerry corrected him.

Erling crossed his arms. "Maybe outlawing every drop makes sense. Not that I'd go around to saloons like that crazy Carrie Nation, busting up places with her ax. But when you hear about whole families left behind. What's poor Mrs. Foxridge going to do now?"

"Learn to run the photography business," Jerry said, with a slight laugh.

Erling didn't laugh. There was a second of uncomfortable silence. "She'll have to do something, won't she?"

Owen felt bad for Mrs. Foxridge, for her kids. He understood being left behind to run things. *Moonshine, rotgut, hooch.* Whatever you called homemade booze brewed up in a still, it was always suspect. At best, a moonshiner produced alcohol from fermented potatoes, barley, corn—natural ingredients. "Minnesota 13," for example, was a reliable, good-tasting moonshine made from corn in Stearns County. But at worst, a moonshiner might add turpentine, mercury, lead, or arsenic. Not only did such brews rot the gut; they killed folks, too—over a hundred deaths a week nationwide. Problem was, the bad stuff was cheap, and since alcohol was now outlawed, there wasn't a speck of regulation to protect consumers. The U.S. government could no longer monitor the production of booze. That's why Pengler was practically doing folks a favor, bringing in high-quality Canadian whiskey from real *regulated* distilleries.

"Fred Foxridge," Jerry said, "must have bought it cheap from some backwoods still. They say he must have stumbled down his stairs, then crawled out on the sidewalk, looking for help. Couldn't breathe. Face turned purple. Somebody sold him poison. *Rotgut.* That's what should be outlawed."

Erling scoffed. "You can try to convince yourself, but I'm staying away from the stuff. I'll be playing ball someday, and I don't need booze to hold me back."

"Real swell for you, Erling," Jerry said.

Owen didn't know his own mind anymore. He'd vowed to quit drinking, yet he was part of selling Whiskey Sixes to help transport booze from Canada. And it was high quality, not the rotgut that did in Mr. Foxridge. That seemed a good thing, since anyone set on drinking was going to find booze when they wanted it. Yet the Eighteenth Amendment and the Volstead Act made it illegal. So how could he justify being on the right side of anything when the laws stated all booze was criminal? It was a bad law. How can you tell the difference between right and wrong when all the legal lines are blurry?

Jerry asked, "Say, any interest yet on your Studeys?"

Owen shook his head.

With a nod of confidence, Jerry said, "I'll tell you what. You drive a model or two out to the horse race next week. Lots of folks show up from all over for that event. You never know who'll be there."

"Yeah," Owen agreed. "Good thinking."

"But that's not why I'm here," Jerry said, leaning onto the counter over the open books. "One Ear. He turned up colicky this morning."

"Cripes." If One Ear was suffering from colic, he could die. A horse could get colic for any number of reasons—too much grain, too much stress, too much early spring grass. With snow still on the ground, grass wasn't the problem. "Did he get into the grain? Overeat?"

"No, he didn't have access. I don't know what got into him. Sometimes you don't know. I walked him for an hour, and when I left he seemed a little better, but I wanted to come right over and tell you. Just in case he can't race. I figured you'd come up with another plan."

13

Something was clearly going on at the tracks as Owen drove into Ranier after his rounds. The train of boxcars was stopped, with several doors slid wide open. Off to the side of the tracks, wooden barrels lay scattered, guarded by a swarm of law enforcement. Sheriff Vandyke and Deputy Kranlin stood nearby, their guns clearly visible.

"A bust!" Owen said aloud, pulling over to the side of the road and stopping. He glanced toward his lot of six Studeys, all shine and chrome, waiting for buyers.

In the opposite direction toward the bay below the tracks, federal agents in their long coats rolled barrels onto the ice. Other agents were busy busting open the casks with axes. Locals gathered, too, taking advantage of the spillage, collecting the amber whiskey with buckets and cups. A dozen barrels were already on the ice, smashed, with more coming. Owen climbed out to look around.

"What a good day to be alive!" one fellow exclaimed, filling his cup.

"The Lord taketh and the Lord giveth," another joked.

Owen laughed to himself.

Frank Hetter, the leading customs agent who lived in Ranier, raised an ax above his head, then brought it down squarely into another cask. *Crack!* He wiped his brow. "It's the law. I'm doing my job."

"Ah, Frank! C'mon, do you have to do this?" one man whined.

"Jeez, Hetter! Whose side are you on, anyway?"

Johnny Schoeller inched closer with his bucket.

"Johnny, you go on home," Frank Hetter ordered. "Now back away!"

But Johnny Schoeller, known for gambling, just laughed. "You can beat me at the silver dollar toss, Frank, but you can't beat me out of this!" The "toss" was a local game of seeing who could toss a silver dollar closest to a crack in the sidewalk. Frank Hetter was unbeatable. Now Johnny spotted an opportunity and darted in, scooped up a bucket of slush and whiskey, and ran off.

Frank Hetter scowled. "Hey!"

The casks kept coming, and the more casks that spurted whiskey, the more men showed up, whooping and laughing as they scrambled to fill whatever they could: buckets, glass bottles, mugs, even their caps. Amidst the cheering and hollering, seagulls hovered, calling, as if anticipating there would be handouts for them, too.

Suddenly, a gunshot went off.

Everyone froze, looking around for what had happened, for who was shot.

"That's your warning!" Sheriff Vandyke shouted, holding a pistol high. He had everyone's attention and shot once more. "Next person who fills a bucket or anything with booze is getting the next bullet in his leg!"

A general air of grumbling erupted, and one by one, the locals backed away, long-faced, buckets and cups in hand. Then a white-haired, bowlegged man—Mr. Dressler—in patched and oversize trousers and jacket, hobbled slowly past Vandyke to a splintered casket. He got on his hands and knees and lowered his head to a puddle of whiskey.

For a moment, the air was quiet.

Owen held his breath. *Don't shoot. God, don't shoot.*

Sheriff Vandyke pointed his gun at Mr. Dressler.

In horror, Owen watched as men exchanged glances, wondering just what the sheriff would do.

Frank Hetter's usually pale complexion turned red as a sunburn. Caught between locals and the federal law, he'd grown up here and was allegedly childhood friends with Harvey Pengler. But the Eighteenth Amendment had put a wedge between Frank and many of the locals. He walked over to the sheriff and mumbled something into his ear.

A brittleness hung in the air.

Like a dog, Mr. Dressler continued to lap, slurping loudly. Then he rose, hands to his knees, and slowly straightened his back. He smiled from his unshaven face and let out a belly laugh. "Didn't say anything about cooling a terrible thirst!"

When a federal agent held up a hand to Sheriff Vandyke, clearly meaning to hold off, the sheriff lowered his pistol, turned, and walked back to the cargo beside the train. Frank Hetter nodded to himself and moved on to the next cask with his ax.

Exhaling with relief, Owen started off toward his truck.

"Hey, Ow-en Jen-sen!" called a man with an oversize bowler hat nearly covering his eyes. He was wobbling along, with two amber-filled glass bottles, one in each hand. "Good thing for you! A guy . . . can't count on tr-trains anymore! Need your rigs for bootlegging, I tell you! How else we gonna get decent booze past these knuckleheads?"

"Whiskey Sixes!" The drunk was following him, as if they were good friends. He must be someone on Pengler's payroll whose mouth grew too big when drinking.

Owen wanted to disappear, to avoid any association with the man, and strode quickly to the creamery truck. But the whole way, he felt the eyes of every federal agent, customs employee, and county law enforcement drilling into his backbone.

He started up the motor, then U-turned away from the tracks, where the train stood idling. The pile of roofing shingles beside the tracks told the story. Someone had tried to hide casks of whiskey beneath stacks of shingles.

Owen steered the truck east and made a long loop home. Prohibition was meant to save families and society from the evils of alcohol, but it seemed to have created a whole new set of problems. With a long history of alcohol being legal, and the ease in brewing it, making it illegal was like holding back the ocean. It seemed absurd to outlaw it. Added to that, there was a general wink and a nod toward moonshining and drinking. County commissioners handing out licenses left and right for "soda fountains" that everyone knew were fronts. Moreover, there were an infinite number of "small cookers" in the county. Everyone had a friend or relative making a little extra cash operating a backwoods still. Owen knew of one farmer unable to sell his last year's potato crop; with plenty of mouths to feed, the farmer turned his surplus of potatoes into booze. And a good amount of cash. Who could blame him?

Yet now that alcohol was illegal, you had folks whose job it was to enforce federal laws. Men like Frank Hetter and Sheriff Vandyke took their jobs seriously.

Everything about Prohibition seemed unworkable, yet it had turned into a game of cops and robbers—with *real* bullets.

Folks say, "March comes in like a lion, and goes out like a lamb."

Sometimes it works that way.

Other times it ambles in soft and sweet, and goes out with the ferocity of a roaring beast.

You just never know.

14

THE SUN LOOMED OVER THE STILL-FROZEN LAKE. ON THE edge of Sand Bay, bonfires roared, and vendors sold mugs of hot coffee; people ate sausages roasted over fires, sandwiches of smoked trout, and cookies. An Ojibwa woman dropped balls of dough into a sizzling cast-iron skillet. Another woman sold fry bread to a gathering line of customers.

It was a good day for a horse race.

A good day for selling a Studey.

Windows rolled down on his shiny, burgundy Studebaker, Owen breathed in the moist air, full of promise. One Ear's bout of colic had disappeared in twenty-four hours, and Jerry had gone back to riding him and getting ready for the race. Now their plan was to draw as little attention as possible: put down as much money as they could come up with, bet high, and keep a low profile until the start of the race.

Folks poured in on horseback, riding in sleighs and Model T trucks, and on "jokers" or tractors. The horse-and-sleigh races and the one-mile horse race drew local families with kids—bundled up in boots, scarves, mittens, wool caps, and jackets—and nearly as many out-of-towners, who arrived on the passenger train in Ranier, turned out in full-length furs, muffs, and fancy hats and scarves. But the sun beamed down on everyone just the

same, creating a shimmer of moisture—as well as anticipation and hope—in the air above the gathering.

Owen parked halfway between the shore and the race-
track, just so folks would stream past, take a look, maybe
ask questions. His hopes rose when he spotted E. W. Ennis
and his wife. Though the Ennises usually rode around in
the latest vehicles, today they were walking away from
their horse-drawn sleigh and driver. They strolled toward
him—toward his Studebaker. Not only was he a towering
man of six and a half feet, but Ennis carried himself like
the wealthy industrialist he was: shoulders back, head
high, and with a broad smile, as if he owned the county and
its destiny. If anyone could afford a top-of-the-line model
today, it was Mr. Ennis.

Owen cleared his throat. His palms sweated inside his
leather driving gloves. He put his head out the window.
"Hello, Mr. and Mrs. Ennis! Fine day for horse races, isn't
it?"

"Couldn't be finer," Mr. Ennis said.

His wife, Owen noticed, walked a half step behind her
husband. Her gaze was everywhere but on the Studebaker.
Her name was Katherine, and their white double-decker
houseboat was named after her.

E. W. Ennis paused beside the Studey and ran his hand
along the front fender, as if caressing it. If anyone might
plunk down money, it was Ennis. Here was the man who
had started as a bookkeeper for a lumber firm in St. Paul
and rose to become a wealthy industrialist. Here was the
legend who only twenty years earlier, along with his head
timber cruiser (hired to scout virgin forests for logging),
had strapped on snowshoes and tramped two hundred
miles of northern Minnesota forests until they reached the
Canadian border and the thundering waterfalls, with all its
promise of powering a first-rate paper mill.

Ennis gave the left fender three solid pats and nodded
to himself.

Owen held his breath. This could be it.

Then E. W. Ennis walked up to Owen's open window. "Owen, glad to see you took the risk—started your own business. Tell you what. I'll buy this very Studebaker today, if you're willing to sell it to me."

"Willing to sell it to you? Why of course!" Owen said, trying to contain his enthusiasm to something business-like. He put his hand on the door handle, ready to step out and visit with Ennis, man to man, but Ennis leaned down and pressed his bulk against the car door. He gazed into Owen's window.

"Wholesale," Ennis said under his breath.

Wholesale? Owen ran a retail business. You buy inventory at wholesale, mark it up to retail price, and hope to make a profit. He wasn't running a charity. Why was Ennis being such an ass? Owen soared and crashed all in a second. "I don't get it. You want it at cost?"

"That's right," Ennis replied, his voice steady, like a steel freighter breaking ice. "If not from you, I have friends in Minneapolis. They'll sell to me at cost. It's entirely up to you."

In a flash, Owen replayed other moments. The past summers when he delivered dairy products by boat to islanders, no one had tried to drive a harder bargain on price than Ennis or his staff. And he never tipped. And then more recently, the news about how Ennis had tried to swindle a widow of ten children out of her land. She'd leased her river property to him, and when one of her boys died she'd asked Ennis for an advance on his rent. He'd agreed, sending someone out with papers for the widow to sign. But unknowingly, she'd signed all her property over to Ennis. She took it to court, and the judge agreed that he'd overstepped his bounds. The contract she'd signed became null and void. If anything showed Ennis's character, it was that. Owen was a mere son of a creamery owner, but that didn't mean he was a pawn.

"You're a businessman, Mr. Ennis," Owen said. "You know I can't stay in business if I don't make a penny of profit. What about supporting businesses here? That way, you help me, I help the community. You know, we help each other." Then he smiled and gave a quick nod to Ennis, as if to communicate to his higher sense of purpose.

But Ennis smiled right back, straightened to his towering height, so that all Owen could see for a moment was the double-breasted buttons on his black wool coat. "Business isn't for the weak of heart," he said, turning away. "Takes money to make money, young man."

Then Ennis pulled his wife closer by the arm—as if he owned her and everything else in the whole world.

Stupefied, Owen sat there, as if the wind had been knocked out of him. He watched as Ennis walked off, head high, greeting townsfolk with his presidential waves and handshakes.

Ennis wouldn't help a local boy on his way up? Didn't make sense. He had money—was supposedly one of the richest men in the country. No wonder Victor Guttenberg was waging such a head-on battle to protect the lakes and wilderness from endless development. Ennis didn't care that his proposed dams would destroy the water levels; he didn't care that higher levels would erase the bays and nesting loons, the craggy inlets and endless scattered islands. He didn't care that his plans would destroy the lake as folks knew it. Ennis saw only one path forward: the one that served his—and only his—needs. There was a name for that. Blind ambition.

If that kind of ambition defined success, then Owen wasn't sure he'd ever make it big in business. He didn't want success at the cost of what mattered.

Soon a gaggle of kids came over, gaping, and wanted to run their mittened hands over the Studey, but their parents ordered them back, as if their children might break it and they'd end up having to buy it. Owen waved. "Someday you'll each be driving one of these yourself," he said to the kids with a smile.

Another fellow smirked as he walked by. "You're just

a kid. You and Pengler got some kind of a deal goin', dontcha?"

"Sorry?" Owen replied, as if he had no idea what the man might be referring to, but the man walked on with a shrug of his shoulders.

"How much?" one large woman asked, taking Owen by surprise and putting her head through the open window. On her breath—booze. And she reached under her fox stole and pulled out several bills—heavy with perfume. She waved the bills in front of Owen's nose.

Owen pulled back, but there was nowhere to go. "Well, today I'm offering a discount, a one-miler special."

Her lips, dabbed with deep red, parted in a smile. "Or better yet, Owen Jensen, you'd like to take a spin with *me*. Find out what a big engine can really do."

He hadn't expected her to know his name, though he recognized her as one of the four hefty women locally known as the "Beef Trust." They, too, worked above the White Turtle. "Uh, well."

"I'm Belle," she said with a wink, and extended her gloved hand, as if she expected him to kiss it. He shook it instead.

Still, she was a potential customer. "Miss Belle," he said, "I'm happy to make your acquaintance. There's no reason you shouldn't own a fine Studebaker yourself someday."

She straightened and backed up from the window. "You're a sweet one," she said, "but you look so lonely. You come see me sometime. I'll give you *my* one-miler special." Then she sauntered away, her ankle-length coat swooshing against her lace-up boots.

Owen tilted his head back and closed his eyes. Hell would freeze over before he'd hike upstairs to visit Belle or any other pay-to-play gal in Ranier. A guy had desires and needs, sure, but he'd heard stories about picking up things worse than lice or bedbugs.

He groaned.

Lonely?

Yeah, Belle had that part right.

But he wanted only Sadie Rose.

When Aasta and Hans Johannsen stopped by, Owen jumped out, glad to see them.

"Hello, Owen!" Aasta exclaimed, a red wool scarf tied neatly beneath her narrow chin. She was as tall as he was, and she looked right through him with sky-blue eyes. "Where you been these days?" she asked. "With our Sadie Rose to college, we don't see you so much."

Hans nodded at Owen. Owen had always enjoyed Mr. Johannsen, a man of few words. He was a skilled carpenter and handyman whom the Bairds often employed on their island. The last time Owen saw him, Hans was repairing the lodge's stone chimney. "Owen," he said. "How you be?"

"Hi, Mr. Johannsen," he replied. "Great. I'm great."

"We have talked together, me and Aasta, and we *vant* to buy Studebaker."

"What?" Owen thought he must be joking. It wasn't that the Johannsens were penniless, but between working as caretaker and cook for the Worthingtons, and Hans doing extra work for the Bairds, Owen had often thought they were hanging by a thread. Though always freshly painted and tidy, their house in Ranier wasn't much bigger than a thimble. He thought he should talk them out of this wild notion. Besides, why would they need a Studebaker? They had use of the Worthington's Model T when the Worthingtons were in St. Paul, which was more often than not.

Aasta smiled and linked her arm with her husband's. "Ow-en," she said, as if to get his full attention. "We are quite serious. It is the first."

It took him a moment to find his words. He still doubted they had any idea what kind of money it would require. "Well, that would be just great. When do you want to buy an automobile? I'm happy to give you an idea of cost. A bit more than a plow horse, you understand."

"*Ja*, we understand," Hans replied a little coolly, and Owen worried he'd offended them.

"Soon," Aasta replied. "We're still saving. But we see one on your lot we like."

"Okay, sure!" Owen answered, reaching out and taking both of their hands in his own. It was an awkward handshake, but his heart was in it. A possible sale! Soon. It would be his first official sale! It was exciting, even if in the back of his mind, a wispy thought arose. Sadie Rose was, after all, their granddaughter. And there wasn't a doubt in Owen's mind that they'd do anything in the world to support her. By buying a Studebaker, they were supporting him—supporting them.

As the Johannsens walked across the snow-covered ice toward the start of the races, Owen caught himself. Did he owe it to tell them that he and Sadie Rose might not be together? Was that his responsibility? Would they change their mind? But then, he didn't even know with absolute certainty what he and Sadie were anymore.

15

HE SHOVED HIS HANDS INTO HIS POCKETS, FOUND HIS pocket watch, and pulled it out. Just a few minutes until the start of the race. No wonder the crowd had all but moved to the track. Owen trotted off toward the horses, riders, and scattered mounds of hay.

Jerry was working One Ear, bareback, in wide circles. The stallion blew and snorted, bending his muscular neck and body, prancing with high steps. His sorrel coat was smooth and glossy; Jerry had been blanketing him at night to lose his winter coat for maximum speed, unlike the other dozen horses, who wore two-inch coats of winter growth.

The other equally glossy horse was Pengler's dark bay, Ace-in-the-Hole, who was ridden by a jockey-sized man Owen didn't recognize. Pengler must have imported a real jockey from somewhere out of the region.

Owen looked for Pengler and spotted him talking with Frank Hetter, who held a pistol in one hand and a megaphone in the other. They stood at the edge of the start and finish line—a black line of paint drawn on the ice. Beyond, a loop had been plowed through the snow to mark the mile-long track.

Hetter lifted the megaphone to his lips and shouted. "Three minutes and counting! All contestants line up for the one-miler!"

Like a school of fish, the crowd shifted to either side of the starting line. Horses and riders sidestepped, pranced, walked, and trotted up to the starting point. One Ear kicked out at Ace-in-the-Hole.

"Hey! Keep your horse under control!" Pengler shouted. "Wait. Jerry Melnyk? You told me you couldn't ride my horse!"

"That's cuz I have my own horse to ride!" Jerry shouted back.

Pengler stood tall in his coat of wolf pelts, arms crossed, running his gloved hand over his chin. "I'll be damned."

A dozen horses pranced and snorted, a mix of large and small, as they lined up at the starting line.

"One minute and counting!" Frank Hetter belted into the megaphone. "This, folks, is exciting! Fifteen horses. One winner takes all."

A white horse reared, and its rider, a square-headed teenager, clung to the horse's neck. But in one giant backward tumble, the horse and rider fell back. The crowd gasped, just as the teenager landed and rolled out of the horse's path. The horse came down with a thud, then scrambled and pulled itself up to its feet.

The teenager shook his head, as if to clear it from cobwebs, then grabbed his horse's reins and climbed back into the saddle. He steered his horse toward the starting line.

The crowd cheered.

"Five, four, three, two, one!"

Hetter shot the gun in the air as Ace-in-the-Hole crossed the line. The other horses skidded and startled. They lunged forward as their riders hung on. One Ear was last to bolt, his haunches churning up snow.

"Go, Jerry! Hang on!" Owen shouted, heart suddenly in his throat. They needed this win more than anyone could know.

The horses kicked up a whirlwind of snowflakes behind

them as they formed a wild herd, racing forward as one. The crowd cheered and whistled and clapped, watching as the horses grouped and then gradually began peeling off. A few horses lagged behind. A few horses gained, striding well ahead of the rest. Now specks, a half mile off, the horses began rounding the midway point. Heading back, at the front of the race, two horses were in the lead: Ace-in-the-Hole followed a length by One Ear!

"Come on, Jerry!" Owen whispered under his breath.

Seconds slowed to an eternity. The horses drew closer and closer. The crowd went silent. Hooves thudded and pounded, and Owen felt the reverberations up through the ice and into his legs. A slight crack sounded. Nothing unusual. Happened all the time with the lake—cracks, whines, and moans—but still, he prayed the ice would hold this gathering of people and animals.

"Ace-in-the-Hole! He's gonna do it again!" a woman cried, clapping her hands together. With that, the crowd erupted anew, as if everyone had been holding their breath and finally chose to inhale.

The last quarter mile.

Something happened.

In the blink of an eye, One Ear and Jerry were down, sprawled across the ice. One, two, then three riders passed. Had they hit a patch of glare ice? Or tripped? Owen waited a second or two to see if they'd rise, and if they didn't, he would start up his Studey and race out there to check on them.

But as quickly as the thought passed through his mind, One Ear scrambled up to all fours, and Jerry climbed on. "Good," Owen murmured. "Thank God."

Ace-in-the-Hole was coming on strong, but One Ear stretched out, powered ahead, and gained . . . gained . . . and passed the third horse, the second, and went neck and neck with Pengler's bay. The two pounded and snorted toward the finish line. The crowd went wild, cheering. And the two bounded toward the finish line, with One Ear and Jerry following by a length.

Pengler threw both arms up. He shouted something, but the crowd drowned out his words.

Owen couldn't believe it. Jerry had proved to be an amazing rider; One Ear had almost won. They were so close.

The horses, after overshooting the finish line, ended up near the woods. Horses and riders gradually made their way back to the crowd. One Ear was lathered in sweat across his chest, flank, neck, and head.

"I'll get a blanket on him before he gets chilled," Jerry said as Owen approached.

Pengler strode up to them in his silvery-gray long coat. "One helluva race!" Pengler barked. "Jerry, you work for me. Now I see why you couldn't ride my horse. I don't like you boys going behind my back like this."

Owen spoke up. "We're trying to pay off what we owe you."

Pengler looked One Ear up and down. "Where the heck did you find this horse anyway?" But instead of waiting for an answer, he strode off to his rider and Ace-in-the-Hole.

Owen walked alongside as Jerry led One Ear back to his Model T truck. Along the way, folks shook Jerry's hand and admired his horse. From the truck bed, Jerry grabbed a fistful of rags and rubbed down the horse's legs and neck until he was nearly dry. Then he secured a wool blanket over One Ear's back, rump, and chest. He tied the stallion up beside a pile of loose hay.

"You almost won—riding bareback!"

"Less weight. I prefer bareback, so I figured if I could stay on, we'd win. But—we hit a patch of glare ice."

Then Owen and Jerry walked over to the table where they'd placed their bet and registered One Ear. The two men on the opposite side both worked for Pengler. The one with a frost-covered beard shook his head and laughed out loud. "Not sure it's so smart to try to beat out your boss, but you boys came close."

"Yeah," Jerry said. "First place would have made the risk worth taking. But second place will have to do. How much did we win?"

The man laughed again. "Win? You didn't win a blessed thing. The race is winner takes all."

"Aw, you're kiddin' me!" Jerry turned away. He booted a chunk of snow and sent it flying. "Winner takes all. If that isn't a kick in the head."

Owen walked alongside him. "Guess we kiss it good-bye."

Jerry kissed the air.

16

THE DAY AFTER THE HORSE RACE, OWEN NOSE-DIVED. He spent all night wondering how they were going to meet their deadline. Maybe he'd get lucky and sell a Studebaker or two, but they still owed a bundle of money.

He needed a break this morning. The thing with a creamery is you never get a day off. Cows keep producing milk, and milk needs refrigeration. Since it was Sunday, he asked Erling to cover for him today. Hands in his pockets, he walked to the Sterling Café.

He headed for a counter stool.

"Joseph!" a man in the corner called. "Care if I join you?"

Owen didn't recognize the tall, thin man with gray tufted eyebrows. He strutted over, bringing with him a half-eaten piece of apple pie and a cup of coffee. He sat down, his legs barely fitting beneath the counter. His eyes lingered a second too long, like a heron watching the shallows, ready to dart in with its long beak.

"It's Owen, not Joseph. But go ahead." He nodded at the free stool beside him. "I don't own the counter."

The waitress stopped by and took Owen's order—coffee, two eggs sunny-side up, biscuits, and gravy.

"So Owen? What is your purpose in life? Where would you go if you could? You have any dreams for your future?

Ever wondered if you might be called to serve the Lord, to spread his Word to the heathen?"

Owen shrugged. "Sorry, mister. I'm not much for talking. Besides, I'm Catholic."

"Well, I'll tell you, young man. I'm ready to shake the dust off the soles of my boots and head on to another county. This is one tough area to reach the lost. But someone from here who knows this area and the folks, he might reach the lost here. And it's a pit of vipers, debauchery, and sinfulness." He leveled his gaze on Owen. "Young man, I have the feeling that someone could be you."

Owen laughed. "You've gotta be kidding."

The man placed his hand over his heart. "God has laid you on my heart. Of course, you must be baptized. Have you been baptized?"

"Uh-huh. As a baby." Owen knew that wasn't the kind of baptism this preacher was likely talking about.

"Oh, but when you give your life to the Lord and go down in the waters of a lake or river, you come up a new man!" The man was now preaching to a congregation—anyone in the café who had ears. "The old ways are left behind, and you're born into a new being! That's right!" He spread his arms wide, bumping Owen's shoulder and spilling his coffee as it met Owen's lips. "Born into a whole new being!"

The café grew quiet. A shifting in a chair, a slight turn of the back, a sinking deeper into shoulders. Backwoods preachers came and went through Ranier. There were any number of ways Owen might live his life, but becoming a preacher wasn't one of them. When breakfast arrived, he bolted it, gulped the last of his coffee, and tipped his hat. "I wish you well. Good luck to you."

The man nodded. "Thank you. God bless you, Joseph."

Owen returned to the creamery for the truck and drove three miles to International Falls. At noon, he took a seat in the middle row of the Broadway Theater, just in time for *The Paleface,* starring Buster Keaton. A western comedy was just what he needed. Keaton, a butterfly collector who unwittingly wanders into an Indian camp, soon earns the title "Little Chief Paleface" and leads the tribe in their effort to stop oil tycoons from forcing them off their land. Owen smiled. Next time he ran into Victor Guttenberg, he'd joke and call him Little Chief Paleface for standing up against the local tycoon.

He sat through the next silent film, *Beyond the Rocks,* starring Rudolph Valentino as the lover in a romantic triangle. Should Theodora stay with the man she was obliged to marry or go with the man she truly loved? The whole movie began to make Owen crabby. All he could see on the screen was Sam-the-Damn-Thoughtful, trying to win the hand of *his* girl.

He closed his eyes during the credits. No, Owen scolded himself. Sadie wasn't *his* girl. She was her own woman. Part of him, he hated to admit, wanted to possess her completely and dictate who she could see and not see. Keep her under lock and key. But that was some primitive part of him. His better self—his better angel—didn't ever want to make someone a slave to his will.

Suddenly, he was back at school, reciting the closing words of Lincoln's first inaugural address:

I am loath to close.
We are not enemies, but friends.
We must not be enemies.
Though passion may have strained it must not break
our bonds of affection. The mystic chords of memory,
stretching from every battlefield and patriot grave
to every living heart and hearthstone all over this broad
land,

will yet swell the chorus of the Union, when again touched,
as surely they will be,
by the better angels of our nature.

No, he would never own her.

She would have to choose to be with him, choose to step closer.

A sweetly sickening scent of booze rose up from behind him. The thing about booze, he thought, was that for many, it had a way of becoming master. Owen had always blamed Dad for drinking away the family's money, but he'd never really considered that Dad had been a slave to something more powerful than himself. It was the booze that had turned him into a monster. And there was Mr. Dressler, brought low as a dog. Yet rumor had it that Dressler had once been a successful Ohio businessman.

He tried to lose himself in the next movie, *Nanook of the North*, a true story of an Inuk, a member of the Inuit people, and his wife and baby in their grueling search for food and trade. This native family carved out an existence in the deep cold of northern Quebec, but the more Owen watched, the more he scorned himself for getting *stuck* in the deep cold with the family creamery. Stuck without hope of ever finding out what he might have been capable of. Stuck with a loan to Pengler and crushing debt for a stupid mistake. With his need to get ahead, to make something of himself, he'd taken risks. He scorned himself for the mess he'd made of things.

In the middle of the film, he couldn't watch anymore. He glanced behind him. A man snored, open-mouthed, and the booze wafted with each exhale.

Owen left.

Outside the theater, the wind had died down. Clouds

pressed down upon the buildings along Main Street. Owen felt claustrophobic, as if he was locked between a thin line of earth and sky. He drew a deep breath, trying to clear his head. Then another. Across the street, the sign for Quality Photography was still there, even though Mr. Foxridge was dead.

Owen pulled the flaps of his cap down over his ears and set off along the boardwalk. He'd read enough about the Civil War to know that when you pit two equally passionate sides against each other, the war turns brutal. Abolitionists knew slavery was wrong and could not be tolerated. Slave owners, however, had grown accustomed to a way of life and would defend what they believed were their rights. Prohibition, too, had two passionate sides: those determined to keep booze out of society against those who believed it was their right to make it, sell it, and consume it. With Canada just on the other side of the river, Koochiching County and the Rainy Lake area turned into something like a border state in the Civil War, where fighting had turned especially bloody. Things were heating up locally and the region didn't show signs of cooling down anytime soon.

Huddled into his jacket, Owen trudged past several taverns, a hotel, restaurant, and drugstore. He stepped into the one place that offered real comfort. And it wasn't a tavern or local church with a tall spire. He didn't fault anyone for going to church. He'd gone enough times over the years to know that he wasn't one to sit in the pew and take guidance from the pulpit. Truth was, he favored Ralph Waldo Emerson's approach in his essay "Nature." It made more sense to him to let his own intuition guide him. He didn't have any answers yet, but he was starting to pay attention. He was starting to listen.

17

AT THE INTERSECTION OF THIRD AND FOURTH, OWEN stood outside the tall building housing a restaurant and soda fountain, along with the new International Falls Public Library.

He turned the handle to the library, but it didn't budge. Then he saw the closed sign. Just his luck. But it was Sunday—he should have known. As he started to turn away, a shadow stirred behind the door's frosted window. The door opened and he was met by a woman five to ten years older than him.

The first thing he noticed were her stockinged legs, which started in shiny navy shoes and tiny ankles and rose to curved calves and ended beneath her knees at the hem of her gray and white polka-dot dress. He tried to look at her eyes, but he couldn't help noticing the way she filled out her dress—in just the right places.

"We're closed, you know," the woman said. Her red hair was fashionably shaped in tight waves on either side of her pale face. "Come back tomorrow. The hours are posted on the door."

"Yes, sorry. I always mean to get here, but my work gets in the way."

"Oh, gosh, perhaps this once I can make an exception," the woman said, stepping back. "If you'd like to look around . . . I'm here catching up on some work."

"That would be swell," Owen said, smiling for the first time that day. He closed the door behind him. Here, in this one-room space, the bookcases and walls were filled floor to ceiling with books. Here, though the space might make another guy feel closed in, Owen felt himself float up. He roamed, running his fingers down the spines of books. Here were ideas. Here was a wealth of learning, open to whoever wanted to learn. If he couldn't go to college, he could at least read everything in this room, cover to cover.

He was suddenly aware of the librarian watching him. He turned.

"I'm sorry, I forgot my manners," he said, walking back to her desk and extending his hand. "I'm Owen Jensen. My family owns the creamery in Ranier." He thought of adding something about the dealership, maybe to impress her, but he held his tongue. "I appreciate you letting me look around."

"It's really no bother. I'm pretty new here, and it's nice to have a little company."

"What's your name? Where are you from?"

"I'm Miss Hamilton. Miss Winnie Hamilton," she added. "I finished school back East, and well, I wanted some adventure. This position became available, and everyone's been very kind and I'm told it will warm up here eventually."

"Don't hold your breath. We'll have several snowstorms before spring arrives."

Her smile dropped. "Several? Oh, I've never been so cold as—"

"Wool," Owen said. "Wear lots of wool and layers." And then he laughed. He tried to picture himself as she saw him just then: wool scarf still wrapped around his neck, wool cap, wool long johns covered by wool trousers, wool hand-knit sweater, with wool-lined leather mitts and wool socks inside his boots.

Miss Winnie Hamilton forced a smile. Over her stockings and dress, she wore a thin navy sweater with tiny white buttons.

Owen shook his head at himself. "Well, if you work outdoors, you gotta dress for it. You look just fine the way you are. But you know, some women work at the paper mill. They wear dungarees and wool, just like the men. Have to, y'know, to stay warm."

The librarian returned to a file of library cards she was apparently updating with pencil. Without looking up, she said, "Well, if I ever take such a position, I'll remember that. Let me know if you have any questions."

"Just one," Owen said. "What college did you go to?"

"A women's college. You've probably never heard of it."

"Try me."

"Smith."

"I've heard of it," Owen said, though it was only a vague reference from somewhere out East.

Miss Winnie nodded. "It's in Massachusetts. Northampton, to be precise. When I received my degree, there were as many students at school as there are residents in this whole town. Isn't that stupendous? And here I am, trying to extend civilization to the farthest reaches, or at least that's what I thought when I first decided to take this position."

"And now?"

"And now what?" she replied, holding her pencil midair. Her nails were trimmed short and perfectly shaped.

"Are you extending civilization?"

"I opened up on a Sunday, just for you, didn't I?" She tilted her head and smiled, though there was a reserve about her.

"Yes, that's so." Owen turned to look at the collection. "Thanks."

He found a small shelf with the label "Newly published books!" and looked at the brightly colored spines and fresh, white pages, waiting to be discovered. He pulled out *One of Ours,* by Willa Cather, one of Sadie Rose's favorite authors, and tucked it under his arm. When he next saw her, it would give them something to talk about.

He pulled out *The Beautiful and Damned,* by the rising star from St. Paul, F. Scott Fitzgerald. Mrs. Worthington called him "Scottie," but Sadie Rose claimed her adoptive mother didn't really know the author as well as she let on. The Worthingtons, with their connections to politics, business, and the arts, tended to show off their collection of acquaintances like expensive jewels. On the other hand, Sadie had never let on how well she knew the young author. She'd said only that she ran into him from time to time.

Another unexpected wave of jealousy swept over Owen. He had no reason to be suspicious or angry with her. She'd done nothing wrong. But he felt helpless. F. Scott Fitzgerald. The mere name of an author she may or may not know, and his gut felt hot with suspicion. He had no control over his own emotions. He was adrift, as if the winds were blowing him off course and he was powerless to get to his true destination. He hated the feeling. He wandered to the back corner of the library and drew a breath to get his heart back to normal, when he noticed the dark curtain partitioning off an area. He stepped closer, peered around it, and spotted a small cot with bedding and a coatrack with women's garments. He withdrew quickly, feeling a mix of desire and guilt, as if he'd stumbled upon her stark naked.

"Oh, I know it looks like I live here," Miss Winnie said from her desk, "but not technically. I have an apartment upstairs, but . . . well . . . with the soda fountain operating all hours of the night, I'm sure you can imagine . . . it's not the quietest—or even safest—place to sleep."

"I wondered," he said, feeling the need to leave, "but it's not really any of my business."

She clamped her hand over her lips for a moment, then dropped her hand and blurted. "Did you read the editorial?"

"What?"

She exhaled through her nose. "Someone wrote to the newspaper last week. Said the library was a fine addition to the town and added, 'but kill the pig.'" She pulled the newspaper out of her desk drawer and held it up as evidence. Her eyes brimmed with emotion as she set the newspaper down and crossed her arms over her chest. Her lower lip trembled. "You're from here. Why would someone say such a thing?"

Her eyebrows twitched with worry, and she reminded him of a skittish red chicken, ready to flee.

"Oh, Miss Winnie. They're not writing about *you*. They're talking about the blind pig that operates here. I mean, a soda fountain—everyone knows they're fronts for 'blind pigs.' Like speakeasies, just not as fancy."

"You mean, it wasn't against me at all?"

"I can't imagine so," he said.

"Oh!" She placed her hand at the base of her throat, and her breasts rose and fell beneath her sweater with her deep breaths. "I'm so relieved! I was ready to resign and take the next train back East."

"That would have been too bad," Owen said, and he meant it. He was coming to appreciate Miss Winnie. He felt alone with her in this sanctuary, and her feminine presence stirred him. But his desire for companionship had its limits. He was still a slave—a willing slave—to Sadie Rose. Whether she wanted him or not.

With purpose, he set the books down on the desk. "I'll start with these two."

Miss Winnie nodded. "Fine writers." Then she pulled a slim children's book from a stack of books on the desk beside her. "And this one?"

Owen looked at the thin book with a rabbit illustrated on its cover. It was a book for kids. Did she think he wasn't capable of reading the novels? That, because he grew up in a frontier area, he was intellectually stunted? "I am capable of reading bigger books, Miss Winnie."

Her petite nose, red with cold, stood out against her pale face. The air in the library wasn't much warmer than outdoors. "It's for children, yes, but it's brand new and shows great promise. I just read it last night and it speaks to adults, too."

With reluctance, he took the book. "I'll read it to my little brothers."

"Oh, good idea!" She smiled. "And bring them with you when you return your books. I have my mission, remember."

"Right," Owen said, as he headed to the door. "To bring civilization to the farthest reaches of the world."

It's easy this time of year for folks to start tilting off center. You see it in people's eyes, as if they're trying not to lose a grip on a saner part of themselves.

We call it cabin fever.

The dictionary says: *A state of being, characterized by anxiety, restlessness, and boredom, arising from being isolated or sharing cramped quarters in the wilderness, especially during the long northern winter.*

Everyone talks about how many snowstorms are yet to come. One night, temperatures drop to seven degrees below zero, and the winds blow in from North Dakota and strike with gale forces, turning a mere seven below to something like seventy below. Mom is coping by scrubbing every floor and crevice until her hands are red and chapped.

When cabin fever is in full swing, taverns don't lose a drop of business.

18

TIPPER INVESTIGATED THE FAR SIDE OF A WOODPILE
while Owen hoisted cans full of fresh milk at the Torgeson
farm into the truck.

Suddenly, his dog let out a pitiful yelp, followed by sharp
whining. Owen spun in the direction of the sound. Three
likely causes, he figured: skunk, trap, or porcupine.

The porcupine climbed up a nearby birch tree as Tipper
raced out from behind the woodpile, shaking his head, as if
he were trying to figure out what happened.

"Dang it! You poor boy! Come here."

A dozen quills decorated Tipper's black nose, golden
snout, neck, and ears. One quill protruded a half inch
above his right eye.

Tipper held back, tail between his legs, whining.

"Come on now." When Owen was four or five, he'd
watched Dad pull quills once from a stray. The quills were
barbed and you had to pull them out at exactly the same
angle they went in or they'd catch on flesh, break, and
cause infection. The stray nipped Dad in the process, but
when it was over, it licked Dad's hand before running off
into the woods.

Tipper dropped to the snow in front of Owen's feet. He
pawed at the quills, shook his head, pawed again, and with
no success of ridding them, grew quiet. It was as if he knew

he'd made a big mistake and he wasn't going to get out of his predicament alone. He was going to need help.

In the toolbox behind the driver's seat, Owen found the flat-head pliers. He closed the doors of the creamery truck and braced himself for the task ahead. "You're gonna have to be brave, Tipper."

He coaxed his dog closer, then cradled him between his outstretched legs, with Tipper's head resting on his thigh. "I need you to be still, boy. It's gonna hurt, but you'll feel better after. If we do nothing, you'll swell up. You won't be able to eat. And you'll die."

Tipper groaned.

With the first pull, Tipper growled. Owen wrapped a leg over Tipper's back, securing him in place. Then he worked rapidly, assessing the angle of each quill's entry and pulling it out—just so—and quickly, despite the whimpering.

"Good boy," he said soothingly, over and over. "You're such a good boy."

As he worked, the Torgeson family, one by one, hovered and watched and talked in soft murmurs. From the farmhouse, a dog barked as Owen continued to work.

He pulled one from Tipper's lip, then lifted the lip to make sure the point of the quill hadn't been left behind in the pink gums.

He left the one above the eye for last, praying he could pull it whole and not leave anything behind that might cause eye or brain problems.

When he finished, he was drenched with sweat as he released Tipper. His dog went directly to the truck and waited at the driver's door.

"You bet," Owen said. "Now we can go home. It's all over."

As they drove away from the Torgeson farm, a gunshot echoed. Owen couldn't blame them. Porcupines, unless cornered, aren't generally aggressive, but apparently the Torgesons weren't taking any chances.

❄

When his first loan payment came due, Owen found Pengler in the White Turtle restaurant with cherub-faced Jimmy, who had been sledding earlier with Owen's brothers.

"Hi, Jimmy," Owen said. "How old are you, big guy?"

Jimmy, sipping a chocolate soda, held up fingers on both hands.

"No kidding? Seven?"

Jimmy nodded, lips still around the straw. He was large for his age, making it easy to think he was much older. He was born to Pengler's housekeeper, who had passed away. And from what Pengler had explained, the woman had been married in Duluth and was originally from there, but when her husband abandoned her, so did her family. She moved with her child to Ranier and took what work she could find. Pengler had hired her to keep house at his farm, providing room and board to her and her son. Over time, she'd become more to him. When she got sick and died, Pengler treated Jimmy as his very own.

Now they sat side by side in the booth, eating meatloaf and potatoes with gravy.

"Sit," Pengler said, motioning to the empty bench. "Bring Owen the meatloaf special," he called to a waitress.

"Thanks, Mr. Pengler, but I already had dinner."

"You're arguing with me? From what I can see, you need a little more meat on your bones."

"Okay. I admit it. I'm pretty much always hungry."

"Of course you are. I remember being your age. My folks started clearing the table soon as I lifted my fork. Always worried about having enough leftovers for the next day. That's probably why I started as a chef. Figured I'd never be hungry."

Owen nodded. In many ways, he realized he was driven by the same thing. Without enough food on the table in those early years, he was constantly striving toward a life he could control. One in which there would always be enough. And look where that got him. Things were spinning out of his control, all because he'd felt so desperate to build a different life.

The plate of steaming food appeared. Owen obliged, digging in with his fork and knife.

"So what's on your mind?" Mr. Pengler asked, wiping his chin with a white cloth napkin.

"My first payment is due."

"You're right."

"And I'm a little short."

"Okay. By how much?" Pengler pinched his thumb and forefinger together. "This?" Then he stretched the space between them. "Or this?"

With reluctance, Owen made a zero with his thumb and middle finger. "This."

Pengler leaned forward on his elbows with palms together. He rested his chin on the tips of his fingers, as if this situation were most delicate. "Hmmm. Not a good way to do business."

Owen's ribs tightened around his lungs. He didn't really know what Pengler was capable of if he was unhappy.

"I'll have to charge a late fee." He shrugged. "But I have an idea. There are just some nights," Penglar said, "when, as a father to Jimmy, I need a little break. Y'know, some adult time. And truth is, Jimmy could use a little more 'family time.'"

And so they bartered the late fee for a month of Saturday nights.

When Jimmy stepped away to go use the bathroom, Pengler confided, "Just wish there was an easy way to legally adopt him. But I'm single."

And running a brothel and a bootlegging operation wasn't going to help, Owen wanted to add, but instead he said, "It's simple. Find a gal. Get married."

Pengler forced a smile. "Not that simple."

What wasn't simple, Owen wanted to say, was coming up with a whopping bundle of cash—in *less* than a month.

The following Saturday, Owen met Jimmy at the kitchen door.

"Come in, come in. We're expecting you!"

"Hi," Jimmy said. "Thank you for inviting me to stay overnight," he added, clearly rehearsed. "But I don't live here."

Owen's mom stepped closer and squatted by Jimmy. "No, of course not. But we are so happy to have you come visit us!" She looked directly into the boy's eyes, as if saying she understood his real mother had died and in no way was she trying to replace her. "Here, let me help you with your jacket."

Owen had hoped that he'd be free to leave, maybe see what Jerry was up to that night, but his mother agreed to Jimmy's overnights as long as he stayed around to help out.

In the small living room, with a fire going in the barrel stove, Owen cracked open the window, just enough to keep out most of the damp and cold, but let in the wild clamoring cries of seagulls. They always returned the last few days of March, soaring above the perpetually open water where the river and lake merged. Once darkness fell, the seagulls were raucous, calling back and forth out on the patch of open water. He had no idea why they made such noise, but he welcomed the sound just the same. It was the first real sign of spring.

On the worn sofa, Owen sat in the middle, surrounded by boys, and read aloud from the children's book Miss Winnie had forced on him. He would have preferred to play cards, but he was stuck.

Little Jimmy fit right in.

He snuggled between Jake, a year younger, and Johnny,

a year older. On the other side of Owen sat Nick, who at ten was trying to act too old for bedtime stories, but Owen knew better. Jimmy leaned into him as Owen read. It was a simple children's story:

"What is REAL?" the Rabbit asked the Skin Horse one day . . .

" . . . When a child loves you for a long, long time, not just to play with, but REALLY loves you, then you become Real. . . . By the time you are Real, most of your hair has been loved off, and your eyes drop out and you get loose in the joints, and you get very shabby."

Owen read on, but he had to admit, there was more truth in the Skin Horse's answer than little kids could possibly understand.

Just another one of the boys, Jimmy shared a cot that night with Jake.

As Owen drifted toward sleep, he thought of Sadie that Christmas with the Worthingtons. Rather than stay at their Summit Avenue home in St. Paul, the Worthingtons spent the holiday in Ranier. Mrs. Worthington, in a plum velvet dress, had never seemed happier. Senator Worthington, usually overbearing, charmed the group by doing magic tricks and pulling silver dollars out of everyone's ear. Aasta sang something in Norwegian, and Hans surprised everyone when he produced a fiddle and accompanied her. He wasn't the best musician in the world, but given that no one knew he played a lick, he won applause and took a bow. And Sadie. Her flapper dress glittered and shimmied with each movement as she swayed, playing the piano. "Something from Scott Joplin," she said with a glance over her shoulder. Then her fingers flew, dancing over the keys and filling the house with ragtime.

Owen couldn't keep his eyes off of her.

About the time Owen thought he should head home, Mr. Worthington announced, pointing to a solitary envelope beneath the Christmas tree, "Sadie, one more present. It has your name on it."

She opened it. Owen expected it would be more money to help with college.

Her eyes drew close as she read. "Oh!" she exclaimed.

"Our only regret," Mrs. Worthington said, "is that we hadn't done this sooner."

"It's official," Mr. Worthington announced, as if to a gathering at the state capitol. "Sadie Rose is our daughter. We signed adoption papers! If she'll have us, that is."

Her smile was ear to ear. Seeing her get the one thing she'd dreamed about since her own mother died melted Owen like wax. How could he not love her? Moments later, champagne appeared; a round of toasting, followed by an arranged ride in a six-seat sleigh. They sat in the last row stealing kisses under horsehair blankets and stars.

19

THE NEXT MORNING, HE LEFT THE POST OFFICE WITH A letter from Sadie clutched in his hand. He climbed into the driver's seat and pressed the envelope to his nose, trying to conjure up her image. But the plain envelope with the St. Peter postmark smelled merely as if it had been stuffed into a canvas mailbag, loaded into a boxcar, and traveled miles north to the border.

Tipper shoved his wet snout up under Owen's right palm—hard—and Owen dropped the letter on the floorboards. "Hey, that's rude."

Tipper thumped his tail. He tilted his head, looking at Owen.

"Yeah," Owen said nonchalantly. "It's from her."

Truth was, his heart dashed around in his chest, the way Tipper raced crazy circles when he was happy. But another part of him was cautious. Wait and see. He picked it up.

Owen had finished his rounds and the creamery truck was brimming with full metal cans and stacks of egg crates. He would return to the creamery after he read the letter in the privacy of the truck.

He ran his finger under the edge of the envelope, ripping it open. The letter was short. Two short tepid, cautious, polite paragraphs. He read those quickly. But the last two sentences—he read those over and over.

"I think we should take a break from each other. Let's see what May brings when I return North."

A raven swooped beyond the truck, followed by another in chase. Late winter was breeding season for ravens and eagles. Even though there would be a few snowstorms to come before spring truly arrived, they were following their purpose. They didn't just turn to one another and say, "Hey, let's take a break this spring, shall we?"

Owen smacked the steering wheel and swore.

Tipper whined, as if he'd done something wrong.

"I blew it," Owen said, his voice softer. He stroked Tipper's floppy ears. And then, before anyone could stop by and put their head in his window and make small talk, he drew a deep and heavy breath, turned the creamery truck around, and decided a short drive would do him good. Besides, he thought, glancing at the library books in a paper bag beside his seat, he had books to return.

This time, the library was officially open. Owen hoped there would be other patrons using the library this morning. He didn't want to be forced to talk to anyone, even Miss Winnie.

But when he walked in, she was on a step stool, a cream-colored wool skirt falling midcalf. She turned her head and greeted him with a big smile. "Why hello, Owen Jensen!" Then her lips turned down in exaggeration. "But I had hoped you'd bring your little brothers with you."

"Next time," Owen said. He set the books on the wooden desk. "Thanks." But before he reached the door, she stopped him.

"But tell me—what did you think of *The Velveteen Rabbit*?"

His shoulders rose and fell. The story, about the high cost of love, had made him think of Dad's last efforts to keep Owen from making disastrous choices. It was his way of showing love, though Owen was only beginning to see that now. The price of love was high. It demanded everything, and in the end, we lose those we love, or they lose us. But he couldn't—wouldn't—spill all that here in the library. "Fine," he said. "The boys liked it."

She nodded, stepped down from her wooden stool, and walked over to her desk. She sat, drawing the books toward her, as if it were urgent she record them "returned" as soon as possible. "I guess the story touched me," she said, without looking up at him, her forefinger resting on the cover of the children's book. She was stalling him. Irritating him. He glanced at the curtain hiding her secret sleeping spot. Or was she looking for something more?

"I'm in a hurry," he said.

"When a person has experienced love and loss," she continued, as if she hadn't heard a word he said, "stories are sometimes the best way of making sense of it all, don't you think?"

Her eyes met his.

And then, before he could edit himself, he blurted, "Yeah, I'm worn down to nubs today."

She waited.

"My girlfriend dropped me."

"Oh, I'm sorry." She picked up a pencil, turned it between her fingers, as if considering her next words. "I lost my boyfriend before coming out here," she said. "It's painful. But sometimes it's for the best."

Tick, tick, tick. The mantel clock on the shelf behind her desk marked off the seconds, as if listening in.

"His loss, Miss Winnie," Owen said.

She nodded. "Thanks. But . . . he was married."

Owen was taken aback. That wasn't the kind of thing people said so openly. But she was new here and probably incredibly lonely.

"I don't know why I told you that," she said quickly, and stood up, smoothing her skirt. "It's just . . . well, please don't spread that around, will you?"

Owen shook his head. "No, of course I won't. You know, everyone has their secrets." He didn't tell her about his debts to a bootlegger.

And then they fell into conversation, and she told him about her socialite family. "'You'll be a spinster if you don't get your nose out of those books!' they said. So what did I do? Spent more time at the nearby library and fell in love with the head librarian."

"Who was married," Owen added.

With a pause, she inhaled, then exhaled one word. "Indeed."

"So it wasn't just about bringing civilization to the uneducated . . . but running away from something, yes?"

"Both," she said. "You know Andrew Carnegie?"

Owen nodded.

"Well, he wasn't always a philanthropist. He started as a steel tycoon, putting money above everything, until a bad choice led to the unnecessary deaths of many townspeople. Carnegie could have kept on making money at any cost. Or he could have run away. He had a change of heart. After that, he used his money to help people."

"And built a zillion libraries around the country," Owen said.

Miss Winnie nodded. "Speaking of libraries—and education—are you planning on college?"

"No."

"Lack of money?"

"Right."

"You're bright," she said. "Good grades?"

He nodded.

"There are scholarships."

What help would a little extra money do if he couldn't come up with the balance for college expenses? And who would run the creamery? Who would pay off the loan for his automobiles? For the lost sugar truck?

"If a college truly wants you, they'll pay your full freight."

"Why would they do that?"

"A student with promise is a feather in a collegiate cap. You rise—they rise."

Her words hung there, challenging him.

He suddenly felt the need to get back to the creamery. He grabbed three random books, turned to her desk with them. "I'll take these ones, please."

She stamped the books on the inside covers. "If you ever apply, you must use proper English and grammar. 'These,' not 'these ones.' You'll have to write an essay. I'll proofread it, if you'd like me to."

"Maybe." Then he headed out the door.

Despite Miss Winnie's encouragement to apply to college, Owen dragged through the day. Every push of the broom took effort. Crates and cans felt heavier than usual. At dinner—over a plate of canned garden peas, salt pork, and beans—his brothers' bantering got on his nerves.

"You stole my socks, Knut, just admit it," Jake said.

"Did not."

"You stinkin' did so."

"Jake and Knut! Shut it!" Owen yelled, something he rarely did.

Everyone around the table fell silent. His brothers looked at each other. With his fork, Jimmy pushed his peas around in circles on his plate. In the uneasy quiet, Mom rose from the table, refastening her apron strings, and returned with a loaf of bread. And for a moment, Owen felt as if he'd just replayed one of Dad's angry outbursts.

All that talk of college and scholarships had gotten under his skin. Who was going to offer him enough money to go to college?

And Sadie's letter.

It was over.

He'd been so consumed by her declaration that he'd nearly forgotten Jerry's words during rounds at Melnyks'. "Something important," he'd said. "Meet me at Callahan's at seven thirty. We need to talk."

❄

Callahan's "soda fountain" was bustling with customers. The tavern was dimly lit, and Owen spotted Jerry sitting alone at a corner booth in back. His bowler hat was listing as he beamed his disarming smile. "Hey, a sight for sore eyes!"

The bartender called over. "Jensen? Whaddya have?"

Before he could answer, Jerry held up his glass. "Same thing I'm having, and it's on me."

"I'm not drinking anymore, Jer, since my dad died."

"Yeah, I figured. But you look like shit."

When the drink arrived, Jerry said, "You either have a drink or I'm going to have to wrestle you to the floor and pour it down your gullet. Think of it as medicine."

Owen tried, but he couldn't muster up a simple laugh.

"That bad, huh?" Jerry said, leaning forward studying him. "Sadie?"

Owen nodded. "Got her letter today."

"No, she didn't," Jerry said, guessing.

Owen nodded. "She's done."

Jerry moved the whiskey-filled tumbler into Owen's limp hand. Owen wrapped his hand around it, lifted it.

"To better days ahead!" Jerry toasted. "There are more fish in the big, wide sea, my friend."

Owen buckled. He threw back the shot. It coursed hot down his throat.

Jerry nodded toward the woman in a red, low-cut dress at the counter. "There," he whispered. "Her dress's sole purpose, my friend, is to contain those two hundred pounds until some wild lover like you helps ease her out of it."

Owen reached across the table and slugged Jerry in the shoulder.

One drink became two, then three. Owen's tongue loosened up, thoughts of Sadie Rose dimmed, as Jerry lowered his voice. "Now we gotta get serious. I got a lead on a shipment from Canada."

"Jeez, Jer! Haven't we learned our lesson?"

Jerry held up his hand. "Hear me out. This could be the break we need. What's gonna save us. And it has nothing to do with Pengler, so don't breathe a word of this to anyone. It's just you and me. So, do you want to hear more?"

Owen closed his eyes and exhaled in a huff.

"Aren't you at least curious?"

Owen looked at Jerry, whose eyes were wide with confidence and belief that this time could be different. "Curious? No. Desperate? Yeah. Okay, tell me."

"We pick up at an island this side of Jackfish—and from there we get it deeper into the States. We make a drop an hour, maybe two, south of here and get cash."

"Enough to pay back Pengler?"

Jerry grinned. "And then some."

Owen whispered, "Pengler finds out we're working on our own, we're dead."

"Yeah, but that's probably our fate anyway if we don't come up with the money. So what have we got to lose?"

Owen asked more questions. The more the whiskey radiated through his body, the more his fears eased, and the more he found himself getting charged up about Jerry's plan.

"So whaddya say?" Jerry whispered.

Owen rounded some kind of bend. "Folks think I'm bootlegging anyway," he said.

"Well, you *were* a few summers ago, weren'tcha?"

"That was different. I was seventeen when I found those cases. I turned a little profit. And then I backed off when I realized it was a bigger game—"

"When you got the crap knocked out of you."

"Yeah, to put it mildly."

Jerry laid out details of the plan. "Top-shelf whiskey, the kind Capone wants on his own serving table. We pick it up, we deliver it. We come back. Easy."

Late March, the seagulls return, followed by trumpeter swans, Canada geese, and pelicans . . . And cormorants, mergansers, golden-eyes, mallards, wood ducks, and loons. They make their long trek north from somewhere warmer, only to wait. They wait for the ice to come off Rainy Lake, wait for winter to lose its final grip so they can begin their nesting season. They wait at the bay in Ranier, where all that lake water eventually flows into a tiny funnel called the source of Rainy River. From there it flows west. West to Lake of the Woods up to Hudson Bay and beyond to the ocean.

Seagulls float on small ice chunks, under the lift bridge dividing the river from the lake. Seagulls float down the narrow, turbulent channel between two shores, between Canada and the United States. And as the sun drops beneath the black and amber horizon, seagulls gather on the big lake, on the edge of ice. Thousands of 'em. Every night in the darkness, they're out there, raucous with carrying on. They call and scream at an indecent volume, as if what they were up to couldn't possibly be legal.

20

OWEN SLOGGED THROUGH THE NEXT MORNING'S ROUNDS. His head felt as if a pileated woodpecker were perched top and center, pounding away. His mouth was dry. It was a good day to go slow. Some guys could pound down great quantities of hard liquor and get up and go to work each day. Eventually, it caught up with them the way it did with Owen's father. But Owen hadn't joined those ranks yet. Three or four drinks and he'd practically crawled home. Daylight pained his eyes. It was time to go back to quitting booze altogether.

When Erling returned from school and suggested they go ice fishing, Owen jumped at the chance. The fresh air might help clear his head.

They hiked past Johnson Boatworks, a brick building with a boat motor repair shop below and an apartment above. Outside the building, wooden boats lined up on wooden supports, waiting to roll down the steel rails into the lake when it opened up.

Erling and Owen walked onto the frozen lake. They followed the shore around the eastern point. "Here," Erling said. With an auger, he hand-churned a ten-inch-wide fishing hole in the ice, its sides glowing blue. "Still over a foot thick," he pronounced, removing his cap. Steam rose from his head.

Eyes on their lines, they sat on their haunches, jigging their baited lines into the black hole as shadows deepened around them and the sun disappeared behind a bank of clouds.

"You miss Dad?" Erling asked.

"Yeah, some," Owen said.

"We used to have some good talks," Erling said. "Sometimes I hung around the creamery just to get him talking."

"Yeah?" The only talking Owen remembered pitted him and his father against each other. Whatever Owen wanted, like college and moving out of the area, Dad wanted something else for him. Yet he always seemed softer on Erling, probably because he wasn't the firstborn.

"Yeah, we talked about baseball teams, and when I told him I want to try out for a team someday and be a professional player, he always made me feel like I could do it."

"Did he say you have to finish school first?"

"No."

"Well, you do. School's gotta come first."

They got a strike, then another. Pretty soon, they'd hauled in two walleyes, one northern pike, and one bass. Things were looking up.

"Y'know," Erling said, "everyone's saying the sheriff and deputy went too far. Do you buy that stuff about the shot bumping off the water?"

"No," Owen said. "They shot him in the back. Nothing about that bootlegger's death was accidental."

"Yeah," Erling agreed. "I'd cry 'foul ball.'"

When they returned home, Erling announced, "Fish dinner!"

Mom, who had dropped to a bird's weight since Dad died, filled a basin of water at the sink with the hand pump. She handed it to Owen.

He took it and headed outside.

It used to be Dad's job to fillet fish—no one could do it better—but now it was his. Owen headed out to the fish house, not much bigger than an outhouse, and cut open the fish one by one on the wooden board. He did his best to pare flesh away from bone, but he wasn't perfect at it. He put the fillets in the bowl of cold water.

As he finished up, Owen thought about how he didn't mind having lost his old job to Erling: cleaning up guts, scales, and bones; wrapping up the remains in old newspapers before adding them to the burn barrel.

In the kitchen, Mom hummed as she dipped fillets in a bowl of eggs and then a mixture of flour, salt, and pepper. Then she added them to the cast-iron skillet, hot and sizzling with lard, until the fillets were browned lightly on both sides and the flesh fell apart with a fork.

To top it off, Mom presented a prized can of peaches from the pantry. "Dessert tonight," she said with a genuine smile—the first Owen had seen in months. "Peaches and cream."

21

"HELLO, MR. AND MRS. JOHANNSEN!" OWEN SAID FROM behind the counter, as Aasta entered the creamery with Hans behind her.

"We want to buy Studebaker," Aasta said, removing her red mittens.

Owen was taken aback by the sudden announcement. "At the races, when you said you were interested, I didn't think you meant so soon."

"*Ja?*" Hans said with a slight grin. "Then you got another think coming."

"Okay then," Owen said. "I'll be just a minute."

He asked Mom to cover out front and headed to the back room. He threw on his jacket, found his wooden lockbox at the back of his locker, then headed with his first official customers over to the lot. The Johannsens walked straight to the cheapest model, a Light Six in deep blue.

The Johannsens sat in the front seat. They sat in the back. They stroked the leather. They patted the steering wheel. They asked Owen to start it up and then show them how. It started like a dream.

But they said very little.

Salesmen, selling anything from hair tonic to a circus act, usually talked on and on to make a sale, as if that was the way to keep their customers on the hook. But Owen felt each Studebaker should almost speak for itself. It was a work of art that would take Aasta and Hans as far as St. Paul to visit their granddaughter when they wanted to. She might be adopted now by the Worthingtons, but she was the Johannsens' flesh and blood. He held his tongue. Under a light falling snow, they circled the car several times.

Finally, Aasta said, "This will do!" Then a smile spread across her face and lit up her blue eyes.

When Hans started to pull a wad of bills from his trouser pocket, Owen held up his hand.

He grabbed the wooden box, which held all the keys and sales papers. "Wonderful! But let's finish this up inside."

Owen ducked under the stuffed moose and led them into the hotel's restaurant.

"We scrimp and save," Aasta said, taking a seat at the table.

"Our first car," Hans added. "Better do this before we get too old."

"You two have plenty of years left," Owen said, and he meant it. And then he needed to be honest. "You know," he said, "if you're buying this to help Sadie—help me in some way—I have to tell you, I don't know if we're together anymore . . ."

They waited.

"I appreciate that you want to make this purchase. As long as you know, with Sadie Rose . . . We're not as close as . . . not that I don't want us to be. But nothing is for sure."

Hans nodded. "*Ja*, that's for sure, especially with women," he said, breaking through the tension. "A fellow never knows one day to the next."

Aasta reached out and put her hand on top of Owen's, stilling his hand. He hadn't realized he was turning the pen over and over in his fingers until she stopped him. "You are miles from each other. No need you worry. I see how she look at you."

He met her eyes, so full of hope and knowing, but poor Aasta really had no idea how far apart they'd grown.

"Thanks," he said.

After they drove off, Owen found Pengler in the blind pig. From the sale, he paid off his late payment, his current payment, and next month's payment in cash.

"Your first official sale! Time to celebrate! It's on me."

"Thanks, Mr. Pengler, but I'll pass. I still have work to finish at the creamery."

"Harvey," he said, clapping Owen's shoulder as he rose to leave. "You call me Harvey from now on. I insist."

Outside the creamery and under a confetti-tossed sky, Owen waited for Jerry. He gazed up at the brightest point—Venus making her debut. For the first time in forever, Owen felt something different. Something like faith, a belief that things could begin to turn around for him.

Owen felt it deep in his being.

This was an end and a beginning.

Spring was just around the corner, and with it would come renewed hope.

Three stars stood out from the others. The Belt of Orion, the great hunter.

He'd spent enough energy fretting and worrying. Tonight's opportunity with Jerry seemed golden. The constellations had shifted.

Things couldn't possibly go wrong.

When Jerry showed up a half hour past midnight, he rolled down the window of a Whiskey Six. "Didn't plan on a flat tire," he said. "But I got it going again."

"Wait," Owen said. "That's one of the cars I sold Pengler."

"So? I work for him. He hands me keys for a Whiskey Six, then that's what I drive. Happens all the time."

"But you said this job wasn't connected to him."

"It's not. Is that a problem?"

"Could be a big problem," Owen said. "If he finds out. He may not like you working for yourself with his wheels. And the truck that went through? We're deep enough in debt as it is."

"Tonight it all changes. But okay. Then we take one of yours." Jerry motioned to beyond the tracks and Owen's lot of vehicles.

"Jerry, I have to say, I'm having serious second thoughts about this whole thing. I shouldn't have agreed to this after a few drinks. And I'm not using my inventory to—"

Jerry stopped him. "Forget it. Let's just head out. We'll be back before anyone knows we left." Jerry adjusted his hat, then gave a cocky smile. "It's going to go slicker than butter on hot toast. You have my word."

They drove past the driveway to Pengler's farmstead and traveled east to the boat landing. When they drove onto the ice, Owen snapped off the headlights.

"Okay, so tell me how to get to Nugget Island. You know the lake better than I do."

At first, darkness wrapped around them like a heavy blanket, but soon Owen's eyes adjusted to the frozen lake, the mainland, and scattered islands.

Owen rolled down his window.

"Isn't it cold enough?" Jerry complained.

"If we're unlucky and go through, I want to escape quickly." The brittle breeze produced drops of moisture at the edges of Owen's eyes. No matter.

"Sheesh," Jerry said. "You could knit a sweater with your worries."

"And I don't get how you can't be worried."

They drove across bumpy whiteness, farther from shore.
They weren't that far from the mainland, but Owen knew
the currents could be strong between clusters of islands.

Unpredictable.

As they followed a plowed path beyond the tip of a peninsula, the sky began to brighten, as if a city had suddenly
sprung up to the north. In minutes, the sky changed. Like
lightning after resounding thunder, the sky was alive with
energy, but this wasn't a flash here or there. The whole
sky radiated pale green pulses across to the north, then
shifted and danced to the east, then flashed back north
again. Against a dark stage, curtains of light moved as if
they were alive. The northern lights, or aurora borealis as
he'd learned in science class, now shifted to strips of pink,
then green, then white, like ribbon candy.

"Incredible," Jerry said. "I could live to a hundred and
never get tired of seeing the sky like this."

"Like ancient spirits," Owen agreed. "Ojibwa call them
'Wawatay,' and believe they're a gift from the Great Spirit."

Jerry laughed. "Whaddya s'pose they're sayin'? Keep an
eye out for feds?"

Ahead, the tiny island was a silhouette with a few pines
dotting its half-moon shape. "There," Owen said, with a
nod.

As they neared the island and the small shack, Jerry
thumped the steering wheel as if it were a drum. At the
shore, he stopped the Whiskey Six and put it in park. "I'll
leave the motor running," he said. "If everything's in
order, I'll signal. You can help load up. But if things go
wrong, take off." Then he trotted off carrying a lighted gas
lamp by its handle.

Owen climbed into the driver's seat, glanced behind,
and saw no lights or shadows of being followed. Studeys
offered deep and comfy seats and engines that purred like
cats lapping cream. But unlike his fresh-from-the-factory
automobiles, this Studebaker already smelled of hard use:
cigarettes, cigars, and sweat.

Above the sound of the motor came Jerry's voice. "Hey, c'mon!" A stone's throw onto the island, Jerry was leaning halfway out the door of the small shack. The lantern in his hand threw light up onto his face.

Owen slipped from the Whiskey Six. The plan was that they would pick up a dozen cases of premium Scotch whiskey, avoid the rails out of Ranier, and drive sixty miles south to the depot in Orr, where it would get loaded for Chicago. Jerry said they would get paid cash on delivery.

Owen broke through ice-crusted snow as he headed to the cabin door. Jerry's lamp had gone out, but he wagged his head. "Of all the luck," he said, disappearing inside, as if he couldn't believe their good fortune.

A wave of stale air greeted Owen.

The shack was dark enough for roosting bats. How could they load up cases if they couldn't see anything? "Light your lamp, Jer," Owen said as he stepped in. "How are we gonna load up if—"

Cold steel pressed against his temple.

A gun barrel clicked in warning.

"Yeah, light the lamp, Jer." A familiar voice, but Owen couldn't place it. "Light it so we can all say hello."

22

Owen wanted to freeze time. Same as a film that gets hung up on its metal wheel, he wanted to stop on the frame. Stop it and rewind.

A match struck twice.

The tang of sulfur filled the air.

A small flame broke the darkness, illuminating Jerry's face and hands as he lit the base of the gas lamp.

The wick caught and glowed and the small room brightened.

Just inside the door, Sheriff Vandyke held a gun at Jerry's back. "Close the door, Owen," he said.

Owen did so. Dread coursed through his veins as he turned slowly toward Deputy Kranlin, who lowered his pistol to his side, his eyes fixed on Owen like a robin after an earthworm.

"Go ahead," the sheriff said, motioning to the crates. "You boys pick up what you came for."

"We were just out cruising," Jerry said. "Thought we'd stop here. Make a fire. Play cards. Hey, Sheriff, you guys play cards?"

They might have had a chance if Jerry would quit talking.

"Pick up the crates," the sheriff ordered. His jaw muscle knotted.

"Whatever you say, Sheriff," Jerry said, in the overly

nonchalant voice that had always gotten him in trouble in school. "Hey, they'll make extra chairs at the table."

Deputy Kranlin motioned Owen with the gun toward the crates. He saw no reason not to oblige. He followed Jerry toward the stacked crates. He lifted one. Jerry did the same. Their eyes met, and Owen shook his head as the weight of their situation hit him.

"Busted," the sheriff said. "You boys are under arrest for bootlegging."

"You baited us!" Jerry said accusingly. "That ain't right."

The sheriff nodded. "Way I see it, you two came here for an alleged shipment of booze. Is that how you see it, Deputy Kranlin?"

"That's exactly how I see it!" the round-faced deputy said, as if this were the biggest joke ever. "Sometimes, you gotta go fishin' and here you are. Hook, line, and sinker. A federal offense. You'll get a quick trial, then spend, oh, anywhere from two to ten years behind bars."

Two to ten? Owen felt sick. He might be twenty-nine by the time he got out. His life would be half over before he even got started. "Sheriff, please," Owen pleaded. "We're local boys. You know our families. My dad's gone. It's just my mom and brothers now, and if I'm behind bars, there's no telling what will happen to them."

"Yeah," Jerry added. "My folks rely on my help on their farm. When the tractor breaks down, I'm the only one who can fix it up again."

"Well," the sheriff said, "too bad you didn't consider the consequences. I could go easy on you, let you go . . ."

"Oh, Sheriff," Jerry said, dramatically dropping to his knees, his hands pressed together like an altar boy's. "Thank you. We promise, we won't ever get into this spot again."

"Coming from you, Jerry, that doesn't mean much. Now Owen, you should have known better." He stared at Owen, as if seeing right through him. "This isn't a game.

You two can set an example for other boys who are tempted to bootleg."

Jerry rose to his feet and crossed his arms.

"Turn around, Jerry," the sheriff ordered. "Hands behind your back."

Then he clamped handcuffs around Jerry's wrists.

Owen watched—their lives and futures pouring down the drain.

"There's one way out of this," Kranlin said.

Owen didn't like the sound of that. There weren't any good options in a situation like this. He held his breath.

For once, Jerry didn't say a word.

"We know you're working for Pengler and doing his errands for him, but he's the one who's making the real money. Not you boys. You're just cogs in his well-oiled machine."

Owen wanted to protest. After all, Harvey Pengler had just practically forgiven the recent late payment; he'd believed in him and given him a loan to start the business.

"So here's your ticket," the sheriff said. "You boys testify against Pengler, say he sent you on this mission, and you two go back to your lives. He serves time, not you."

"But he didn't send me on this mission," Jerry said. "I caught wind of this one all on my own. Thought I'd make a little extra money and—"

"Jerry, shut up," Owen said. Jerry wasn't helping them out by handing over his confession on a silver platter.

"Doesn't matter," the sheriff replied. "You can testify just the same. Let Pengler take the credit and blame for this one. We know it's not your first run for him."

"You want us to lie," Jerry said.

The small room flickered from the lamp's single flame, and shadows played off the walls and rafters.

Owen didn't like that Pengler hadn't been completely up front with him about the initial order of autos, but he'd treated Owen fairly enough. Worked with him when Owen had fallen short on his first business payment. He wouldn't lie about Pengler, no matter which side of the law he was on. It was all so damn complicated. The only thing Owen knew was that he'd made a colossal mistake tonight going out on such a shaky limb for money.

"Toads," Jerry said. "You're asking us to be toads."

The sheriff snorted in reply.

"Yeah, you'd be toads," Kranlin agreed, "but you'd be *free* toads, not ones behind bars."

"Like I said," Jerry continued, "we were just cruising the lake. Guys out for a drive."

"Too bad you already confessed, Jerry. Too bad for you your drive ended here," the sheriff said. "Honestly, for your sakes, I'd rather see you keep your noses clean and do the right thing with your lives."

The wind picked up from the north, sending a chill down Owen's sweaty neck and back. With both hands free, Owen did as he was ordered. He lugged crates of booze from the shack to the back of the Whiskey Six—the Studebaker he'd sold to Pengler. With each trip back and forth, he wanted to kick himself. He'd acted so sure that he wouldn't get involved in bootlegging when he accepted the loan. Dad had been right, more than Owen cared to admit.

As Owen carried the last crate out of the shack, the deputy followed with the lantern, which illuminated footprints in the snow across the island and away from the shack.

When Owen loaded the last crate, he looked for the sheriff and Jerry. "Where'd they go?"

His answer came in the form of bouncing beams of light as the sheriff's car appeared around the point, headlights on. When it stopped beside the Whiskey Six, Sheriff Vandyke slipped from the driver's seat, but Jerry remained in the back of the sheriff's Model T.

"So you parked on the north side of the island," Owen said, "and walked the cases over so we wouldn't see tracks."

"That's right," the sheriff answered. "Couldn't give ourselves away. Now, you and Deputy Kranlin will drive to town together, and Jerry will ride with me." He held out another set of handcuffs. "Owen, turn around."

23

THE THOUGHT OF DRIVING ACROSS THE ICE WITH HAND-cuffs suddenly made Owen's nightmares of going through the ice seem vividly possible. "Please, I'm scared to be handcuffed while we're crossing the lake. Don't make us wear them until we get on land, Sheriff. We won't cause you any trouble. Promise."

"Yeah, he's right!" Jerry hollered, his voice carrying through the sheriff's open driver's door.

"Jerry, you'll be just fine," the sheriff replied. "Makes me feel better if you wear 'em. On the other hand, Owen has never caused me trouble." He put the cuffs away. "Deputy, you keep an eye on Owen while he drives, yes?"

Kranlin lifted his pistol in agreement.

As Owen started up the Studebaker, he expected they'd head directly back toward shore, but the deputy directed him to the north side of the island and out toward the frozen channel where the water ran deeper . . . the course boaters followed in the summer to avoid submerged rocks and shallows.

"Hey, we don't want to go this way," Owen said. "Trust me, let's turn around."

The deputy laughed. "Think I'm going where you direct me? Keep going. Straight ahead." He held the pistol a few inches higher.

"This way—the current runs stronger," Owen said.

Deputy Kranlin kept his gun visible. "I said we don't take your route. You might have friends waiting along the way, making sure your shipment doesn't run into trouble."

"Nobody's waiting. We got into this mess on our own. But please, you need to hear me on this. On extra-cold nights like tonight, the ice gets brittle on top, but underneath it's not hard. It's been softening up for some time, which makes this a dangerous time to be out here," Owen said, hoping to say something to convince Kranlin, who was new to the county . . . probably hailed from some big city where his biggest worry had been slipping on icy sidewalks.

"You talk all you want, kid, but we checked the ice a few days ago. It's plenty solid."

Lake ice boomed and groaned.

"And that doesn't scare me," the deputy said. "It's been doing that all winter long."

Owen glanced in his side mirror. The sheriff and Jerry followed, lights bouncing up and down as they traveled between ice ridges and remaining snowbanks and over patches of black ice. Owen was tempted to turn the wheel sharply, or maybe stop suddenly and try to grab the gun from the deputy's hand. But what good would that do? He'd only get into more trouble. He slowed his pace but kept driving.

With the next boom, an ear-splitting crack followed. Owen sensed the ice giving way. He grabbed the wheel tighter as the bottom fell out from beneath them, and the car dropped with a jolt.

"Oh no!" Deputy Kranlin hollered.

Water poured through Owen's open window and sloshed on his trousers and onto the floorboards.

"I can't swim!" the deputy shouted.

Owen had only one thought: *Get out!*

Climbing out his window, he was met by blood-stopping icy water.

Water seeped into his clothes and his skin, waterlogging his jacket and trousers, mitts, socks, and long johns.

Water filled his boots.

He thrashed, but water weighted him down. The lake dragged him below until his nose was barely above the surface.

He kicked and paddled for everything he was worth. Inch by inch he pulled himself up and headed toward an edge of ice. Behind him, Kranlin hollered and grabbed the edge of Owen's jacket, shoulders, neck. The deputy clawed and cried out for his life and, in his panic, pushed Owen under.

In blackness, Owen gasped, and bitter cold rushed into his lungs. He flailed and slugged and thrashed for something, anything to grab on to, and came up. He sputtered and wheezed, and his lungs ached for air.

Kranlin's gloved hand rose from the water.

Owen grabbed it and the man surfaced. "I can't swim!" he wailed.

"Hang on," Owen said. "Don't panic." Then he pulled the deputy to the edge of the ice. "I'll crawl forward, see if it'll hold. Hang on to my foot." He belly-crawled forward, slowly, cautiously, across the ice. Beneath them, the ice groaned and complained.

A sharp crack sounded and traveled under Owen's belly. He stopped crawling and flattened, distributing his weight as evenly as possible. His teeth started chattering and his body shook.

But the ice held.

Again, Owen inched ahead. The only way to go was forward. Not until Owen and the deputy made it a safe distance from the breakthrough did Owen look back.

Just behind them, the lights of the sheriff's vehicle flashed on them for a moment, then shifted skyward, as if trying to merge with the northern lights. The Model T, lettered "Koochiching Sheriff" along its doors, was pointed nose up, like a breaching whale. To Owen's horror, the vehicle sank rear first.

Ice cracked as it went down.

Helpless, Owen watched.

Muffled shouts.

The driver's door cracked open just as the vehicle dropped beneath the surface with a *whoosh* and disappeared.

Darkness engulfed Owen.

The truck was gone, but cases of booze floated at the surface, as if mocking their high-minded quick-money scheme.

For the moment, Owen didn't want to move forward for fear of breaking through again. A numbness started to envelop him, almost warming him. His mind downshifted into some low gear. Shock. Disbelief. None of this could be real. He stared into the darkness, unable to move.

A voice startled him. "I'm here!"

Owen's mind jerked into alertness.

"Jerry! Where are you?"

"Here!"

It was the sheriff's voice.

"Where is he?" Kranlin asked.

Owen's eyes began to adjust. He rose to his hands and knees and scanned the patch of black ice where both vehicles had gone down. Finally, his eyes adjusted to a vague outline of a head and hands, clinging to an edge. The sheriff flung himself forward, but with each effort the ice broke and the sheriff fell back into the water. He surfaced and sputtered, "Help! Need a hold of something!"

"We're coming!" the deputy called back, motionless.

Owen needed something—anything—to help. His fingers were numb, as if they belonged to someone else. He worked off his jacket. He crawled as close as he dared, then he held one sleeve of the jacket and tossed the jacket toward the sheriff. The sheriff grabbed on, and Owen crawled backward, keeping his weight low. Slow, steady, and sure, he pulled against the sheriff's weight until he was out of the water and sliding on his belly, and eventually crawling away from the hole.

"Jerry!" Owen called, scanning the otherworldly landscape. "Jerry!" he called over and over.

He'd surface. If anyone had a thousand lives in him, it was Jerry. Heck, he'd surfaced after the sugar truck disappeared. Owen had been sure he was a goner, but he'd come to the top, ice picks at the ready.

And then he remembered.

Jerry was handcuffed.

24

THE FIRE CRACKLED WITH LIFESAVING WARMTH IN THE stone hearth. Wrapped in wool blankets pulled from storage closets, Owen huddled with Vandyke and Kranlin beside the flames. They sat as close as possible to the heat without setting themselves on fire, but Owen was still cold to his core. At his back, the air was freezing, so he turned himself bit by bit like a sausage on a stick, heating up one side, then the other.

At first his teeth chattered as if they'd fly right out of his head, and shivers came in convulsive shudders. But as his body gradually warmed, and minutes or hours passed—he really didn't have a sense of time—his brain started to emerge from its survival fog.

He was alive.

He'd survived. Miraculously.

And then the horror returned.

Jerry.

His friend was entombed at the bottom of the lake.

Owen felt a knife pain of loss.

It couldn't be. Only an hour or two earlier, they were driving under the northern lights, hoping just one whiskey run would solve their problems.

Baird's Island was the nearest possible shelter. Soaked

and shivering, Owen knew they couldn't waste a minute out in a bitter wind. They had to get warm before they froze solid. There had been no lights to guide them, but Owen recognized the outline of the island to the west, where he knew Trinity's cabin waited.

As they neared the island's shore, Owen led them a few hundred yards to the square log cabin, boarded up for winter.

He knew where the key was hidden, just inside the lid of the wood box. Protected from snow and ice, the key was there—thank God.

He turned the skeleton key and the bolt gave way. Stepping inside, he was overwhelmed by memories of the nights he'd cut his motor, drifted in, and tied his boat to come see Sadie Rose. They'd talked and touched until the sun chased away shadows and he had to leave for the creamery. He'd barely slept during those two weeks, but he'd never felt more alive or happier. He'd surrendered his heart to her then, or as much as he was capable of surrendering. Now he breathed in the cabin air, stuffy with being shut up all winter. His feet were numb. His hands felt like ice blocks. He wanted—more than anything in the world—to sleep.

And he knew he had to ignore that urge, or it would spell his own death. What he needed to do was to get a fire going—fast—before hypothermia completely overtook his thought process.

Fumbling in the darkness, he found stick matches above the stone fireplace and struck one against a stone. When it lit, he spotted the copper barrel nearby filled with dry birch logs, cut and split, and ample birch bark.

His mind wasn't working right. He was numb, but he forced himself to stay in motion. He started a fire using birch bark beneath crisscrossed logs, but when the draft backfired and filled the room with billows of smoke, he realized he'd forgot to open the chimney flue. He pulled the lever on the hearth, and the chimney drew air. The fire roared to life, bright and hot. The smoke-filled room began to clear as the sheriff and deputy coughed and clustered by the hearth.

"Take off your clothes," Owen said, jumping to his feet.

"Hell I will," Kranlin said.

"Suit yourself," Owen said, as he shrugged off his shirt and pants, long johns and socks. Then he wrapped himself in a striped wool blanket and huddled by the fire.

"He's right," the sheriff said, speaking slower than usual. "Wet clothes. Keep in cold."

Before long, the deputy and sheriff stripped off wet clothes and cocooned themselves in blankets.

Owen gradually warmed.

The fire illuminated Trinity's easel and oil paintings of flowers, of her family, of herself. He knew Baird's Island—two islands, like an hourglass, joined by a strip of sand beach. Trinity's cabin was on the southern half, and a main lodge and cabins graced the northern half. He'd made countless dairy deliveries by boat, visiting with Mr. and Mrs. Baird, with Trinity, and with Sadie Rose when she'd abruptly left the Worthingtons and headed out on her own with barely a dime. She'd managed to go under a different name and find work at Kettle Falls, not as one of the working madams, but doing maid work—until Senator Worthington got wind of her whereabouts and tried to track her down, but Owen gave her a lift to this island to stay with Trinity.

Warming up in Trinity's familiar cabin, in this amber patch of necessary warmth with Kranlin and Vandyke—with Jerry gone—was a bad dream from which he'd soon wake up.

His mind drifted half in and out of sleep. Thoughts of Jerry struck in powerful waves. Tears filled his eyes and poured down his cheeks. He couldn't stop them. Didn't have the will to stop them. His friend was gone. Not just a close call this time, not an amazing recovery from another dire situation from which Jerry would escape.

This time was different.

"Why did you have to handcuff him?" he cried out.

Neither the sheriff nor the deputy responded. They both stared into the fire, huddled in their wool blankets, almost as if no one had spoken. It was a nightmare . . . one he may never forget. Here they were, stripped nearly to their skin, beneath blankets to stay alive, at the mercy of a flame lapping at a few logs. Without the fire, they'd be dead. Their last breaths would have frozen on the wind. But because of a simple shelter and a simple fire, they might survive.

Because of simple handcuffs, Jerry was dead.

Owen imagined him, struggling as the sheriff's Model T went down, filling with ice-cold water that rose over Jerry's mouth and nose, trapping him as he dropped inch by inch, foot by foot, beneath the surface. And the moment Jerry might have called out, might have gasped for breath, his lungs would have been met by an intake of deadly cold water, closing off his lungs forever.

"He was . . . ," Owen began, dropping his head to his blanket. And then he began to sob. His shudders turned to a wail that he couldn't contain or hold back, and in that instant, he understood the howl of the lone wolf, rising with such melancholy on the air. At his very being, Owen understood. He ached. He hurt at his core for the presence of his friend. For his father. The wail was primal, calling from somewhere so deep in his being that it seemed to come from someone else.

He seized a breath.

He got control.

He pressed his fists to his eyes.

He lay down on his side, tucked into a blanketed ball before the fire, and let sleep and silence overtake him.

He turned from the cold, remembering.

He turned toward the warmth, and dreamed.

It was summer, warm, balmy, heavily scented with pine and blossoms. And Sadie Rose was pressed into him, murmuring, kissing his earlobe. They were at a place of their own, a little cottage overlooking the water, and Sadie was talking about someday how she'd love to have a pet elephant, just like the baby elephant she'd seen at the circus in Ranier, but Owen wasn't sure where they'd keep it. It would grow and get quite big. That's what he was trying to tell her. And then, Trinity showed up, saying she needed to paint in their cottage, that if she couldn't paint she would die. And so they let her paint a portrait in the corner, and she promised not to be in the way, and she painted and painted and painted. And when Owen finally was permitted to look at what she'd accomplished, she turned and smiled, and moved out of the way. And there it was, a portrait of Jerry. "Because he was your friend," Trinity said, her blonde hair cut short, giving her a fashionable air, but her eyes filled with understanding, of knowing, that this portrait would bring solace, as well as sadness for Owen.

It was a portrait, exquisitely rendered, of Jerry, capturing his eyes, so full of life, and his cockeyed smile, the way he was always caught between doing good and mischief. "It's perfect," Owen said in the dream.

And then he woke up.

They'd burned through the stash of wood and the fire was dying down to coals. Owen forced himself to stand and checked his trousers and jacket hanging on the back of a chair, but they were still too wet to put back on. In boots and underwear he headed out, blanket wrapped around his shoulders and torso, and gathered an armload of wood from the fire box.

He hurried back in and built the fire up until it blazed. Though most of the heat went up the chimney, the air in the cabin and the braided rug beneath them began to warm. He pulled the chaise lounge closer to the fire, tucked under another blanket, and closed his eyes. The fire snapped and roared. Life was like a fire. All it took was a spark to set off an inferno. Full-of-life Trinity, who dared to jump off the highest cliffs on Rainy Lake. She'd studied art in Paris, had a yacht named after her—the world at her fingertips—and yet she'd come close to taking her own life. Something in her brain went haywire. Jerry, who could charm the horns off a bull, who had a good family, and who could have set up shop as a mechanic—he was that good—needed to take risks. It was something that drove him until, ultimately, he took one risk too many. And for Owen, maybe it was his need to make something of himself, to prove he could be more than his father, that would be his undoing.

His Achilles' heel.

It took him a moment to register the sheriff's voice. Vandyke was talking at him. "And so as far as I'm concerned, Owen, you say nothing about last night and we'll forget this night ever happened."

Owen sat up, straddled the chaise lounge, leaning forward in disbelief. "My friend's dead," the reality of his words falling on him hard. Saying it aloud took it out of the land of dreams.

"I could press charges on you," the sheriff continued, "but I won't. You saved our lives. You acted. You led us here. I'll never be able to repay that debt."

"You want me to be silent. When folks ask questions, when his parents ask questions, you want me to be silent." Owen couldn't believe it. It was terrible enough to lose Jerry, and now he was supposed to lie? Pretend it never happened?

"He went through the ice," the sheriff replied. "That's what happened. You survived. That's the truth. I'm not asking you to lie."

Owen didn't know what to say. His gut coiled in anger.

Deputy Kranlin spoke up. "You needn't tell everything, that's all he's saying. Not the whole truth."

"And if I do?" Owen said.

The sheriff sighed, then said, "Honestly, if I were in your shoes, I would just go home and sleep it off. Last night never happened. Start talking about it and lots of folks might blame me, blame the deputy here, maybe even blame you—for surviving when Jerry did not. They might ask questions, and there would be no good answers."

Owen felt the snare tightening, holding him there, as much by his own choices and actions as the sheriff's ultimatum. "He asked you not to handcuff him! You didn't give him a chance."

No response.

The fire burned and a red spark landed on the rug. Reflexively, Owen jumped up and ground it out with the heel of his boot.

Finally, the sheriff stared at the fire. "Believe me. I'd do anything to change that decision now."

From the regret in the sheriff's voice, Owen believed him.

"Prohibition," the sheriff continued. "Hell of a thing to enforce."

"It's the law," Kranlin said, as if those words absolved them.

Vandyke said, "When I worked as a timber cruiser, the job was straightforward. Just me and a cook tromping around the woods. My job was to find timber, calculate how much was available for logging, and report back to Ennis. The cold in the winter, the bogs and the bugs in summer, I would never call it easy. But that job was black-and-white. Easy compared to sheriff. Every other Joe and his grandmother has a backyard still, turning normal folks into criminals."

"It isn't easy, but you're doing your job, Sheriff," Kranlin said. "And I'm doing mine."

A long silence passed before the sheriff spoke again. When he did, he turned his head to meet Owen's eyes. "I don't want to strong-arm you on this, Owen," he said, "but you know I could send you to prison for bootlegging. You'd get two years, if you're lucky, ten if you're not. So I have one more demand."

Owen waited.

"I need you to tell me what you know. About Pengler's operations. About bootlegging that's going on in the area. You hear something, I want you to tell me."

Owen clenched his fists. He wasn't about to be a squealer and play both sides of the fence. He struggled for air, his chest in a vise. "And if I don't?"

"Let's just say, what good will serving prison time do anyone? What would that do to your creamery, your dealership? Oh, and when Pengler learns that you were busted because you and Jerry went off on your own—you think he's going to support your mom and brothers then?"

What a damn fool he'd been! The sheriff had him bound and gagged, but he was caught in a trap of his own making. *He* chose to go out with Jerry, ignoring his own misgivings. *He* chose to go for the extra cash opportunity. He'd take the secret about Jerry with him to the grave.

There wasn't anything more to say on the subject.

Silence was his answer, and the sheriff didn't mention it again.

Owen drifted to sleep, waking once to hear the door open and close as someone stoked the fire again.

When his eyes next opened, a pale light filled the cabin.

Three words clanged in his head: *Jerry was gone . . .*

How had he slept when his friend was somewhere beneath the ice? Guilt caught in his throat. Why had he survived when Jerry had not? Why didn't he put up a fight with the sheriff and insist that Jerry not be handcuffed? And what would he say to the Melnyks when they asked about their son's whereabouts?

The cabin was almost too warm. Owen checked his long johns, now nearly dry. He put them on, clenching his jaw against an overwhelming swirl of emotions. As if he were right there, Dad's voice sounded in his head: *Don't say I didn't warn you.*

Owen pulled the cotton curtain back from a window. Throat aching, he looked to the southeast. Five wolves traveled in single file across the ice between islands, their tails outstretched, their bodies dark silhouettes. They trotted north, oblivious to the international border between two countries. Likely in pursuit of deer, they disappeared. Owen felt a kinship with them and hoped they'd escape a trapper's snare or hunter's bullet.

He'd seen as many as thirty pelts tacked to a shack's outer walls. Wolves, like people, are driven to eat, to mate, to feed their young. They live in packs, with leaders and followers, much like families. On occasion, they take livestock, to the outrage of farmers, who in turn shoot the wolves to protect their livelihood. He understood that. Still, he wished people and wolves could find a way to coexist. There was a hefty bounty on the wolf, paid out by the state of Minnesota for every shot, poisoned, or trapped animal.

He'd heard trappers' stories. Caught in a trap's steel jaws, a wolf will chew off its own paw, trying to escape. He squeezed his eyes shut. Right now, he'd do just about anything to escape last night's events.

The sheriff and deputy stirred behind him, waking up.

The day was about to unfold.

Owen opened his eyes.

Dawn broke in a rim of red, a glowing orb behind the tops of pines.

Owen dreaded every moment of what lay ahead, unsure how he could possibly put one foot in front of the other.

DREAMS OF
SUMMER

Unlike other signs of spring, the mass of ice on the big lake hangs on.

New growth of pale green paints spruce and balsam, aspen, birch, and maple. Pollen floats on a warm southerly wind. On the north side of buildings, boulders, and towering pines, the last snowdrifts melt into puddles. Water trickles into rivulets, streams, and rivers that flow into the lake.

You wait an eternity for the actual event, and then one day in late April or the first or second week of May, it happens.

An arctic air mass rushes in.

Clouds blacken.

Lightning flashes.

Winds howl and gust.

Where the ice has melted along the shoreline, ripples turn to waves, and waves turn to whitecaps that wash over the ice and push from beneath. Water sloshes into hairline cracks, softening them until they widen and the surface of the lake breaks into giant fields of ice.

All night long, violent wind drives ice downstream.

An act of nature, and afterward—everything is changed.

25

Nights, Owen dreamed of Jerry.

Jerry floated, facedown, amid sheets of ice. "Jerry!" Owen called out to him, and Jerry lifted his head and started swimming toward shore. Owen was beyond relief. He broke out crying, "I thought you were dead!"

"Can't keep a good guy down," Jerry said, laughing, and then, as if he were a dog, he shook off the icy water in a blast. Instantly dry.

"Hey, that was good. Tipper can't even dry off that fast. You're a magician!" Owen felt such happiness at seeing his friend. He wanted to wrap his arms around him in a bear hug. "I just can't believe it."

He dreamed of going through the ice, clawing at anything to keep from sinking into the utter darkness.

He dreamed of Sadie Rose, handcuffed by some outrageous mistake in the back of the sheriff's Model T. She called out for Owen, and though he tried to reach her, his legs wouldn't budge from the ice and the vehicle slipped out of sight before he could save her.

When he woke, the real nightmare always returned.

He turned on his light, pulled a book from his bookshelf, and read "A Scandal in Bohemia," about the only woman who challenged Sherlock Holmes intellectually. For Holmes, she is always *the* woman.

And for Owen, there could only be Sadie.

Enough. He sat up and slapped his hands down on either side of him, startling Tipper out of a deep sleep. Tipper jumped up on all fours and started yipping.

"It's okay, fella," Owen dropped his voice. He wrapped his arms around the golden dog. Tipper leaned closer into Owen's side, then he snuck a quick lick across Owen's chin.

"Gee, thanks." Owen wiped it away.

He got up and went down to the kitchen. The hands on the wall clock read three fifteen, about the same time he found himself in the kitchen every night since . . .

His gut churned in anger. Anger at the government and the Volstead Act that made Prohibition the law of the land. Anger at Dad for leaving him to figure everything out on his own. Anger at Sadie Rose for being distant. But more than anything, he was angry at the needless loss of Jerry.

In his coat pocket, he found his flask, took off its cap, and put the flask of brandy to his lips. Deadening the pain would feel good. He could drink and drink until a numbness settled over his whole being. It would be like running away from everything. Only problem was—when he sobered up, he'd have to face his life. Sure, he might handle booze now, but over time, he might not be so lucky. Some families grew alcoholics the way a field sprouted buttercups. He screwed the cap on and put the flask away.

He opened the icebox, pulled out a jug of milk, and poured himself a tall glass. He found fresh sugar cookies in the ceramic cookie jar he'd bought last Christmas for his mother. It was a round, smiling, red-aproned man with a white chef's hat. Maybe that's how Pengler dressed when he worked as a chef in Chicago, before starting a new life up north. At the Palmer House, known as a top-shelf restaurant, Pengler must have met all kinds of powerful people in Chicago. What made an ambitious guy leave all that behind? Was he running from trouble? Or had he simply wanted to strike out on his own and be his own boss?

Convinced that he couldn't go back to sleep or, worse yet, that sleep would only bring more nightmares, Owen grabbed his jacket and stepped out into the damp air and cacophony of seagulls calling from ice floes.

As if they hadn't a care in the world, cows produced milk right on schedule. Day in and day out. Owen forced himself to keep his foot on the gas pedal and turn the wheel into Melnyks' long driveway.

When Mr. Melnyk flagged him down from his blacksmith shop's open doors, Owen slowed the truck and rolled down his window. His throat went dry. He swallowed hard and forced the words out: "Good morning."

With blackened gloves and a knee-length heavy apron, Mr. Melnyk stepped up to the truck. Behind him, coals glowed red within his shop. Smoke curled around the door frame and rose toward the gray sky.

The sight of Mr. Melnyk was almost too much. Owen liked Jerry's father, who always carried a raw potato in his pocket to ease his stiff joints. Jerry used to laugh about many of his father's "Old World" superstitions, which included burying a strip of raw bacon near the house as a remedy for getting rid of warts. If only there was a remedy for bringing back sons. Mr. Melnyk lost one son already in the trenches between France and Germany; it was beyond comprehension that he would lose a second son. And he didn't even know.

"Owen, I am wondering. Have you seen Jeremiah?"

Owen pretended to wipe sleep from his eyes. "No, haven't seen him in over a week. Why?"

"This is not the first time he go away, you know." He

nodded to himself. "He will come back. I am sure. You have good day." And then Mr. Melnyk turned back to his anvil and continued hammering.

No, he won't come back, Owen wanted to say. He wanted to tell Mr. Melnyk everything about what happened. Jerry's father would fly into a rage and go directly to the sheriff to give him a piece of his mind, and the sheriff would draw up charges on Owen, maybe make him an accomplice in Jerry's death. Who knows how the truth might get braided with falsehoods?

Holding back a dam of emotions, Owen drove on.

Later that day, as he worked in the back of the creamery, topping off glass quart bottles with fresh milk, the entry door chimed.

"Owen here?" Harvey Pengler boomed.

"Yep, he's in back. I'll get him," Mom replied.

With the push of the swinging door, Harvey swept in, removing his fedora. "You're here. Good. I've been meaning to talk to you, but you've been hard to track down."

"Harvey," Owen said with a nod of greeting. "I've been awfully busy."

Harvey eyed the creamery. "You do a good job here. Neat as a pin. Your dad would be happy to see the way you've kept things going."

Owen waited.

Harvey eyed the wooden stool by a worktable. "May I?"

He hadn't come by for a simple chitchat.

"Help yourself," Owen replied, as casually as he could manage, but the nauseous feeling returned. Sooner or later, he would be asked about Jerry.

Pengler sat down, legs wide in gray trousers, elbows to his knees as he turned his fedora around and around in his hands.

Owen braced himself. He'd give anything to be able to spill the truth. But telling the truth to Pengler? There was no telling how Pengler would react if he learned he and Jerry had decided to bootleg on their own. Not to mention that in the process, they'd lost one of Pengler's brand-new Whiskey Sixes—along with Jerry.

"Have you seen our friend Jerry?" Pengler asked, his voice low.

Owen swallowed, forcing out words. "Not for a while." He turned from Pengler's gaze and began filling jars from the vat of buttermilk.

"It's not like him to disappear. He had a job last night. Never showed up. Haven't heard a word from him. Haven't seen my Studebaker, either. He had keys. I trusted him."

"Huh."

"Yeah. That's what I say. I like Jerry, so I don't want to start being suspicious. But some guys, they see all this booze and bucks and they get ideas. So I'm wondering. Did he take off and try to start a little bootlegging on his own?"

Owen shrugged and raised his eyebrows. Had Pengler caught wind of their activities?

"He doesn't seem like the type to put a knife in a guy's back. I figure you might know. If he skipped out, he might have said something. Might drop you a line. Make a phone call."

Owen shook his head.

"Unless he was out driving on the lake and went through somewhere, where the ice was—" He stretched out a hand, fingers splayed, and tilted it back and forth. "That would be the craps."

The memory burned. Owen's eyes felt hot. His throat closed up. The emotion must have shown on his face, because Pengler stood up and clapped a hand on Owen's shoulder. "Hey, sorry. Didn't mean to upset you. Anyone who can ride bareback, crash, and nearly win a race has more lives than a cat."

Then he put on his hat, tilting it slightly over his right eye. "Y'know, I worry already about Jimmy. Just a few years and he could be doing stupid things. I know I sure did when I was a kid." He laughed. "But you. You're different. You got a real level head on your shoulders. Like you actually use the brains God gave you. That's good." Then he stood, gave a nod, and added, "You hear from Jerry, just let me know. And if not, guess I'm going to be forced to buy another one of your Studeys. A good deal for you. Not for me. This time, I s'pose I'll have to pay full price."

And then he left.

Owen's stomach churned. Sure, he wanted to move his inventory. No doubt about it. But he didn't want to make a sale because of Jerry's death.

Pengler hadn't said a word about the big sum of money due in a few weeks. And it certainly couldn't have slipped his mind.

26

OWEN WAS SWEEPING FLOORS WHEN ERLING BURST through the creamery door.

"I'm gettin' tickets!"

He yanked off his raincoat, sending a shower of sleet across the floorboards. Then he raced to the back room, calling out from behind the swinging doors, "I'm gonna see Babe Ruth play!" When he emerged, he ran his hands through his hair, which he'd recently trimmed short along the sides, leaving the top long and wavy, much like Owen's. He was turning into a pretty handsome young man, with Dad's squarish face.

"When?" Owen asked, broom in one hand, dustpan in the other.

"Not 'til August, but boy oh boy—I can't wait! They just announced their tour and I bought tickets over the phone. All I have to do is send a check! I mean, to see the Babe in action, even if it's a promotional tour, the Babe—playing against local folks. Still, he's a legend, and—oh, just about forgot." He disappeared in the back and returned with an envelope. "Stopped by the post office. This is for you."

Like a bird riding an updraft, Owen's heart rose in his chest. A letter from Sadie. He didn't want to get his hopes up. "Thanks."

The envelope was damp, and the ink on the return address was smeared, but he managed to make it out. The letter wasn't from Sadie but from Trinity Baird. He exhaled in disappointment, wondering why Trinity might be writing to him. It was a first.

He finished up the floors, then found the letter opener and read her words:

Dear Owen,

It has been much too long since I last saw you. I wanted to let you know that Sadie Rose and I will be arriving soon by train for the summer. She plans to stay at Worthingtons', and I will head to the island. But I will get there two days before my parents arrive. Could you be a sweetheart and take me out to the island by boat? I hope your answer is yes, because I'm counting on you already.

Your forever friend,

Trinity

The mention of the island—Baird's Island—set off an avalanche of memories: peeling off stiff and frozen clothes; the mindless dark tunnel of hypothermia; the lifesaving fire in the hearth; Jerry at the bottom of the lake. Suddenly, with this round of memories, his body went haywire.

His heart kicked into high gear, racing in his chest. His ears rang and everything seemed muffled. He felt sick, as if someone were turning a wood auger into his gut. He had to get outside. He had to get some fresh air before a customer walked through the door. He wondered if he was having a heart attack. "Erling, cover for me."

"What'd she say? Is she in love with you? Is something wrong with Sadie?"

Without answering, without grabbing a raincoat or umbrella, Owen hurried outside. He stood there, face into the driving rain and sleet. Through blinking eyes, he watched wind chase slate-gray blankets of freezing rain across the open bay. He gulped in breath after breath. He didn't know what to do. He couldn't head home. Mom would pester him. But he couldn't stand in the sleet either. He shivered, wet to the skin, and headed across the tracks to the White Turtle.

Haloed by a cloud of smoke, Izzy nodded at Owen as he stepped in. She held her cigarette holder between two fingers and waved her cigarette in greeting, before taking another puff. Owen nodded back, then headed into the hotel's restaurant. He could use a drink to calm him—a hard drink—but he stayed on this side of the soda fountain. He found an empty table and ordered coffee.

Seconds after his first sip, a screech of automobile brakes sounded outside, doors slammed, and the lobby filled with the voices of men.

Sheriff Vandyke's voice rang out. "Where's Harvey? Where's the boy?"

"Should be here soon, Sheriff," Izzy answered. "We've got a swell breakfast special this morning, fellas. Switching over to lunch in an hour."

Vandyke and Kranlin took seats at the table nearest the entrance. The sheriff glanced around the restaurant at the few tables of patrons, then spotted Owen a few tables away.

"Owen," the sheriff said.

"Sheriff."

And that was it. If they'd been friends, they would have sat together, leaned in and talked about the recent night out on the lake, how they'd barely survived. But instead, they'd pretend that night never happened . . . Owen realized his right leg was vibrating from the ball of his foot to his kneecap, bouncing up and down beneath the table. He forced his foot flat on the floor and willed himself to be still. He drank his coffee, added an extra teaspoonful of sugar, and tried to focus on the newspaper someone had left behind.

He tried to read, but his thoughts were on Jimmy. He wasn't just "the boy" to Pengler; he was his son.

With a clatter of chairs, the sheriff and deputy shot up from their seats as Harvey entered the restaurant. Jimmy was at his side: red plaid jacket, collar turned up; windburn patches on round cheeks; gray cap and mittens.

Sheriff Vandyke stood with his legs wide, as if ready to take punches. "We've come to put this child into the protective custody of the Minnesota Welfare System."

"Like hell you are," Pengler said, pulling Jimmy toward him and resting both hands on his shoulders. "I'm his father."

"Not according to the law, Harvey, and you know it. You don't have any legal ground to stand on."

"It was her wish. She told me so. I'll adopt him legally. Soon as I'm allowed."

Vandyke snorted. "Now, let's make this easy on everyone. Hand him over."

The pain that crossed Pengler's face turned to anger. As the deputy reached for the boy, Pengler snapped his fist into Kranlin's face and blood poured from the deputy's nose. He grabbed a napkin from the table and pressed it to his nose.

"Don't let them take me!" Jimmy's face contorted. "Daddy! I don't want to go with them!"

Owen stood up. "Hey, if it helps, I'll vouch for Mr. Pengler. He's good to Jimmy. Treats him like any parent would do. In fact, when Jimmy has spent overnights with us, he seems very well adjusted. Happy. Seems like things are working fine, from what I see."

The sheriff motioned Owen closer. "What d'you mean, 'spends overnights'? The kid gets moved around, house to house in Ranier? What kind of parent would do that?"

"A responsible one," Owen said. He might not like everything about Pengler, but he saw no gain in ripping Jimmy from the only father the boy knew. "There's times in any family when you need a night out, need someone to cover—"

"A night out, my ass," Vandyke said. "Yeah, to manage his bootlegging operations from here to Kettle Falls."

Pengler didn't say a word.

Vandyke continued, "One of these days we'll press charges that'll stick. We'll get someone to testify against you, just wait."

If the sheriff couldn't get Pengler one way, he'd get him another. Through Jimmy. The sheriff was willing to bend the laws of morality to get what he wanted.

"You're under arrest, Harvey Pengler, for obstructing justice and assaulting an officer of the law." The sheriff snapped handcuffs on Pengler.

The deputy put his hand on Jimmy's shoulder, but the boy spun away, wide-eyed. "No! I won't go! Daddy! Don't let them take me!"

"He's welcome at my house until things get sorted out," Owen offered.

"You're saying you're a blood relation?" the deputy asked.

"No, but we could care for him until this gets figured out."

But before Owen knew what else to say, the deputy lifted Jimmy, legs flailing, and pinned the boy's arms down. He carried him outside.

Pengler walked ahead of the sheriff into the lobby. "In front of my son. That's awfully low, Vandyke. Just not right."

"He's not your son, Pengler. Get that outta your head and this will be easier on everyone."

Sick to his stomach, Owen watched from the window with other customers and staff. Pengler and Jimmy sat in the backseat of the sheriff's brand-new Model T. He'd replaced the one that had gone through the ice. Owen wondered what kind of report he'd filed. The new Model T made a sharp U-turn and headed toward International Falls.

"I don't get it," Owen said.

From the lobby counter, Izzy caught Owen's eye. She put her forefinger to her lipstick-red lips, then motioned him closer as the lobby cleared.

"Why take the boy?" Owen said. "Why not let Pengler be his foster parent, at least till he gets married to some gal and can make it legal?"

Leaning across the counter, Izzy whispered, "I'll tell you why. That son of a bitch knows how to get Pengler where it will hurt. Hey, they've made busts here. 'Course, the sheriff knows there's bootlegging. He just can't make an arrest stick. Vandyke has tried every which way to get each and every one of us to testify against our boss."

"And nobody will?"

"That's right. We'll take the fall, serve time if we have to, because he'll cover expenses until we get out. One fella's doing four years for serving booze, but while he's locked up, his wife, his five kids, they're fed, got a roof over their heads, money for clothes, shoes, you name it."

"That's some kind of dedication," Owen said.

Izzy tapped the side of her head. "Smart business, too," she added. "We lose one employee behind bars, things keep going. But we lose Pengler behind prison bars, we lose our livelihoods—and fall like dominoes."

27

SHORTLY AFTER THREE IN THE MORNING, OWEN WALKED the streets and alleys.

The world between night and dawn is a netherworld, a purgatory, or Frank Baum's "Oz," where anything is possible. It's a world between real and unreal, heaven and hell, a world where few humans travel, and those who are out at that hour are either drunk or disturbed. It's a world where Bram Stoker's *Dracula* might truly exist, where Mary Shelley's *Frankenstein* is a reality, with a monster lurking around the next corner, escaped from its creator's laboratory.

His mind felt disengaged from his legs and feet. He wandered past taverns. Some were still open, but only a few drunks loitered outside. An occasional light remained on in the upstairs quarters of women who earned late-night income. He wandered toward the depot, then followed the railroad tracks heading southeast out of town.

In the rays of a half-moon, the rails gleamed, challenging him. Arms out, Owen stepped onto the steel rail, and like a tightrope walker in a circus, he thought of nothing else but putting one foot in front of the other, looking ahead at the steel tracks stretching off into infinity. If he teetered, he struggled for all he was worth to right himself again, and by intense concentration, he managed to wobble less and less. He breathed in the night air, crisp with pine, damp with melting snow. He kept his gaze on the rail ahead, didn't look down at his feet, and slowed his breathing. He felt he could follow the rail forever, until a train from the south approached.

A single light shone in the distance. The ground trembled and, within moments, began to shake under his feet. The oncoming locomotive bore down on him, its light glaring. Owen hopped off the rails, slipped down the gravel railroad bed to a ditch, and broke through a thin sheet of ice into thigh-deep cold water.

Thundering, the black locomotive powered toward Ranier, pulling dozens of cars and a last yellow caboose. Shortly after it disappeared, it sounded its horn, announcing its entrance into town. By then, Owen was a mile or two away as he climbed out of the bog, back onto the tracks, and stood still. A haze of light glowed to the east, though the sun was at least an hour or more away from rising. He looked at the silver rails heading south to Virginia, to St. Paul, to Chicago. A guy could hitch a ride on a boxcar, start over somewhere. Start a new life where he wouldn't be reminded every moment about Jerry. Where he wouldn't worry about someone discovering his secret. It could be a fresh start without any tethers of history, family, or relationships. But he couldn't convince himself.

He turned back, his boots squishy with ice water, and trudged between the steel rails, counting the creosote wooden ties set in gravel.

The sky changed from black to slate gray. A stiff wind bent bare tree limbs and swept sleet-spitting clouds across a pewter sky. A rooster crowed somewhere in Ranier. Ravens flapped overhead. A door slammed. For the life of him, as the morning's curtains parted and the stage was set for another day, Owen couldn't masquerade any longer. He couldn't lie. He couldn't pretend nothing had happened. When a familiar truck motor started outside the creamery,

Owen said aloud, "Bless you, Erling." His kid brother was up and going, ready to make the morning run without him. Maybe he was wrong. Maybe Erling *could* manage things if Owen were gone.

For once, Owen was going to let him. He reached in his pocket, jingled some spare change, and headed to the café near the depot. He didn't remember when he last paid for breakfast somewhere, and suddenly, he was starving.

Train workers sat at one end of the counter, and Owen sat down at the other. At a corner table sat two drunks, hunched over their cups of coffee. Dad would have spotted them, left, and returned with a bottle of fresh buttermilk. "Here you go, fellas. This will help clear your heads, help you remember what matters in life."

But Owen wasn't his father.

In fact, when he considered how Dad had changed in those last few years, Owen realized he wasn't nearly as good as his father. Dad had found a way to change for the better.

Owen kept falling further and further from his truest self.

He hadn't forgotten who he was.

He just didn't know how to find his way back.

One night, his walk ended at dawn.

Juju stood before him at the counter, pen and tablet at the ready. The last time he'd seen her was at Kettle Falls.

"Morning, stranger," she said with one fist against an ample hip. "What'll it be?"

He ordered sausage and eggs and buttermilk pancakes and toast. He ordered orange juice and coffee with sugar and cream. And as a last thought, he ordered a giant cinnamon roll. Then he counted out his change to make sure he had enough and slid the coins across the counter.

"Big spender this morning," she said with a wink. "Gambling winnings?"

He shrugged.

"Hey, did you hear about that gambler named Noel?"

"Yeah, I know he runs a gambling operation—a movable operation—off the east end of Dryweed Island."

Juju leaned closer. "Well, folks say he just disappeared. His gambling boat must'a got frozen in, cuz when the lake broke up, it landed on the mainland. I hear Victor Guttenberg is buying it, going to fix it up for his island."

"That so?" Why did hearing Victor's name send him spiraling even further downward? Owen really didn't have anything against him. In fact, he counted him as a friend, even if he hadn't seen him most of the winter. Victor usually lived out on his island, but not as much lately with his fight against Ennis. Sadie Rose saw far more of Victor than Owen did. And that, he figured, was why he felt irksome toward the Harvard grad. It wasn't Victor who was the problem. It was himself.

He was the one who lost her.

He glanced at the drunks. They were here the last time he was in, too. One was leaning his head against the wall, snoring. And for some reason, Owen suddenly recalled splitting wood with Dad. He was only six, but he'd wanted to prove he could do it. By mistake, he'd glanced the ax off his knee but fortunately didn't take his kneecap with the blow. It hurt, but he was lucky not to lose it altogether. When Dad asked why he was limping, Owen had told him, and that's when he and Dad trotted out to the splitting block beside the woodpile. Legs wide, ax back, and eye fixed on the log, Owen did as Dad coached him. When the steel head came down with a crack, it was as satisfying as hitting a home run. "There you go. Now you're getting the hang of it." And that afternoon, Owen split enough wood to make his dad proud. He split until he could barely lift the ax; Dad stepped in and lifted the ax from his shoulder and hands. "That's plenty, son," he said. "You sure are a good worker."

The memory split something in him.

He stared at the counter, stared at his folded hands, holding himself still, as if any movement might shatter him into a thousand pieces. When breakfast came, he wasn't hungry, but he ate it reverently, as if it were his last meal, down to licking the cinnamon and white icing off his fingertips. Then he thanked Juju, left the last of his change for a tip, and headed out of the café under a sky of deepening pinks and oranges. This time, he turned west and followed the tracks toward the lift bridge.

He walked past the "No Trespassing" sign, almost halfway over the river to Canada, and stopped at the deepest part of the current. Pigeons lifted from steel girders and swirled in circles overhead.

A series of sharp caws sounded as blackbirds harassed a bald eagle riding the air currents. The eagle flew off, following the winding river westward.

Ten to fifteen feet above the water, Owen balanced on a single rail. Beneath him, the vast lake shot through this narrow funnel, transforming from "lake" on one side of the bridge to "river" on the other. The water rushed headlong, folded in on itself, and tumbled into widening whirlpools, spraying white foam into the air.

Water boiled, roiled, and raged beneath him. Shooting out from beneath the bridge, sheets of ice lifted and glinted like massive plates of glass in the emerging sun. Ice chunks the length of rooftops crashed together and broke into glass tabletops. Smaller pieces clinked together like infinite goblets of crystal.

Seagulls rode ice sheets, then flapped upward as the ice swirled and churned in the current's eddies.

Owen stared at the water.

It was as if he'd already been sucked down into the deep current, pulled under into its darkness, which wouldn't let go until it squeezed the last bit of air from his lungs. Spring was here, but he was stuck in a bleak winter that would never end. It had all been too much . . . Dad lying lifeless beneath a bedsheet . . . Jerry trapped in a watery coffin . . . Crushing debts . . . Sadie Rose moving on.

Despair ran through his veins like lead, weighing him down. If he jumped, the cold and powerful current would end his pain. His chest tightened, making it harder and harder to breathe. Beneath him, the water and ice churned and clanked and clanged, filling his head, beckoning.

He loosened his grip on the support cables.

He wiggled his toes in his socks.

He let go of the cable and balanced on a single steel rail.

Fall forward.

Let go.

End the pain.

End it all.

He closed his eyes, asked God for forgiveness, and filled his lungs with one last breath of air. But when he opened his eyes, something passed beneath the bridge, startling him. Owen nearly fell headlong but instinctively reached for the cable with one hand and caught himself. He looked again. Yes, there was definitely something riding along on top of an ice floe. A big dog?

Giant pieces of ice turned and flipped in the current, rising vertically to catch the sun and reflect it back with blinding light, then dropped to the water again. It was like watching the last breaths of someone before the end. Fleeting moments of the exquisite in the face of imminent decay and dissolution.

And then, there it was. Not a dog at all, but a doe, standing on its split hooves, balancing on a giant plate of ice as it made its way under the bridge to the source of the river. The miniature iceberg floated, following the swirling current, and the doe rode the ice, as if in a death-defying performance. Maybe she had been trying to cross from island to island when the ice beneath her hooves broke loose from the whole. Rather than jump, she rode the small glacier downstream.

Suddenly the deer jumped into the river. The moving ice, in all its gathering jigsaw pieces, was closing in around her. I worried the doe would be crushed. But she kept her head high and swam hard. I felt like God, watching from above, wishing her well but unable to intervene. Her choices, too, had consequences.

I cheered her on. C'mon!

A turn here, an opening there, she found her way through an ever-tightening maze of ice and swam the last few yards of open water to freedom. The moment her feet hit shore, she bounded into the thicket and disappeared.

28

Owen stared at the Ranier Bank calendar on the creamery wall.

The day had arrived and he gritted his teeth.

April 13.

The deadline.

Yet everything had changed with a single deer.

In those moments at the bridge, when in a fraction of a second he was willing to end it all, he'd been distracted by a doe. He'd watched her struggle and survive. And with that—turning from the roiling, numbing waters below that promised silence for his pain—he'd walked home. He'd made a clear decision then. And he needed to make a decision now. He needed to face Pengler—no matter the outcome.

When he didn't find Pengler at the White Turtle, he drove east to the farmstead and parked between the house and barn. A chickadee called from the bare branches of an apple tree—*chick-a-dee-dee-dee*—as Owen pounded on the door of the two-story farmhouse.

There was no answer.

Then Pengler yelled. "Top of the morning to ya!" Owen turned.

Teetering high above the ground in the barn's hay door, with a pitchfork in hand, Pengler shouted, "Over here, Owen!" His voice was overly enthusiastic.

He was drunk.

Outside the barn and within the fenced paddock, Ace-in-the-Hole and three other horses pranced and whinnied in anticipation. Pengler tossed down a pitchfork of loose hay. The moment the hay hit the ground, the horses dropped their heads and turned to eating. "There ya go!" Pengler called.

Owen headed to the barn and stepped inside, just as Pengler started down the loft ladder.

"I can't pay for the sugar or the dump truck!" Owen yelled to Pengler's back.

"That so?" Pengler's boots touched the barn floor. He turned, eyebrows furrowed, hand still gripping the pitchfork handle, its sharp prongs angled at Owen. "You and Jerry owe me. And it's no small sum."

"I know, Harvey. But today's the deadline, and if you have to have the money today, then just knock me off. Get it over with!"

Pengler huffed. "Too early in the day for that. Haven't even had my coffee yet." Then he set the pitchfork in the corner and headed out of the barn toward the farmhouse. "Well? Are you coming?"

Owen followed him into the kitchen, a cheery shade of yellow. Pengler percolated a white enamel coffeepot over a new gas stove, filled two blue-and-white cups, and sat across from Owen.

How was he supposed to have a cup of coffee while bracing himself for the worst? Threats to his family. A grisly beating and eventual death. The kind of stuff he'd read about in big cities.

"I'm a wreck," Pengler said with a sigh. And it was true. Beneath his eyes, gray pockets had formed. Stubble covered his chin and he smelled of sweat. "I never knew how much Jimmy meant to me. It's like losing his mother all over again. I'm not sure how to go on."

This wasn't at all what Owen had expected. He didn't know how to respond.

Pengler extended his arms wide. "I'm building an empire up here, with a landing strip out beyond my fields for my plane to come and go. More product and demand with every passing day. But what the hell does any of it matter? Why do any of this if you don't have family, someone to live for?" His eyes watered and he leveled his gaze at Owen. "Y'know?"

Owen nodded. He understood more than Pengler could know.

When Pengler rose and opened a cupboard, Owen's guard shot up again. Maybe this was it. Pengler was drunk, but not too drunk to remember the mountain of debt. He was probably going for his pistol.

Instead, Pengler returned with two glasses and an unopened bottle. "Best homemade gin you'll find south of the border. I've come up with a perfect formula. Have a drink with me."

"No thanks," Owen said. "And Harvey, from the looks of you, you've had plenty to drink."

"No I haven't—" he began, then stopped himself. "Yeah, I have—ever since that blasted Vandyke took Jimmy. He could have ripped my heart out of my chest, it would have been the same thing." Pengler started to cry.

Owen went to the icebox, which was nearly bare. He pulled out cheese, salami, and a jar of pickled herring. He found hardtack and set it all out on the table. "Eat something, Harvey. Then go back to bed and get some sleep. You're never going to get Jimmy back looking and acting like this."

Harvey obeyed as if he were a child.

"I'm not saying I won't cover my debt," Owen said, sitting back down. He wanted to leave, but he also wanted to make sure Harvey ate. "But it's not going to be today. It might take me a year, it might take me ten. That's just the way it is."

Harvey looked up at him, without a hint of malice or

judgment in his eyes. "You're being square with me. I appreciate that. So . . . okay."

"Okay?"

Harvey nodded. "Now get outta here before I change my mind." Then he reached for the bottle of gin.

As Owen drove back to town, anger built like hot steam in his belly. If he and Jerry had talked to Pengler and told him they didn't have the money, things would be different. If he and Jerry hadn't been so desperate to come up with cash—scratching around in the dirt like chickens—Jerry would still be alive.

The enormity of it hit him hard.

He swore out loud as tears rolled hot down his face.

Once the lake sheds its frigid layer, you never know what its shoreline will reveal: boards from docks, a wagon wheel, a dead dog, a bottle of rotgut . . . Eventually, scavengers—human, animal, and bird—come along and clean it up.

At the end of the pier, I wait for the distant rumbling of the train. On the water, ducks of various breeds put on their annual spring show. Two goldeneye males, each with distinctive black and white markings, chase each other across the water until one sends the other packing; then the winner tosses his head back and forth in triumph. Goal achieved, he settles in, side by side with his rather plain partner, paddling off together like a couple on a morning drive.

A mallard drake with iridescent emerald feathers quacks and quacks until he mounts his brown mate, seemingly drowning her. But not long after, she bobs up to the surface, and they drift off together.

A half dozen male mergansers with tufted heads chase each other, flapping across the water, diving underwater and popping up again at some distance, while the object of their affection swims calmly, seemingly indifferent to the commotion she is causing.

Now that the lake is open, loggers will move another harvest down the lake, sluice timber under the lift bridge, and send their winter harvest downriver to the mill.

You try to take comfort in the commonness of it all, to quiet your nerves as the dock beams vibrate below, announcing the train's arrival, only minutes away. It will bring the season's first tourists; they'll take the steamer to their summer places. The wealthiest lake people will have already hired staff to open their lodges and cabins, air them out, plump the pillows, prime water pumps, and clear fallen trees from paths.

If Trinity hadn't written about a boat ride to her island, I wouldn't be here. She's traveling with Sadie Rose, of course, who's returning from college for the summer.

My heart flips and flops like a fish yanked from water. Sadie and I haven't written a word to each other or spoken over the telephone in nearly two months. Any sane person would assume it was over between us, but I can't help myself. I want to see her.

Brakes screech.

Pistons hiss.

I take off my cap, the wool too hot in the midmorning sun, wipe my palms on my trousers, and set off to meet them.

29

Late morning, the third week of May, the north-bound train rumbled and wheezed to a stop in front of the depot.

Owen hung back in an alcove near the ticket window.

In a floral sheath that skimmed her breasts and hugged her hips, bobbed waves softly framing her heart-shaped face, Sadie Rose stepped off the train and onto the platform.

At the sight of her, Owen's heart seized up.

Carrying two suitcases, head high, she scanned the crowd. Anyone else would have seen a young, confident woman, just back from college. She carried herself well: shoulders back and a cutting fashion. Yet her gray eyes held uncertainty, as if she'd been preparing for this moment.

He longed to catch her in his arms, to feel her warm breath against his neck as she pressed her head under his chin. But everything was different now. He remained in the shadows, leaning against the wall.

"Sadie Rose, dear!" Mrs. Worthington called out, waving a pleated fan in the air. "Over here!"

Spotting the Worthingtons and her grandparents, Sadie's eyes brightened. Her cautious expression gave way to a smile. She looked around again—as if waiting for someone else—then stepped off the platform.

Trinity followed. The silver headband encircling her short blonde hair matched her dazzling smile. She waved. "Owen! You didn't forget me!"

Sadie turned her head in his direction. When her eyes met his, she lifted her hand in a simple wave and mouthed something to him, but he couldn't read her lips.

He lifted his hand and waved.

Then Hans was at Sadie's side, gathering her luggage from her hands and leading her toward the Worthingtons.

An aching hollowness filled him.

He longed for her. Yet it was something more than their being apart for so long. He'd changed. Where she'd once filled his heart, something cold and impenetrable had settled in. It was as if he'd gone through the ice with Jerry, only he was still breathing, his heart was still beating, with no hope of surfacing again. He felt as if he were watching himself stand there, numb and unable to respond.

Trinity left her luggage by the platform and ran up to him.

"Owen Jensen!" She stood on tiptoes and hugged him. Though she came from a well-to-do family, she never put on false manners or airs. It was something he'd always liked about her. "I'm a modern woman, but I hope you're not going to leave me alone to handle *all* my luggage. Could you give me a hand? It's over there."

She pointed to the small tower of luggage, topped off with a cherry-red hatbox.

He nodded. His words came out as if someone else were in charge now, pretending to be him. "Sure. I'll get a cart."

In minutes, he loaded one of the available carts, rolled it over to the pier where he kept his boat, then returned it to the depot. By the time he got back to the dock, he was both saddened and relieved to find that Sadie Rose and her family were gone.

Owen started his boat motor and left the pier with its bustle of passengers boarding the steamer. As he motored with Trinity out into the bay, the bow cutting through the glassy surface, he began to settle back into his own skin. He began to breathe a little easier. The lake had a way of making the surrounding gray clouds fluff into giant popcorn clouds of white high above. *Lake clouds*. Of course the scientific reason had to do with temperature, humidity, and barometric pressure, but Owen liked to think the lake had its own mystical power to drive away the darkest moods.

He filled his lungs with pine-fresh air, rich in oxygen and moisture. The morning sun painted the water in dabs of peach and blue. Pelicans, scattered across the bay like white sails, lifted one by one to the air, until they were drifting overhead.

As the bow cut through the water, a loon surfaced off to their right, eyeing them with its red eye, before disappearing below again.

Wrapped in a powder-blue sweater, Trinity glanced over her shoulder at him and smiled. "I love being home!" she called above the motor.

Owen nodded and smiled.

Then she faced forward again.

Though a bit terrifying to think about, Owen hoped that her time at the asylum had helped her. He'd liked Trinity's spirited ways, but after her outburst two summers ago, he'd felt cautious around her. Not afraid, just wondering when she'd find her way back to her old self. This morning, he was hopeful that she had.

He drew in another breath of lake-scented air.

A guy didn't have to spend time in an asylum for mental treatment, or go away to college, or live in a big city to appreciate being on the water. Life on the mainland was one thing; being on the water was another. He'd forgotten how much he loved cruising the lake. On the open water, he could leave everything else behind.

He met a white tugboat pulling its lasso of logs, destined for the mill, and veered wide, then continued east on Sand Bay past islands, peninsulas, and the American shore. Not until he spotted Baird's Island and Trinity's log cabin did it hit him. The ice and snow were gone, but the memories returned in full force.

"Let's drop my things off here," Trinity said, motioning to the small cove beside her cabin. "Then we won't have to carry them over."

"Uh, sure," he said, slowing the motor. It made sense, not going to the other side of the island to the long dock, where the family kept the yacht named *Trinity*.

The boat pulsed slowly forward into the cove. A pair of mergansers scuttled out from the shore, then beat their wings over the water and flew off.

Trinity jumped off the bow, deftly grabbing the line, and secured the boat to the low cedar. Then she disappeared to the front of the cabin, which was still boarded up. Owen sat there. He pictured Vandyke and Kranlin, the fire they'd built, how they'd managed to warm up and dry off to survive. He turned his gaze in the opposite direction, beyond the next peninsula and what lay at the bottom of the channel.

"Owen? Are you okay? You look a little seasick." Trinity's voice brought him back to the present.

"Oh, my thoughts were somewhere else." He tried to shake it off. *Leave it,* he told himself. *Don't think about it.*

He grabbed her luggage and handed it over the bow, piece by piece, and she set them on a broad slab of rock. Then he climbed off the bow and moved her luggage inside her cabin.

"Somebody's been here," she said, looking around.

The fire, long cold from that night, left a mess of ash and dead embers. They'd moved the chaise lounge away from the fire, and the extra lamp they'd lit sat on the floor. "Must have been some teenagers looking for fun," she said. "Doesn't look like they did any real harm."

Hardly fun, Owen thought. *And there was harm. Unspeakable harm.*

"Well, no matter." She pushed the chaise lounge back to

its original position, set the lamp on the fireplace mantel, and then suddenly grabbed Owen's upper arm with both hands.

"Oh, how thoughtless of me! Of course you're not feeling well. Not until the train ride north did Sadie say anything about a distance between you two. And then, when we arrived, you two didn't say a word to each other. Owen, you should talk with her."

He inhaled stuffy air. Exhaled hard. "While you get unpacked, I'll help you open things up." He stepped outside, undid latches, and removed the heavy wooden panels from all the windows. Inside, he opened windows wide and let a soft, warm breeze cleanse the tiny cabin. He cleaned up the fireplace, refilled the wood bin from the outdoor woodpile, and swept the cabin floor, all the while feeling as if he were making amends.

"There," she said. "Good enough for now. Let's get a drink, shall we?"

"A drink? You want to go back to Ranier?"

"No, you silly sailor. *Here*. On the island. My father's stash. Believe me, he has more than one hiding place. I'll show you."

"That surprises me."

"That he hides booze, or that he and my mother drink it?"

"Maybe both."

"Oh, they're social drinkers. On the boat, Father keeps a bottle of top-shelf Canadian whiskey for law enforcement for whenever he goes across to Canada, and he keeps special booze on hand for the feds and police here when he's on the island or in American waters. He's a businessman. He wants to keep everybody happy."

"He's a bootlegger?"

She laughed. "No! But he has been known to take a load of whiskey down to Davenport, Iowa, to give to friends. Once when his trailer went off the road and into the ditch, a policeman came by and asked what was wrong. My father, with a straight face, said he needed help getting his 'trailer full of whiskey' back on the road again. The officer thought he was joking, never looked at what he was hauling, and helped winch the trailer out of the ditch and sent him on his way. Can you believe it?"

Owen knew Mr. Baird to be a jovial man who got what he wanted for the cheapest price possible. Somehow he'd talked Owen's dad into selling dairy products to him at a penny above cost. He'd given Dad a song and dance about trouble with cash flow, but sitting here on the sandy beach, with the log lodge and outcabins, the boathouse, and yacht, the only thing for certain was that Mr. Baird was a character.

They followed the path to the top, then dropped down to the sandy peninsula joining the two islands into one. Trinity had her shoes and stockings off and walked out into the water, screamed, and kept going up to her knees. "It's freezing!"

"What did you expect? The ice just went out a few weeks ago. It'll be weeks before it's warm enough for swimming."

"Oh, it's never warm enough," Trinity said, laughing. "But I have to dive in anyway." Then she put her hands over her head, dove under, exploded out of the water with another scream, and lunged through the water back to shore.

The sun was at its pinnacle and sizzling warm. As they sat side by side in the sand, Trinity's goose bumps disappeared and she stopped shivering. "Oh! Just what I needed!"

"Yeah? Good."

They watched tiny mallard ducklings, who couldn't be more than a day old, skittering around their mother.

"This year, I attended college along with Sadie."

"I didn't know that."

"I took an apartment off campus, but I went to classes.

Mostly art. The year before at the asylum, well, I don't want to ever return again. I mean, there were truly crazy people there. It was frightening at times. But I had good doctors and I got the rest I needed. I don't think I'll ever go off the deep end again like I did here on the island when Sadie was here. But thank goodness she was. If she hadn't heard me that night, I might have ended my life."

He thought of the bridge, of his own moment, but wasn't sure how to discuss it.

"Did the doctors ever tell you what happened, why—"

She nodded. "Artistic types," she said, "often suffer from highs and lows. Dr. Strattus said that mania and melancholia often show up during teen years or early twenties. Many famous composers and artists, apparently, from Van Gogh—well, he *was* crazy—Tchaikovsky, too, suffered from the same psychosis, to greater or lesser degrees."

"So . . . you're cured now?"

"I can't be cured of who I am!" She laughed, bright and cheery as a robin. It was his favorite thing about Trinity, her sometimes irrepressible spirit, and he was relieved that her therapy hadn't erased it.

"I'm glad," he said, and he meant it.

She leaned her head onto his shoulder, just for a moment—just long enough for Owen to wonder where this was going—but then just as quickly, she sat up again. "It feels good to talk about it. I don't really have anyone to tell about it, other than Sadie Rose. She's a charm. But I *do* have to watch my moods. I have to make myself go to sleep at a decent hour, no matter *how much* I might want to stay up all night. And not drink too much or smoke too much or have too much fun." She turned to him with a tilt of her head and an exaggerated pout. "Or be around big crowds for too long or spend too much time alone for long, long stretches. And paint. I absolutely *must* keep painting. Keep creating. It helps me be at my best, whatever that is. And that's why, at the end of this season on the lake, I'm heading to Paris to study at the Sorbonne. The sheer light of that city makes me feel better, and wherever I turn, there are artists and writers and musicians. I may go there this time and never return."

"That's amazing! I'm glad for you—and proud of you, too."

"Thanks." For a moment, her eyes turned teary. "That means more than you know."

"Good. And Paris sounds great, but I hope you return. At least for summers."

"You do? Truly?"

"I wouldn't lie." And as the words slipped from his mouth, he wished he could tell her all about that night. It was strapped like a heavy stone to his chest. He carried it around from the moment he opened his eyes until he finally fell asleep. To tell someone, anyone, would lift the burden, at least a little. Bless Trinity, she was good-hearted, but she could also be a chatterbox in her happy moods, and he couldn't risk the truth spilling out with just one-too-many drinks.

"I better get going," he said. "I have a job. Two jobs, actually."

"I think opening your own automobile business is the bee's knees."

"But do bees have knees?" he asked.

" 'Course! Same as cats have pajamas!"

She hopped up. "Before you go, let me show you something."

He followed her up to a small cabin overlooking the water. He hesitated. Trinity wasn't known for being bashful, and if she was looking for something more than friendship, he couldn't be that for her. Not while there was a thread of a chance with Sadie Rose.

But instead of heading inside, she walked to the back corner, bent down, and pushed aside the branches of a bush. "See this?"

Owen stepped closer.

She held a wire loop in her hand, connected to a wire that was attached to the cabin. "Abracadabra!" She gave it a small pull. "Now, for the magic."

Curious, he followed her to the front step of the cabin, stepped inside the screen porch, through the heavy door, and past two twin beds to the closet. She pushed back the leaf-patterned curtain to the closet with built-in dresser drawers. "Voilà!"

She pointed to the trapdoor, now lifted and revealing below a wooden crate brimming with bottles of whiskey.

"Yours?" Owen asked, just a little bit worried. A volume of booze like that wasn't going to help Trinity stay on course.

She laughed. "My father's, silly!" Then she pushed the door back down until all you could see was a tongue-and-groove floor. "He won't put a rug over it, because that gives the feds reason to look closer. But all the lake people drink."

"Townsfolk drink, too," Owen said, "but sometimes the rotgut brew they drink kills 'em." He told her about the photographer who died earlier that winter, leaving behind a wife and kids.

She closed the hatch and crossed her arms. "That's exactly why I support bootlegging from Canada. Real distilleries that make real liquor, not poisonous backyard concoctions. We lake people need our cocktails and parties!"

Yes, Owen thought, from his two summers making deliveries on the lake. What would the upper class do without their booze? All summer long, they have cocktail parties, themed parties, costumes and playacting. Victor is always invited to gatherings. He may not have money, but he's better educated than anyone on the lake, and though he doesn't drink, he's far more interesting than most.

Trinity laughed. "I can't wait to see Victor over the summer. He's the best storyteller. I could sit and listen to him all night long, and the way he plays his violin, with so much emotion that I could melt and—"

"You're still soft on him, aren't you?"

She nodded. "I suppose I am, though I have no reason to expect my schoolgirl's crush to ever be returned. You know, when I was away . . ." Her pause told him she meant at the asylum, not at college. "I met several young men who, well, they were interested in other young men. Their families sent them there for treatment to try to change their tastes, but . . . well, we are who we are, don't you think?"

He thought of his secret, like a stone tossed in the water, and the ripples that followed. Ripples of isolation. He wanted to put an end to it and tell Trinity everything, but he held his tongue. He was being blackmailed into holding back the truth. Keeping Jerry's death a secret was like a poison he swallowed every day. He should return to his work, because if he spent too much time listening to her secrets, he might be tempted to reveal his own. And that would lead to no good for his family.

"Have you heard a single word of what I've been saying?" Trinity elbowed him. "She's all you can think about, isn't she?"

He shook his head. "No, actually I was thinking you're right. We can't change the past. We're stuck with who we are."

When they returned to her cabin, Trinity had hatched a plan. "I've got it. I'll plan a picnic—you, me, Sadie Rose, and Victor—just like old times."

"I don't really have free time these days," Owen said as he untied his boat from a tree and pushed off from shore. He clambered to his seat and started the motor.

"I insist!" Trinity waved good-bye. "And Owen! Thank you!"

30

"WE HEAR NOTHING FROM JERRY," MR. MELNYK SAID AS he helped hoist the steel cans into the creamery truck. "We hope you hear something."

If Owen could carry out his work without any reminders of the past, he might manage. His face tightened into a mask. He willed himself to swallow, to try to find words to reassure Mr. Melnyk. To outright lie to Jerry's father! *Saint Christopher!* He wanted to tell the Melnyks the truth.

Jerry was dead.

He was never coming back.

But he couldn't.

Treetops fluttered in the breeze, sending pollen adrift and leaving a dusting of gold across the truck. A tickle rose in the back of Owen's throat. He sneezed, then shook his head in answer to Mr. Melnyk's question, then sneezed again, glad for anything to distract him from having to open his mouth and lie.

"We know," Mr. Melnyk continued, "he goes on wild goose chase, but always—he sends letter or makes the phone call. So we don't worry." Mr. Melnyk's eyes and lined face showed plenty of worry. "But this time. Two months go by. We worry."

Owen nodded, shrugged, then climbed in his truck. Arm on the edge of his window, Owen felt an overwhelming need to make Mr. Melnyk feel better. "I'm sure he's fine. Bet you'll hear something any day now."

His own false words made him sick.

Mr. Melnyk nodded. "Hope you are right, Owen." Then he turned away and headed back to his dairy barn.

Before returning to Ranier, Owen stopped by the library and set a small stack of books on Miss Winnie's desk. "I owe something," he said. "I don't mind paying the fine." Paying a fine. Going to prison. Making restitution of any sort would be better than living this life as a lie.

Miss Winnie was deep in a ledger when she looked up from her desk; a smile spread across her pale skin and rosebud cheeks. "Owen, how nice to see you!" she whispered, an unofficial signal that other patrons were in the small library.

Out of the corner of his eye, Owen noticed the slightest movement. Behind a book rack, someone. A jolt of electricity surged through him. He knew the outline, the curves, the profile of the face, the full lips, the eyes. Behind her somber eyes existed a perpetual melancholy, a world only she could enter.

Sadie Rose stepped into a ray of sunlight pouring through the window. Owen knew social custom required them to act polite.

She hesitated and forced a smile. "Hello, Owen."

That moment of hesitation, that instant before smiling, told him all he needed to know. If he'd had any hope— now that she was back—that moment told him everything. She could no longer feel easy with him. The break was not temporary.

"Oh, so you two know each other," Miss Winnie said brightly. "I'm glad, because I'm terrible at names and introductions. The thing I've learned about a small town is that everyone knows everyone. But to a newcomer, it's quite overwhelming."

Sadie directed her attention to Miss Winnie, as if looking at Owen brought her discomfort. "Well, you'll start to put names and faces together before you know it," she said, as if they were good friends. "Owen and I—" she began, then stopped abruptly.

Owen finished the sentence for her. "We both grew up in Ranier. When Sadie's father went from mayor to senator— Senator Worthington—"

"Is that so?" Miss Winnie said, her eyes widening, as if seeing Sadie for the first time.

Sadie nodded, a little too vigorously. "Yes, since then I've spent most of each school year in St. Paul. I just returned from college in St. Peter."

"Oh, where's that?"

"Southwest of Minneapolis and St. Paul. My college is there. Gustavus Adolphus."

And soon Miss Winnie was starting a discussion about the differences between a college for young women, like Smith, and a college that included both men and women. And Sadie was explaining that she would be tutoring in the area over the summer before returning to college in the fall.

A shoulder width from Sadie Rose, Owen listened. Like smoke wisps rising from the start of a birch-bark-fed fire, her familiar scent drew him and conjured up memories: the day she first stepped into the creamery, communicating through her slate board because she hadn't yet found her voice; riding double on a neighbor's horse and falling off together in a heap when the horse startled at a garter snake; boating and cutting the motor . . . floating under sheets of pink and green. Now, instead of enjoying the warmth of her company, he felt he was standing too close to the fire. Her presence was more than he could bear.

Instinctively, he backed away, guessed on his library fine, added a few extra coins, and headed quickly for the door.

"Wait," Miss Winnie called. "You paid too much."

Without looking back, he waved her concern away and

stepped out, as if dreams, college, girlfriend—none of it had ever mattered.

May rolled into June. Warming days, cool nights, and cold water.

Between questions about Studebakers, test-drives, and keeping the creamery running, Owen was glad his days were too full to think. At high season, he certainly couldn't afford to be away from Ranier. So the first week of June he took his brother Knut, who'd just turned fourteen, out to learn how to make "lake rounds" in the small cruiser.

They got an early start. White pillows of clouds gathered at the edges of the lake. Behind the closed bow, Knut, who was small for his age, sat proudly at the boat's wooden steering wheel. Head high, his face held an expression of intense seriousness. He reminded Owen of himself the first summer he'd launched the idea of lake deliveries as a way to earn a little extra money, filling two long boxes along the boat's ribs with Jensen Creamery products.

Owen gave Knut the basic speech Dad had given him. "You have free rein to go where you want, as long as you don't hit rocks, get lost, or spend more money on gas than you make in dairy sales."

"But how do I know where the rocks are?" Knut asked, scrunching up his face. Rainy Lake, with countless underwater rocks and shoals, was hard on boats and propellers. Owen pulled out the charts, rolled up and tattered, that were stored in the bow. "You study these before you head out. And you stop when you're uncertain, and you look again. And you'll learn the channels from other boaters. You gotta pay attention."

"Okay," Knut replied, looking at the map.

"Also," Owen added, "you need to make twice the price of gas in sales. That's the deal. But if you just go to all the lodges and resorts I've already served, you'll be fine." He smiled. "There's nothing like making the run clear down to Kettle Falls. Forty miles off. Just you and the water and an occasional other boat. We'll go there today. I'll introduce you to Darla, who runs the hotel, and every other owner along the way. You'll get the hang of it in no time."

Knut beamed, as if Owen were giving him the keys to a new Studey. Knut looked so young, Owen wondered if he could handle it, but then he'd been the same age when he'd come up with the idea and pitched it to Dad. That was the difference between being a worker and an entrepreneur. One showed up and followed routines, the other started with good ideas and a willingness to take a few risks to see what might be possible.

They set off, with Knut at the wheel and Owen giving directions. "Steer clear of that point." "Swing left in this channel." "Avoid the sandbar over that way."

They stopped by Baird's Island and Owen introduced Knut to Trinity's parents and their caretaker, who ordered a week's worth of milk, eggs, cheese, and buttermilk.

They stopped in the channel between two pencil-thin islands. Victor Guttenberg met them at the dock beside the small library building at the water's edge.

"Hello, Owen!" Khakis rolled up to midcalf, tanned limbs and face, and elf-like smile, he grabbed the bow as it floated in. "My mother is going to be delighted to see you. You're a godsend."

"This is Knut," Owen said, as he jumped out of the boat and onto the dock. "He'll be making deliveries this summer."

Victor shook Knut's hand. "Well, good for you, young man! You have some big shoes to fill," he said, with a nod in Owen's direction. "Speaking of shoes to fill, I'm sorry about your father. How are you all holding up?"

Owen chose his words carefully. "That's partly why Knut's taking over on the lake. I need to be around more in town."

"Of course. I hope you can get away for the picnic Trinity is planning on sometime next week. She gets her mind made up about something, and well, there's little that can stop her."

Owen smiled. "I gave her a ride to her island. She seems good. Talking about Paris in the fall."

"So she says. We might cross paths. I'm hoping to do a lecture tour next fall in England."

"Really?" Owen couldn't imagine being asked to lecture on a subject in another country, but then he didn't have Victor's credentials. "What are you going to speak about?"

"Photos I took of moose on my trip up to Hudson Bay. People often need a glimpse of the wild before they can appreciate it. Before they think it's worth protecting. This summer, I'm hoping for a steady flow of visitors to the island—a university in the wilderness—so they can begin to know what's at stake, what could be lost forever, if we don't win this battle against Ennis and his plans for development." He looked to the east and Owen followed his gaze.

The lake stretched on forever.

They motored to Ennis's nearby island, with its dockhands, lodge, and surrounding cabins and the two-story houseboat, *Katherine,* moored in the bay. Mrs. Ennis waved from its upper level, where she appeared to be having tea with a few women under the shade of the porch roof. Owen and Knut waved back, delivered a sizable order to the Ennis kitchen staff, and then set off toward Kettle Falls.

Late that day, as the sun dropped into shadows of gray, Owen tied the boat's line to dock cleats at Johnson Boatworks. Walking home, Knut said, "Thanks, Owen. I'm not going to let you down."

I'm not going to let you down. The words stung.

Poor Jerry hadn't had as much as a funeral or memorial service. His fate was a mystery to everyone in the world, except Owen, the sheriff, and the deputy. Not even his family knew what had happened to him.

Knut slowed his pace, and Owen saw that he was waiting for an answer. A reprimand perhaps. A lecture. Something.

Owen swallowed hard and found a few words. He rumpled Knut's hair. "Hey, Knut. Don't worry. You'll do just fine."

Summer solstice. By the third week in June, the sun climbs so high you almost think it might decide to stay up and never come down. Working class or upper class, everyone wants to be on the water: swimming, fishing, touring, sightseeing, rowing, canoeing, or trying out the latest new boat motor and watercraft to explore bays and inlets, islands large and small.

Rainy Lake. She's a beauty.

Towering rock ledges. Quiet lily-pad-covered inlets. Winding rock-filled narrows. A bald eagle lighting on its nest; a wolf gazing down from a craggy ledge; spring peepers in full chorus; a moose swimming across open water; a doe with twin fawns at the shore; a black bear standing on its hind legs, sniffing the air; a family of otters chasing each other down a well-worn slide into the water; dragonflies emerging in mass; loons yodeling under a painted canvas of stars . . .

You know, Victor's right.

How can anyone from a city appreciate wilderness without first experiencing it?

31

ALL SUMMER, MOST FOLKS TALK ABOUT FISHING. THE
trophy catch. The type of bait or lure they caught it on. The
best fishing hole ever.

Not Erling.

He talked about nothing but baseball.

Stats. Games around the country. Going to see the Babe
in August. Going professional someday. Every evening,
he gathered with local boys to play sandlot baseball. He
started in again as they unloaded the creamery truck and
hauled milk cans inside.

"I'm going to get his signature, either on a ball or maybe
my bat."

Owen didn't need to ask *whose*.

Evenings, Owen spent time at his lot of cars, waxing and
polishing. He threw himself wholly into the task, until his
arms ached, his fingers were stained from car wax, and his
mind went numb. All there was left to think about was how
beautiful these machines looked in the shadows and amber
light at sunset.

When Pengler reported that a few of his Whiskey Sixes
were having carburetor problems, Owen went to the
library and read everything he could in national newspapers. A guy named Burt Miller of Detroit had just started
up a company called Wonder with a product called "Magic
Oil." It allegedly fixed the problem of clogged jets. Owen

jotted down the phone number and ordered a supply. Turned out, "Magic Oil" countered the high lead and contaminants in gasoline, but it also improved gas mileage and minimized engine wear. Owen was realizing he not only had to sell cars, but he was going to have to learn a lot more about how to keep them going, too. If Jerry were around, he'd be a whiz at repairs.

A single thought and images rushed in.

Jerry, arms deep in the engine of the Melnyks' vehicle they called "joker," because it was half tractor, half car and never worked. He'd toss his head to get his sandy hair out of his eyes. "This thing will never be more than a piece of crap. Every time I work on it, feels like I'm polishing a turd."

Jerry, in sixth grade, racing around at recess with pretty little Annie Dorner on his shoulders, while Owen carried another girl, not quite as cute, and definitely not as light. Owen ran behind Jerry, until his buddy rounded the corner of the schoolhouse and hit a mud slick. His legs went out from under him; Annie flew into the building, skirts and petticoats to her waist, and broke her arm. For the rest of the year, Jerry and Owen were banned from recess. Fortunately, it happened in April, not September.

Jerry, vanishing.

Trinity's plans for a picnic kept getting postponed. Rained out. Company her family said she must help entertain. But eventually, the first week of July, the day arrived. Clear skies and a breeze light enough not to stop them from getting to Kettle Falls; breezy enough to keep black flies away.

Owen had crossed paths a few times with Sadie Rose, but they hadn't been forced to talk. For him, the day promised pain.

"Mom, I'll help out here today, instead," he said.

Hands on her hips, chin high, apron strings gathered

around her small waist and tied in front, she almost made
Owen laugh. "You have done nothing but work for as long
as . . . ever since—"

He nodded. True enough.

"Look at you. Dark circles under your eyes. You don't
look well, Owen. Go. I'll be fine."

Owen gave her a hug. "Okay, okay. I'll go."

Then she buried her head in Owen's shoulder and cried.
Owen didn't pull away. He let her sob. And when she finished, Owen pulled a clean handkerchief from his trouser pocket and handed it to her. "You always say, we may
not have much money, but you'll always keep us in clean
handkerchiefs."

Tears streaked her face and her eyes were puffy, but she
smiled. "I didn't mean to start crying, for Pete's sake!"

"It's okay, Mom."

At two minutes before ten thirty that morning, sleek as a
seagull, the fifty-foot white yacht *Trinity* appeared around
the point in the east. Tipper waited beside Owen on the
pier.

After the porcupine, Tipper's head had swelled—even
his tongue—but eventually, the wounds healed and he was
back to his old self. Having him along on the picnic, Owen
figured, would be a good distraction. Tipper's head swung
toward the other end of the dock. Owen followed his gaze.

Sadie Rose strolled past Erickson's Grocery, where
Mr. Erickson was busy tossing meat scraps from a box to a
flurry of seagulls. She continued to the pier.

"Owen!" she exclaimed, walking straight for Tipper and
kneeling beside him. "Hey, Tipper. Have you been hiding?"
she asked, stroking him under his neck. She glanced at
Owen. "Have you?"

"No," he said, lying.

She walked to Owen, her head high, and grabbed him

above the elbow with both hands, as if to emphasize their friendship. "We haven't had a chance to talk."

"Oh, there's not much to talk about. But we'll have the whole day."

"What I mean is—"

"Ahoy, landlubbers!" Trinity called out.

"Catch the line, will you?" Victor added.

And with that, the white rope uncoiled from Victor's hands into Owen's. He pulled the boat close enough for Sadie to hop on. With line in hand, he pushed off and stepped on. A touch-and-go landing.

Under the captain's roof, someone new was standing at the wheel. About the same height as Owen, and roughly the same age as Victor, with a sculpted chin, no-nonsense eyes, and cigarette in the corner of his mouth, he lifted one finger. "Hello!"

"Sadie, Owen, meet Henry Densch. His family is building a small castle—"

"Not a castle," Henry said, the cigarette bobbing up and down. He pulled it out and put it in the ashtray. "Nice to meet you. Hope you don't mind an extra!"

"Not at all," Victor said. "We're all friends."

Sadie glanced at Owen. He once felt he could read her gray eyes, see to the depths of her. But not now. As the boat swung around, pointing east, Sadie sat with Trinity on the bow. Barefoot.

The day was underway.

At the stern, Owen and Victor chatted at a small table with red-cushioned wicker chairs.

"Margaret will be delighted," Victor said, and nodded toward the blueberries. "She makes the most delectable blueberry pies." At their feet lay five buckets, full of blueberries they'd picked along the way, stopping at islands where the water was deep enough to tie up the yacht.

Winding through the craggy channel toward the dam linking Namakan and Rainy Lake, the roar of rushing water turned deafening. Only two summers back, Owen had met up with Sadie Rose behind the hotel here in the cedar-scented icehouse. In the near darkness, he'd drawn her close and kissed her, nearly as surprised by his own actions as she was. From that moment on—he'd found what mattered most in life.

Owen pulled himself back to the conversation. "And if he gets his way," Victor continued, "Ennis would like to hear the roar of dams—at least a dozen more—through the North Country. Forever change these lakes as we know them. That's why the fight has to go beyond local to national, why we must advocate for legislation that will protect this region for future generations."

He nodded toward Henry at the steering wheel. "Someone like Henry, he's educated. Connected. Adding his voice to the cause will help."

So far, Owen had learned that Henry was from a family who made their money in manufacturing. Like Victor and his mother, as well as the Bairds, Henry's family had ties to Davenport, Iowa.

As the boat rounded the next point, the dam came into full view. And with it, Owen couldn't help but admire Sadie, on the bow with Trinity, soaking up sun—all bare legs and arms—in her skirted wool swimsuit. He'd love to roll up his trousers, take off his shirt, and sit beside her in the sun.

Instead, he hopped up, jumped off as the boat approached the dock, and caught the line. He tied off bow and stern to steel rings, offered Trinity and Sadie Rose a hand down, and then followed up the long boardwalk. The white two-story hotel with its red-and-white striped awning rose against a backdrop of sparse pines.

32

WHEN OWEN STEPPED INSIDE THE HOTEL LOBBY—WITH its stairs leading to rooms upstairs where certain ladies plied their trade, and its restaurant to the right of the counter and display cases filled with trinkets, cigars, and cigarettes—he was startled to see Harvey behind the counter, shoulder to shoulder, with Darla, who ran the hotel.

Harvey beamed when he looked up and a smile spread across his freshly shaved face; a dot of shaving cream remained on his earlobe. "Owen! What brings you here today? And such lovely ladies!" he said, extending his hand toward Trinity and Sadie Rose.

"Hi, Darla," Sadie said, casually, though Owen knew their past ran deep. Before running Kettle Falls Hotel, Darla ran a boardinghouse in Ranier where Sadie spent the first five years of her life.

"Why, Miss Sadie, I haven't seen you since last summer with the Worthingtons."

Sadie leaned toward Darla. "Yes, and I want to tell you, I'm sorry for your loss. My parents told me last winter. Pneumonia?"

Darla put her palm to her ample cleavage, barely contained by her old-style corseted dress, and nodded. "Yes, poor man." Folks said Darla's husband spent most of his time in Chicago, but no one had ever seen him. Owen guessed the husband didn't exist, that he was more likely a ruse for a shrewd businesswoman like Darla to operate more freely.

Pengler reached across the counter and shook hands with Victor and Henry. "Gentlemen, welcome to Kettle Falls Hotel. What's your pleasure today?"

Trinity answered. "We've been out picking berries. Hoping for dinner in the restaurant before heading back. And after, perhaps something cool and refreshing at your soda fountain!"

"You've come to the right place!"

While they ate in the restaurant, Pengler leaned down by Owen and whispered in a hushed voice, "Heard from Jerry?"

It's one thing to keep a secret to yourself, to use all your mental energy to tiptoe around locked doors in your mind. They'd come east by boat, and he'd managed to focus in hard on the conversations, rather than think about the channel and its deep water between specific islands and the mainland. When there's something you dread thinking about, you can manage, unless someone else suddenly dredges it up.

"Can't say I have." Perspiration rose on his forehead and around each follicle on his head. A droplet formed and ran down his spine.

"Hoped by now he'd have dropped you a line—something."

Sadie sat across from him. If anyone could tell he was lying, it would be her. He purposefully pushed his chair back from the table, and as if to continue the conversation in private, he motioned for Pengler to follow him so they could talk elsewhere. They went out to the screened veranda, serenaded by a soft hum of black flies, mosquitoes, and deer flies.

"He owes me a vehicle," Pengler said, his expression turning serious. "Not that he's your responsibility, but it's not right—taking off like that without squaring up with a guy."

In the bar someone started up the nickelodeon player, then a man sturdy as a bull ambled out along the porch. "Harvey, Harvey! Come on. When are you going to join us for a drink?"

"Owen, meet Mr. Clayton Vittorio."

Owen stretched out his hand, and the man grabbed it in his beefy paw and squeezed hard. "Friend of Harvey's? Then you're my friend, too."

Pengler continued, "Mr. Vittorio is visiting from Chicago. He and a friend of his. We have some business to attend to, so if you'll excuse us." He motioned back to the bar, but before they took a step, Owen blurted, "Ever meet Al Capone?"

The two men looked at each other. Pengler shrugged. "Don't worry. He's good. He's not a fed."

"You can never tell." Then Mr. Vittorio tilted his head back and laughed, his mouth wide as a rain gutter. "Capone. Sure I know him. But don't believe everything you read in the papers. They don't tell *half* the story." He laughed again. "Things are probably much worse! Not like here where it's real peaceful." Then he fake-punched Pengler in the shoulder. "A guy could get used to doing business up here. Heck, it could be Little Chicago."

On the boat ride back to Ranier, Owen managed to catch bits and snatches of conversation.

"It's what comes through the eyes that's the hardest to capture," Trinity was saying. For a moment, as he sat with her on the bench seat behind the captain's wheel, he couldn't piece together what she meant, if she was talking about him and his lying.

"The iris," she said. "When you really look at it, you'll

see whole worlds in its tones and hues. Then you realize, no matter how hard you try, you can never fully capture it. Eyes. Like trying to paint the universe."

They were approaching the channel. Jerry—at the bottom of the lake. By now, fish and crayfish would have nibbled away at him. His flesh. His eyes.

Owen moved back to the table at the stern, and Tipper followed, settling at his feet. He was glad for a little time alone, until Sadie sat down in the opposite chair. In the past, just being near her would make everything in him smile.

"I wanted to tell you that my work tutoring in the county is going well," she said, meeting his eyes for a brief moment, before he had to look away.

A familiar rock ledge rose up on the mainland. The islands were off to the right. They were getting closer to *the spot* on the channel. His stomach seized up, but he had to say something. "That's good."

"There's a family visiting on the lake for the summer with two children. They're bright enough, but the parents don't want them to fall behind in the summer, though my guess is that they're just looking for a dignified excuse to get a babysitter a few days each week. Truth is, they seem more interested in the butler and what he's serving up for their next round of cocktails."

Owen nodded, but not even Sadie Rose could hold his mind in the moment. She talked on about how she tried to bring music into each student's world, even if she was asked to tutor only general subjects. "Then, on the other extreme," Sadie continued, leaning forward on her elbows, as if she truly wanted to engage him, "I've worked with a few families that can barely clothe their kids or feed them. Farmers, who are spending morning 'til night tilling clay until their oxen or horses break, or their plows, or both. One family asked me to take their two youngest children. Not for a spell, mind you, but to 'take' them home with me.

Adopt them. Of course, that wasn't going to happen, but on my next visit, I brought food and clothing for the little ones. I mean, how can anyone possibly try to concentrate or learn something if they're starving? They can't possibly focus in such a state . . . Owen, have you heard a word I've said?"

"Sure, I'm listening . . . your tutoring . . ."

"You don't look like you're feeling well."

He tried to laugh, but it came out more as a huff of bitterness.

She flinched and backed away, as if rebuffed.

"Sorry," Owen said. "I didn't mean . . . I'm not feeling quite right. Seasick, maybe."

"That never bothered you before. You boated everywhere."

They were closer now, approaching the spot. His mouth turned chalky sour with remembering. The surface water glistened in the late-day shadows, black as oil. "Things change."

Sadie smoothed her sundress to her knees. "Let me get you a glass of cold water. Maybe that will help."

But when she returned, he was leaning over the stern railing, emptying his stomach. Hand on his back, Sadie waited.

He wiped his mouth.

Drank the glass of water.

The wake receded into frothy white as they motored on.

"Owen, we haven't really talked since I returned from school."

Owen studied the water, the ever-diminishing wake of roiling white.

"There's not much point," he replied, not meeting her eyes. He was being a fool, he knew, not to seize this moment, but if he started talking, he might not stop.

He'd made a deal with Vandyke, he reminded himself, and didn't say another word.

33

BABE RUTH.

It was Erling's only topic, right up until he boarded the train one morning in late summer. "You know, Owen," Erling said as stepped onto the train with an overnight suitcase, "Babe Ruth started out as a pitcher for the Red Sox before he was traded to the Yankees."

"Yeah, that's what I hear," Owen replied. So many nights, while Owen read books in his bedroom, the muffled sounds of baseball games played from the radio. He and Erling came from the same parents, slept under the same roof, and lived in the same border town, but their interests were wide apart. Owen wished he could go through life with one singular love, such as baseball. But his interests ran the gamut from business to history to politics to science to . . . Sadie. There was nothing wrong with baseball, but it just didn't hold his interest the way it did his brother's.

"And then," Erling continued, with a shake of his head as if he still couldn't believe it, "he became an outfielder and shattered, by wide margins"—he stretched his arms wide and knocked the travel case against the side of the train—"shattered all the batting records. Knocked 'em out of the ballpark!"

"So tell me," Owen said, hand shading his eyes from the morning glare, and looking up at Erling. "How did a little town like Sleepy Eye snag someone as famous as Babe Ruth?"

But Erling had a ready answer. "I guess the Knights of Columbus asked him to put their town on his tour."

Owen shrugged. "I don't get it."

Erling's eyes went wide in disbelief. "He's Catholic, that's why! How could he say no? I mean, he has to be more Catholic than most. His parents turned him over to the church to raise him when he was seven years old. That's when he says he learned that 'God is Boss.'"

Owen nodded. "Hard to go higher than that."

The train whistled, and the conductor herded the last customers aboard the train. Steel on steel, it chugged away, slowly picking up speed, and rumbled down the tracks with its passenger cars, cargo cars, and yellow caboose.

Owen turned back to the creamery. The ground stopped humming beneath his feet. Soon the rumbling was replaced by crickets pulsing in roadside weeds. Ahead, seagulls called from the pier.

If *God was Boss,* then perhaps Jerry was called home so that others might learn through loss and suffering. Or maybe God needed someone like Jerry around to crack a joke and break up the monotony of eternal worship. Or maybe Jerry was called because of unconfessed sin. He'd racked up his share of trespasses—and Owen knew only half of them. That would put Jerry in purgatory, that dreaded limbo between heaven and hell. Or he was burning up in the fiery furnace itself.

But if *Darwin was Boss,* maybe Jerry was culled because of his risk taking, a trait that in the end might not have helped further the evolution of mankind. If so, Owen wished he could take up that theory with Darwin, because if anyone seemed to add to the quality of life, it was Jerry.

God, he missed him.

That morning, after Erling left, Owen felt weighted down as he went through the creamery's ledger. Profits were thin, but there would be enough to keep the Jensen family going another month. Enough to pay the utility bills, enough to buy a pair of new shoes for each of the boys before school started, enough to keep food on the table.

Erling would come back with big dreams and plans. He'd eventually leave Ranier and turn his passion for baseball—and no small talent—into a career. Owen wouldn't try to hold him back or ask him to stay.

He startled when the creamery door opened and Sadie Rose stepped in. Everything about her was soft: her rose-colored dress and sheer overlay across her neck and shoulders, hair in soft waves, her hesitant smile. The sight of her sent a team of horses galloping through his chest, but he expected she always would have this effect on him.

"Hello," he said.

"Hello," she said, with equal courtesy.

He hated the stiff politeness, when what he really wanted was to sweep her into his arms and whisper in her ear everything he'd dreamed about her. "What can I do for you?" he asked. "Aasta usually stops."

Sadie Rose shrugged, and there was something in her shoulders, her uncertain smile, that made him wince. It was as if she felt sorry for him.

"Oh, I wanted to come by today. I had to get out of the house. She needs a pound of butter, a quart of buttermilk, and—oh no. I forgot. She insisted I write it down. I insisted I would remember. But suddenly . . ."

Owen knew Aasta's routines by heart. "Bet she needs two kinds of cheese, a dozen eggs, a quart of buttermilk, a—"

"That's exactly it. How did you know?"

"It's what I do," he answered with a shrug. He marked the ledger under "Worthington," then filled a bag and set it between them. "Thanks. Nice to see you."

"You too," she replied, balancing the bag on the counter. "Before long, I'll finish my degree." Then she went on to talk about her summer of tutoring. How needy families had opened her eyes, that Koochiching County was still a frontier, and it was hard to attract teachers to the area. "I intend to teach here," she said, "when I finish my degree. We need good teachers."

"True." He nodded.

"And cars, too," she added. "How's your Studebaker business going? You know, Aasta and Hans love the car you sold them. Whenever they have a free moment, they take it out for a spin."

"I sold one a few days back."

"You did? To whom?"

"A tourist and his wife. They'd arrived by train, spent some time out at Kettle Falls, and when they returned, they decided to take a romantic drive back to Chicago in a new Studebaker."

"That's sweet," Sadie Rose said, her eyes closing slightly with a soft smile. "Makes me miss—"

With a dismissive wave of his hand, he cut her off before she could go any further. He picked up her bag and opened the door with his shoulder. She followed, and he placed the bag in her arms.

"If I don't see you before you leave, have a great year at school," he said. "You deserve it, you know."

She chewed on the nail of her middle finger, then shook her head, as if there was so much more she wanted to say. "You're the one who deserves to go to school. You're taking care of your family, doing all this for others. I admire that, but I know you've always wanted to go to school. You *love* learning! If there was a way that I could change that, I—"

"I'm fine. Really."

He didn't need sympathy. He needed to move on. All summer he'd worked on letting go of her. And now, he almost had. Then, before she could protest, he turned around and went back to work.

For the next hour, he tried to concentrate on the ledger, but he couldn't. He closed the book with a loud snap, told his mother he was stepping out for a moment, and walked to the end of the village pier.

Some things weren't meant to be.

Water surged around the pier. A warm breeze brushed his face. Shrieks of laughter carried from kids swimming at the sand beach. Beyond the dock, playing follow the leader, a dozen juvenile mallards cruised, heads high and alert, now that they'd outgrown the need for a mother's watchful eye. But still, there were risks. Northern pike lurked beneath the surface, with rows of razor teeth, ready to grab a young duck and pull it below.

There wasn't a damn thing he could do to change what was.

He couldn't change that he'd survived and Jerry had not.

He swallowed past the knot of guilt.

He sucked in a deep breath, filling his lungs until they hurt, until he could feel the limits of his rib cage, the utter limits of a single breath, as if it were his last, as if it were Jerry's last breath.

And when he could hold his breath not a second longer, he exhaled hard, gasping for oxygen.

His heart pounded.

He was here.

Alive.

Alive, but good as dead.

He was sick and tired of feeling miserable, sick, and no more human than Frankenstein's monster.

Jerry wouldn't want him sulking around. He'd slap him and say, *C'mon, pull it together!*

He owed it to Jerry . . . to live.

Then and there, he made a vow. He swore to the air on

his skin, the water swooshing and flowing around him, and the earth that kept him tethered . . .

He swore to everything above, below, and between . . .

He swore to the past, present, and future . . .

Going forward, he'd make each day count.

34

READING THE *CREAMERY AND MILK PLANT MONTHLY* wasn't Owen's idea of entertainment, but if he was going to run this operation, he needed to stay informed. He thumbed through it as he stood at the customer counter. Studies showed that milk helped with intestinal disorders. (Dad hadn't been far off with his buttermilk-to-drunks program, after all.) Studies in Wisconsin showed that malnourished schoolkids benefited from a midafternoon snack of a glass of milk and crackers. There were ideas on how to make European cheese, right here in the States, from Brie to Roquefort. And there were always ads for the "Buflovak," a newer and better milk evaporation machine for making powdered milk. Maybe they'd purchase one . . . someday.

With a wide grin and ruddy cheeks, Erling lumbered into the creamery, dropped everything—traveling case, signed baseball cap, bat, and ball, and half a bag of popcorn—rushed over to Mom behind the counter, lifted her up as if she were a porcelain doll, and spun her around. "What a time!"

"Oh my!" Mom exclaimed, before her sturdy shoes touched the floor again. "Don't tell me you went off and got married or something foolish."

Erling raised his arms to the ceiling. "I have seen

the Babe in action! I shook hands with the legend himself. I don't need to go anywhere again for my life to be
complete!"

At first Owen was sure the last statement was an exaggeration, but over the course of the day, Erling seemed as
happy as a clam. He settled into his routines, mopped the
backroom while whistling baseball songs, and showed his
signed souvenirs to every customer.

Owen envied Erling's contentment with what seemed
so little.

The same afternoon, Mr. Boshelink came into the creamery. Dad had been easy on the wiry small man, a relatively
new immigrant with a thick accent. Now he ran his tongue
across his dry lips. "My ship, how you say, came in. You
good to me. I want to settle up." Then he plunked down a
blank check, asked how much he owed, and paid off his bill
in full.

When Owen went to deposit the check later that day at
the teller cage, the clerk—with a birthmark beet-red on his
forehead—held up the check, then pointed his forefinger
in the air, as if he had an epiphany. "I'll be right back."

When he returned, he adjusted his spectacles and announced, with all the gravity of an undertaker, "I'm sorry,
sir. But the check is no good. Whoever signed it forged the
name. A few checks got by us before we realized what was
going on."

"The man's name is Boshelink," Owen said. "Same
name as on the check."

The clerk nodded. "Yes, but the real Boshelink works
at a lumber camp. Someone stole his checks and is passing them off as his own." Then the clerk produced another
piece of paper with a signature at the bottom. "This is the
real signature. See? They're not even close."

"You're telling me it's no good. That the creamery is stuck for it?"

"You might take it up with the sheriff."

Outside, Owen gripped the medal at his neck and let off a stream of swear words under his breath. He'd been taken. Hook, line, and sinker. He'd fallen for Boshelink—or whatever the man's name was—his whole story about the anemic wife and firstborn and how he didn't have any money. Owen had felt pity for him. Now he felt cheated.

Owen waited for a Chrysler touring car to pass on its way across the tracks, then crossed the street to the White Turtle and took the entrance steps in two strides.

Izzy was busy blowing smoke rings from her stool behind the counter.

"Izzy, have you had trouble cashing checks lately?"

"Yes, as a matter of fact. Just yesterday."

"Boshelink?"

She crossed and uncrossed her stockinged legs, then shook her head of curls back and forth. "That's who he claimed to be anyway. Oh, he got you, too? He had false identification to go along with it."

"Right." Owen let out a bitter, short laugh. "I'm not going to let him steal from me!"

Pengler stepped out of the restaurant and stopped beneath the moose head. "Owen, I've been doing some asking around." He motioned behind toward the restaurant and blind pig. "Just found out where he might be holed up, that little weasel. Folks work hard for their money around here."

"I'm going to talk to the sheriff," Owen said. "See if there's any way to get money out of him."

"Well, if you do, here's directions to where the guy might be." He handed Owen a scrap of paper with writing on it. "Give this to the sheriff. He and I aren't exactly cozy, so it's better you don't say where this came from."

Then Pengler motioned Owen closer. "Look at this," he said. He closed his fist and extended his arm right to Owen's eyes. Had he learned about Jerry? About their night on the lake and trying to make quick cash on their own? Owen closed his eyes, drew a deep long breath, bracing himself.

"C'mon, Owen! The ring."

Owen opened his eyes. A gold band circled Pengler's ring finger.

"You got married?"

Pengler nodded, a grin on his face. "Yup. And I have you to thank! You told me I needed to get married, and it was just what I needed to hear. Didn't have to look farther than Darla. We've always gotten on, and well, she said, 'Sure. Why not?'"

"Good for you," Owen said. "Now you'll be able to get Jimmy back."

"Gotta go to court first," he said, "but how can they keep him from me now?"

Owen didn't want to dampen his enthusiasm, but to a court, there were the not-so-tiny matters of bootlegging, brothels, and gambling.

"Thanks again for this," he said, tucking the slip of paper with directions in his shirt pocket. The sheriff was a family man with a wife and kids. He would have headed home for the day. Owen decided it could wait until morning. He'd stop by the sheriff's office after his rounds.

35

TIPPER GROANED AND PRESSED HIS HEAD AGAINST OWEN'S leg.

"I know, boy," Owen said, gazing through the filmy windshield. "One last stop, I promise. Then we head home."

"Forging checks," Owen said, scratching Tipper behind his floppy ears. "Same as stealing. How'd you feel if someone stole a bone from you—right out from under your paws?"

Tipper moaned in reply.

"That's what I thought."

Milk cans clanked as the creamery truck rumbled. Flannel shirtsleeves rolled to his elbows, arm out the window, one hand on the wheel, Owen glanced at his side mirror.

In clouds of roiling dust, the sheriff's Model T Ford trailed behind.

After his last morning delivery, he'd dropped by the sheriff's office to report being swindled and to share a tip on the culprit's location. Vandyke listened, mug of coffee between his hands. "If this fellow broke the law," the sheriff replied, "then he'll pay. There's always a price to pay."

Owen met Vandyke's eyes. An unwelcome understanding sat there between them, as prickly as a porcupine. Owen's gut churned. He couldn't change what happened that god-awful night. He couldn't change a thing. He stuffed down his feelings. There was plenty he could say to the sheriff, but this was about the here and now. He held his tongue and handed over the directions on a slip of paper.

But Vandyke took one glance and waved the paper away. "Heck, Owen. It's on your way home to Ranier, isn't it? Just lead us out there and you can confirm the guy's identity."

Truth was, Owen had never been to Boshelink's shack, but he'd gotten directions from a reliable source. All he wanted was to see the swindler arrested, to turn out the man's pockets and return what was owed to the creamery.

Again, Owen checked his mirror.

As he drove alongside Rainy River, a tugboat pulled a boom of logs. On the south side of the road loomed stock-piles of pine, cedar, and spruce, all destined for the paper mill or to be shipped south by train. He drew a breath of air, earthy with fresh-cut lumber and the decay of summer.

He glanced at the small photo on the dashboard, which always sent a zigzag of lightning through him. He'd hoped the summer might have drawn him and Sadie closer, but there were too many ghosts between them now, too much left unsaid. Any day, she'd board the train south and return to college in St. Peter. Time to move on.

After he crossed the tracks, he looked for the crooked white pine with a doughnut hole in its middle—following the directions Pengler had scribbled down—and took a right turn, hand over hand.

At a slab-wood barn and pasture, Owen took a right. Two gray draft horses grazed, resting from pulling logs from the woods, hauling ice blocks from the frozen lake, and plowing fields. At the next turn, the gravel road snaked through a dark grove of cedars. Branches scraped along the sides of the creamery truck. Moose antlers topped a wooden post, and several yards beyond, he took a left. Long grasses swished along the truck's underbelly as it made its way along muddy ruts. At a clearing, Owen slowed and pulled off to the side. He wanted to give himself plenty of room to turn around. He waved the sheriff and deputy ahead toward the small log shack with a front porch.

The sheriff parked halfway between the creamery truck and the shack, then he and the deputy walked to Owen's truck.

"Okay," the sheriff said, poking his head into the passenger window. "Should be quick. We'll cuff him and you can finger him."

Deputy Kranlin added, "Wait for us." Then he trotted after Vandyke.

Fingers drumming his steering wheel, Owen waited with a good view. The sun was high. Set against a backdrop of dense black spruce, the shack was surrounded by spindly young aspen, stretching up toward the patch of sky.

Kranlin knocked three times on the wooden door.

Something inside the small shelter crashed.

A muffled sound of footsteps followed.

"Open up," the sheriff said, pressing closer to Kranlin. "We just want to have a word."

Boshelink probably didn't even have a wife, Owen mused. Just rotgut or moonshine for companionship.

The sheriff nodded toward a nearby shed of boards and wood. The deputy trotted over, grabbed a long board, and returned. Then he wedged the board into where the door and frame met.

The sheriff's hand slid onto his revolver.

As Owen watched, a sick feeling—an unexpected knowing—rose in his chest.

The sheriff and deputy were met by sharp, resounding shots from a large-caliber rifle—*Crack! Crack! Crack! Crack!*

Startled, Owen jumped, slamming his head into the truck's ceiling, then he slid to the floor as Tipper cowered beside him, whining.

Owen peered out the passenger window.

Sheriff Vandyke and Deputy Kranlin were down, silent heaps on the porch in an expanding pool of blood.

He caught a glimpse of Boshelink—or someone—fleeing from the back of the shack and into the dense woods.

He couldn't move or think. He couldn't remember why he'd come there in the first place. Light streamed down through the treetops, creating flickering patterns of light and shadow.

Gunshots echoed in Owen's head.

The sheriff and deputy are down.

Willing his legs to move, he walked in eerie silence to the porch, peering around for anyone who might be watching him, ready to shoot. He had no gun. No way to defend himself. But he had to do something. He drew a breath and braced himself—he'd never seen someone shot before—and stepped onto the porch.

A ragged hole in the sheriff's chest.

Eyes wide open.

Owen leaned down.

He listened for a breath.

There was none.

Hand shaking, he closed the still-warm eyelids with his fingertips.

Owen exhaled, turned away, and doubled over, vomiting.

Then he turned to the deputy's facedown body. He carefully rolled him over. Like a gut-shot deer, blood poured from the deputy's belly.

"Get help," the deputy croaked, his eyes unusually bright, and with those two words, blood spilled from his lips.

In the quiet, a chickadee called out: *Dee-dee-dee!*

Owen would be the last one to be seen with these men. The secretary had watched him leave the sheriff's office. She'd wished him a good day.

Everything in him tumbled. Half blind, he stumbled through the grassy clearing back toward his truck. He hadn't planned any of this to happen. And now, what if everything about Jerry's death rose to the surface? It wouldn't be too hard to find motivation to pin all of this on him. Who wouldn't feel anger and the need for revenge after losing a friend? He'd be locked away—or worse. He'd lose everything he'd been working toward—everything in this world that mattered.

He swore, jumped into the truck, willed his left hand to grip the wheel. Willed his left foot to the clutch, his right to the gas pedal, his right hand to the shift. He cranked the wheel, backed up, then jolted ahead. Tipper, who'd always hated the sound of gunshots, whined from the truck's floor.

"It's okay, boy, it's okay," Owen said over and over, as he sped away. He had to get help. Though he knew . . . nothing in this world could help the sheriff and the deputy now.

FATAL SHOOTING OF Sheriff AND Deputy! COMMUNITY IN SHOCK!

This morning, at approximately 10:45 a.m., Koochiching County Sheriff Vandyke and Deputy Kranlin were fatally shot in the line of duty. They were following up on a complaint registered by Owen Jensen of Ranier, who alerted law enforcement that his family's creamery had fallen victim to a forgery. When Jensen led the sheriff and deputy to the suspect's location on the edge of woods, the suspect, now identified as Peder Skogland of Minneapolis, shot through the walls of his shack, killing the sheriff and deputy, and then fled into the woods. The witness, Owen Jensen, immediately drove to the International Falls Police Department and reported the heinous crime.

As word of the event spread, local outrage erupted. By midafternoon, a search party of over 200 men had gathered to comb the woods east of the suspect's shack. By day's end, the suspected murderer had made it on foot as far as Ray, 20 miles south. But when Skogland tried to check into the Ray Hotel, the hotel operator, Samuel [Sammy] Blackwell, reported that the man asking for a room seemed "exceedingly nervous." When Blackwell confronted the man with the morning's murder, gunfire ensued, and Blackwell shot Skogland in self-defense. The community of International Falls and surrounding county are shocked at this unthinkable tragedy and are in deep mourning.

36

THE SUN ROSE HIGH AS OWEN RETURNED HOME, CLIMBED into bed, and pulled the gray wool blanket to his shoulders. Tipper jumped up, padded in circles at Owen's feet, then lay down with a groan.

A few minutes later, Mom climbed the attic steps and sat on the edge of his bed. "There's nothing then?" she asked. "Nothing I can get you, Owen?" She set the newspaper with its front-page article on the bed.

As he read the story, Mom fluttered over him, and he clenched his teeth. It wasn't her fault. None of it was her fault, but at this moment if she didn't let him be . . .

"Owen? I'm worried about you, honey. Everybody says it couldn't be helped, but still I can't imagine. Having to see such a tragedy. Maybe a cup of tea with a bit of honey would—"

"Mom, please!" he said too harshly, but he couldn't help it. "Let me be!"

The mattress sighed as she stood up.

"If that's what you want, but sometimes . . ."

To his relief, she left and headed down the attic stairs. At least his brothers were all off to school. He needed sleep. He'd been up all night.

After the murder of Vandyke and Kranlin, he'd sped

back to town to the police department. Within hours, news spread and hundreds of men were out combing through bog and brush to find Boshelink.

Three deaths in fewer than twenty-four hours. And he'd set it all in motion. How could it not somehow be his fault? Under the blanket, he closed his eyes, but he couldn't stop replaying what had happened.

In the dark predawn hours, he'd stood over the third body at the makeshift morgue in the basement of the police department. The sheriff and deputy were laid out on tables, draped in white sheets. On the other side of the room lay Boshelink, his trouser legs ripped and muddy, his face covered with a burlap feedbag. Owen lifted the burlap from the face of the small man, his eyes open. "That's him. Boshelink is what he called himself."

Then Owen spent hours answering questions from police, questions from the local newspaper reporter, and was told to be ready for more questions soon. Outside investigators as well as reporters would soon make their way north from Duluth, St. Paul, and Chicago.

Chicago.

Now the word clanged in his head until it formed a sentence, until it took on life—blood and bones and breath—until he could hear his father's last words as clearly as if he were standing at the foot of his bed.

The word churned in his brain and his gut.

"Chicago," he said aloud.

After Kettle Falls and his encounter with Mr. Vittorio, he had no doubt about Pengler's connections to Chicago.

What if the death of Vandyke and Kranlin were some plan of Pengler's? Had he orchestrated it all? Had Boshelink been on his payroll? Get Owen to go to the sheriff, lead him out to the shack, and with gunfire, end Pengler's problems with the sheriff?

Owen hated Vandyke for blackmailing him into silence,

chaining him to secrecy about what happened to Jerry. Owen would resent the sheriff forever for it. But that didn't mean the sheriff—and the deputy—deserved to die.

He bolted to his feet.

"Harvey Pengler!" he yelled, storming into the White Turtle's lobby.

"No need to shout," Pengler said, standing right behind the counter. "I'm right here, son."

"Don't call me son. And don't make me do your dirty work for you! You gave me directions to that shit-bag's shack. You knew where he lived! So I'm asking you straight up. Straight up and—" Owen's voice was on the verge of breaking, but he was enraged, and he needed that anger now. "You gotta answer me. No spins or twists. Did you set me up?"

"Set you up? I have no—"

"Did you set me up? Lead the sheriff to Boshelink's to get murdered? It would make your life easier, wouldn't it? Get the vigilante sheriff out of the way of your operations—payback for taking away Jimmy."

"What in God's name are you talking about?"

"Boshelink! Was he on your payroll, too? Like Jerry and half of Ranier? Did you have a plan—a scheme, to see them killed? It was you who gave me directions to his shack!"

"Hold on, hold on! After we got scammed here, I asked around. Someone knew where he lived. I wrote it down."

Pengler stepped out from behind the counter. Like a bear scenting something foreign on the wind, he stopped, head high. "Honest to God, Owen, I had no idea anything like this would happen."

"He took Jimmy, practically your own flesh and blood, right out from under your nose. Put him in foster care. Has to make you plenty mad."

"Yes, I'm mad. And I don't like you putting me on trial. Accusing me!" Pengler's eyes pierced Owen's. "I'm mad as a hornet at Vandyke! Each time Jimmy runs away from some damn foster home, Vandyke puts him in another. Poor kid!" He cussed. "But mad enough to get the sheriff killed? God no! No matter what you might think of me, I'm not that kind of man."

"Isn't that how they do it in Chicago? How about your friend at Kettle Falls? The one who's on a first-name basis with Al Capone."

"What are you, some lawyer, for God's sake? Yes, in fact, I've had Vittorio at my farm. But this is Ranier. I treat folks right and expect the same in return."

All the air was suddenly gone out of Owen. He believed Pengler. "Then who? Why?"

Pengler motioned for Owen to follow to the blind pig. At a table, they sat across from each other. "Someone gave you a bad check. You did your job to report it."

"Yeah, but had I known—"

"I didn't always agree with how he did things, but the sheriff was doing his job. Sometimes bad things happen."

The shack. The sheriff and deputy. Pools of blood.

Owen closed his eyes and winced.

"Can I get you something to drink?" Pengler asked. "You don't look good."

When the ice water came, he gulped it down.

"I don't believe in Prohibition," Pengler said, lighting a cigar. "Never will. So I'm not law-abiding in that sense. But in everything else that matters under the big sky, I'm not a bad man. There are men like Boshelink. They're not serving anything higher than themselves. How can you lie and pretend to be something you're not? Pretend to be good, then steal from the ones you're fooling? That's another kind of criminal. I'm moving booze. I don't deny it. But I'm never going to lie to you or intentionally hurt anyone."

The room felt too dark, too smoky, too much like its

walls were closing in on Owen. He had to get out of there. He had to get some fresh air.

No.

He needed to tell the truth. He couldn't hold it back another second. With the sheriff and deputy dead, he didn't have to pretend any longer. "I know what happened to Jerry."

Pengler's visage darkened. He looked hard at Owen.

Then Owen told Pengler everything about their desperation to come up with money to pay off the sugar truck. How they'd fallen for bait to pick up cases of whiskey and deliver them south of the area. How the sheriff wanted them to lie and say the stash was Pengler's—to testify against him.

"You wouldn't lie about me, even with your necks on the line?"

"No." And then, drawing a deep breath, Owen forced himself to continue. He told Pengler about both vehicles breaking through the ice—the sheriff's Model T and Pengler's Whiskey Six—with all the cases of booze and "planted evidence." Somehow, miraculously, three of them survived.

"And Jerry?"

Owen answered with a slow shake of his head.

"I'm truly sorry," Pengler said, his whole countenance softening. "What a waste. What a blasted shame."

Owen suddenly felt overcome by telling the truth. As he exhaled, his shoulders shook. He wiped back tears.

"Why didn't you tell me all this sooner? You boys could have worked extra for me. We could have worked something out."

"Harvey, I didn't know that. Early on you made it clear. And besides, I don't want to work for you. I don't want to be part of bootlegging or anything that comes with any more favors. Jerry and I, we thought we could make quick money—it was *too* easy, I know that now—but it was a way *out*. Figured we'd pay off what we owed you. Get free of all these strings."

"You really think Jerry would have moved on to anything different? He was a natural for taking risk. He wasn't going to be happy running that mechanics shop he talked about."

Owen shrugged. "Maybe. Maybe not. He never got the chance."

Owen pressed on.

"Vandyke didn't want any backlash about a local boy going through the ice with handcuffs on. He swore he was just doing his job. And I guess he was. But he told me if I talked, he'd press charges on me for bootlegging. Promised I'd serve time. I couldn't put my family in that kind of bind."

Pengler listened. "So what are you going to do now?"

"Make a deal with you," Owen said. Pengler had money, but a thin reputation in the eyes of the law.

"And what's that?"

"I've already said you gave me the directions to Boshelink's shack. You'll be questioned soon enough about motive regarding the sheriff's and deputy's deaths. When that happens, I'll stand up for you. And if you have any trouble in court getting Jimmy back, I'll stand up for you on that, too."

"Okay. And in exchange?"

Owen had never imagined how far he could go down a wrong path, how badly things could fall apart. He'd never imagined that he would barter Jerry's death to get out of debt to Pengler. A guy couldn't fall much lower.

"A favor," Owen continued. "You'll forgive the debt on the sugar truck. Part of doing business. You sent me out to follow Jerry and help unload. He took a shortcut and lost the truck. In trying to pay you for it, I lost my best friend. I'm begging you—pleading to your better angel. Moving forward, consider us even."

"Hmm." Pengler looked sideways at Owen, as if trying to see his opponent's cards. "That's it?"

Owen nodded.

"I can't believe I'm agreeing to this." Then Pengler extended his hand across the table. They shook on it.

Owen added, "And I owe you a Studebaker."

37

Late afternoon, the air was heavy with regret.

As Owen climbed out of his truck at Melnyks', the sun beat down on his head. His shirt stuck to his back.

He wiped sweat off his forehead before it ran into his eyes.

He had to face Jerry's family and tell them the truth.

He asked to speak to Jerry's mother and father in private. It was the hardest thing he'd ever done. He told them about that night in March.

The handcuffs.

Everything.

"You knew for months and you no tell us the truth?" Mr. Melnyk shouted.

"You lied to us," Mrs. Melnyk whispered through tears.

No apology could ever change their opinion of him. He had lied. He had gone to the farm, gathered their milk and eggs, and pretended he knew nothing of what happened to their son.

Maybe someday they'd forgive him. And maybe they *never* would.

Maybe someday they would let him back into their lives as Jerry's best friend.

Maybe with time.

When he returned to Ranier, he was drained with deep exhaustion. He parked the creamery truck in the shade of an oak beside the creamery. He sat there until the sun was low and red and dusky. Beside him, Tipper panted. When Owen finally noticed saliva dripping from the dog's pink tongue into a small pool on the truck's floor, he pulled out of his stupor.

"You need water. We need a swim," Owen said, and peeled himself off the seat and out of the truck. Tipper followed.

But instead of heading to the sandy cove where locals gathered, or jumping off the pier into the cool waters of Rainy Lake, Owen started walking. It was as if the deepest recesses of his being knew what he needed, even if his mind was murky, overwhelmed by heat, by the events of the past two days. Tipper walked beside him, veering off to mark a telephone pole or bush, but always returning to his side again, panting.

They crossed the railroad tracks, the smell of hot creosote rising from the railroad beams. From somewhere in Canada, a train horn sounded as it wound its way toward the border to cross into Ranier with its cargo.

The candy shop's Closed sign was on its window, but music and laughter drifted from the screened windows on the second floor.

The bank, with its arched Tiffany glass windows, was closed.

The Empire Club, Callahan's, and the White Turtle drew a few horse-drawn buggies, and saddled horses were tethered to hitching posts. But more and more, cars were parked outside the "soda fountains." He had a few more Studeys to sell. He'd get his business loan paid off soon. Then he was switching to Fords. Factory built, sure, but they were the wave of the future. A vehicle everyone could afford.

Instead of checking on his remaining inventory, he walked on.

Sadie Rose.

She'd stopped by the creamery—on the pretense of running an errand—but she must have wanted to say good-bye to him. And he'd been cold toward her. He didn't want her to go away to college with that as her last memory. He wanted to wish her well, to say good-bye properly.

He turned up the street past the community building to the Worthingtons' cedar-shingled cottage. The Studebaker he'd sold Aasta and Hans was parked out front, gleaming, as if Hans had spared no elbow grease in keeping it up.

When he knocked on the door, Aasta, lean and towering, met him with her silver-blue eyes, which smiled, even if her lips did not. With a nod, she read his mind before he had to form any words. She drew in a quick breath. "While Worthingtons are away, we stay over. And . . . *ja,* Owen. She is down at the dock then. She wanted her feet to put in water—one more time before she catches train tomorrow morning, *ja?*"

He nodded his thanks, then walked past the garden shed and the side of the house. In deepening shadows, he spotted Sadie Rose silhouetted at the end of the dock. Beyond, the train rumbled across the bridge, drowning out any attempt to be heard.

Expecting she might startle, he walked up beside her. He cleared his throat. "Sadie?"

She turned in her sleeveless dress and looked up at him, as if she'd been expecting him. Her face glowed in the last remnants of light. Her skin was made of peaches and cream. Her dress skimmed her knees as she swung her feet in the water.

"Mind if I join you?" he asked.

"Please," she said, motioning for him to sit beside her. He sat down, but not too close. He didn't want her to think he was trying to start things up again. He respected her need to move on, even if it was the last thing in the world he wanted. Tipper flopped down between them.

"You leave tomorrow morning," he said, gazing out at

the bay. In shades of silver and black, the current swirled in eddies and flowed westward into the river's arms.

"I heard what happened," she said, stroking Tipper's back. "It was in today's paper."

He stared at the water. What could he possibly say in response? There were no words.

"Yes," he managed.

As a loon popped up halfway between the dock and the bridge, the dam in him that had held everything back broke loose. He told her about the events of the past seven months. About his fight with his father and his death. About Jerry. He told her about being held to secrecy or else risk his family's welfare and go to prison. Despite a brief onslaught of mosquitos, he recounted what happened before and after the sheriff and deputy were shot. When he finished, as if a heavy beam had been lifted off his chest, he drew in a deep, full breath. "I don't need to keep silent anymore."

She put her hand on his arm. "That's why you've been so . . . so far away all summer."

The loon broke into a wail, aching with melancholy. The song pulsed several beats, then stopped.

"I should go," he said, standing up. "But I want you to know, I'm ready to let go of you now." She gazed up at him. The moon rose above the spruce tree and lit up her face and the water at her feet. He had to leave. Lingering, even a few seconds longer, might kill him.

"I think I'll always love you." He half laughed. "How could I not love you?" Then he grew serious again. "But there's someone else out there for you, Sadie. Someone who can take you to heights I can never reach."

"Owen, don't say that."

He stepped away before she could touch him. "No, it's fine. I don't want you to feel sorry for me. That's not why I came over."

"Then why did you?" she asked, meeting his eyes.

He would always love her dark, brooding eyes. He'd hold this picture of her in his heart, wherever life took him. "To say good-bye."

She jumped to her feet, grabbed both of his hands in hers, and squeezed them hard. "Damn it, Owen. I don't want you to let go. I don't want you to say good-bye. When things were crazy for a while at school, I know I said I needed a break. But all summer, I thought you were angry with me. Or tired of me. You've been distant and cold, pushing me away every chance you've had and—" She began to cry.

He pulled her in, drawing her to his chest, his face buried in her hair. She nuzzled her nose into his shirt.

"Owen," she said, her voice muffled, until she turned her head. "*This* is where I want to be!"

"Here? Not returning to college? No, you can't do that. Not when you have the opportunity to—"

She stopped him, pulling back and looking into his eyes. "No, of course I'm returning to school. Oh! You're making this so difficult. I want you, Owen. You."

"You do?" he whispered. "Not Sam, not one of those attorneys who could offer you—"

She rose to her tiptoes and kissed him deeply, her lips silencing him. They kissed, quieting in him, for the first time in many months, his grief and hopelessness.

He pulled away, and with more certainty than he'd ever had about anything, said, "Marry me."

Her lips trembled; then she smiled. "Yes."

"Yes?"

She nodded. "Soon as I finish college."

Tipper whined and nudged his nose between them.

"I think Tipper likes the idea, too," she chuckled.

Owen looked toward the house. It was completely dark without a single light on, as if Sadie's grandparents had retired early to give them privacy. "Think they'll approve?"

"They love you," she said, fingering the Saint Christopher medal around his neck. "I know they'll approve, even if you're Catholic."

"Let's swim. No one can see us."

In growing darkness, they removed their clothes and let them drop in heaps onto the dock. They slipped into the water without a sound. Tipper followed, paddling around them, until Owen found a floating stick and tossed it out farther for Tipper to retrieve.

To the north, swaths of pale green swept back and forth.

"Northern lights," Sadie whispered.

"A good sign," Owen agreed, then dove into the dark, cool, forgiving water. He had the oddest sensation of being baptized . . . of going under into the cleansing water, leaving the past behind and coming up new.

When he broke the surface, Sadie Rose emerged nearby. She wiped water from her eyes and smiled.

Out of the shadows, Tipper paddled straight for them, teeth clamped around a stick, as if he'd never let go.

Letter of Intent

On the Minnesota–Canada border, when Rainy Lake sheds its winter coat of ice, we call it "ice-out." Some years it happens after a season of warm spring days: the sun beats down, turning one hundred miles of ice into a vast honeycomb of black, until the ice gradually yields to open water. But most times, ice-out is preceded by a violent storm. Sheets of ice, like huge glass windows, crash forcefully against the shoreline.

In a similar way, a gale-force wind struck my otherwise uneventful life. In a half year's time, I lost my father to ill health and my best friend to Prohibition (through a preventable drowning) and witnessed the cold-blooded murder of a sheriff and his deputy. These events busted my insides into shards of ice.

Set me adrift.

And changed me forever.

I understand now how fleeting life is. Each of us is here for only a season.

For better or worse, this season is mine.

I can't turn back Prohibition. I can't rescue and bring back my friend, or raise the local sheriff and deputy from the dead. Along with my father, they are all gone and will never return. But their deaths clarify and sharpen my purpose. More than anything, I know now that I want to work toward a fair and just society. I believe mercy and justice should go hand in hand; and I want to see this sort of justice carried out across our state, including in small towns on the northern border. With the hope of something better—something higher than what I have witnessed—I am reclaiming my dream of attending college, with the intention of completing law school and eventually returning to Koochiching County to practice law.

Therefore, please consider my application to your institute of higher education.

Sincerely,

Owen Jensen

AUTHOR'S NOTE

WHEN I FIRST THOUGHT ABOUT A YOUNG MAN TRYING TO make something of himself during Prohibition—an era on the northern border when no one seemed to hold the moral high ground—I turned to stories of my own father's youth. My father was born in 1929 in Chisholm, Minnesota, and like Owen, his early years were hardscrabble. As a boy, and at his mother's instruction, he trailed his father from bar to bar, gathering his father's loose change. To earn money, he and his friend raised, trained, and sold white rats. As a teenager, he stopped his father from strangling his mother. Indeed, similar to Owen's father, my grandfather was so stunned by what he had done in his drunkenness that he stopped drinking. After my father returned from the

navy, he met and married my mother, and they eventually left northern Minnesota for St. Paul, where they raised ten children. A successful businessman, my father always had a heart for people.

Whenever they could, my father and mother

My father (left) often spoke of his best friend, who died in World War II.

packed ten kids and family dog in the station wagon and headed north to our grandparents' cabins: one on Eagles Nest Lake near Ely, the other on Elbow Lake near Cook. Those childhood trips instilled in me a deep appreciation of wilderness, which I still share with my husband, Charlie. It's why we moved north after college. He took over an insurance agency in International Falls; I began to write.

During most of our time on the border, we've lived in a historic home in Ranier across from the lift bridge joining Canada and Minnesota. The bridge was built in the early 1900s and still operates today, lifting to allow passage to large boats in summer and carrying trains year-round. From this place of confluence, where two countries converge, where the lake and river meet, where seasons play out with quiet drama, I have watched the seasons come and go. One spring, during ice-out, I couldn't believe my eyes when I spotted a deer riding a large ice raft under the bridge and into our bay. I might still wonder if I'd imagined it if another resident hadn't spotted the deer, too.

How much of my novel is inspired by actual events?

Honestly, most of it.

That said, for me as a novelist, the key word is *inspired*.

This postcard captures Ranier, Minnesota, as a frontier town in the early 1900s—but unfortunately misspells the town's name.

I have taken creative liberties with actual people, places, and events to weave a story that I hope is entertaining; that compacts events to convey how an era might have felt; and that explores moral dilemmas that everyday people, like Owen, might have encountered during Prohibition here in 1922.

For those who want to know more about what's factual, here's a partial list of actual events that occurred here during Prohibition:

- A truck with a load of sugar, destined for stills somewhere on Rainy Lake, went through the ice. Its driver surfaced and survived.
- When a Koochiching county sheriff was dismissed because of charges of corruption and bribery related to bootlegging, Sheriff VanEtten was appointed.
- A bootlegger was arrested on the lake and handcuffed; when the vehicle went through the ice, law enforcement officers survived. The bootlegger did not.
- When casks of whiskey were discovered under shingles in train cars, federal agents broke the casks with axes on the bay in Ranier. Locals showed up with cups and buckets; some lapped it up on their hands and knees.
- When a man's body with a bullet hole in his back was found floating near the dam, Sheriff VanEtten claimed the bullet ricocheted when he shot the bootlegger fleeing across Rainy River to Canada. Many locals were outraged at the sheriff's actions.
- In 1922, following up on claims of check forgery, Sheriff VanEtten and his deputy went to a shack east of town and were shot dead. The culprits fled. One was shot by someone in a local search party of two hundred men. The other was shot after a confrontation at a hotel south of International Falls in Ray, where he appeared "exceedingly nervous."
- The area's most prominent bootlegger, Bob Williams, first worked as a chef at the Palmer House in Chicago and moved north to run his own restaurants and taverns.

- As Prohibition built momentum, Bob Williams and VanEtten did not see eye to eye, especially regarding Williams's "son," whom VanEtten seized and put in foster care. Eventually, by marrying a woman who ran a Ranier candy store (and brothel upstairs), Bob was able to adopt Charlie Williams legally. Lil and Bob Williams bought the Kettle Falls Hotel, and the Williams family ran the Kettle Falls Hotel for decades. You can still visit and stay at the hotel today, which is on the Historic Register and within the boundaries of Voyageurs National Park.
- Horse races on ice-covered Rainy Lake entertained onlookers and gamblers. Often favored to win, Bob Williams's horse Hamline "J" ran the one-mile race in two minutes twelve seconds.
- Sleepy Eye, Minnesota, hosted Babe Ruth, but in October (not August) 1922.

I am indebted to the research and recent books by Mike Williams and Peggy Vigoren, both descendants of the Wil-

A federal agent breaks up a wooden barrel of whiskey, likely found on a train passing from Canada into the United States through Ranier, circa 1920s.

liams family. Mike Williams's book *My Life at Kettle Falls* creates a rich portrait of the early years of bootlegging as well as a day-to-day glimpse of life at the Kettle Falls Hotel, located between Canada and the United States. He writes: "Overnight lodging, food, beverages, prostitutes, and gambling were all available at Kettle Falls. . . . With prohibition and smuggling, you had the perfect recipe for notoriety." Mike grew up in Kettle Falls, where he claims he caught walleyes as fast as his mother could serve them to the restaurant's customers. He and his wife, Mary, later owned and operated the Thunderbird Lodge on Rainy Lake. A respected fishing guide, Mike now also works as an interpreter for Voyageurs National Park.

In her book *The Adoption of Charlie Keenan,* Peggy (Williams) Vigoren documents her family's earliest connections to the area. In a narrative blend of fiction and nonfiction, Vigoren creates a complex picture of her grandfather, Bob Williams, mastermind of the region's bootlegging. Williams owned the fastest boat on the lake at that time. He cleared an airstrip on his farmstead for planes to transport liquor. He was visited by Chicago mobsters, yet he was never convicted of bootlegging and won the admiration and support of many locals. When I imagined Owen Jensen, a fatherless nineteen-year-old in 1922, how could he not cross paths with Bob Williams—or at least a fictionalized version of him?

Other real historic figures who inspired my cast of characters include:

- E. W. Backus, the leading paper-mill industrialist of northern Minnesota.
- Ernest Oberholtzer, originally from Davenport, Iowa, and Harvard educated, who lived on Mallard Island and almost singlehandedly ran the fight against Backus. The Wilderness Society met in secret in St. Paul, with many young attorneys risking their jobs to be in attendance.
- The librarian is entirely from my imagination, but the International Falls Public Library was housed in 1922

in a building with a "soda fountain" (also referred to as a "blind pig") where illegal liquor flowed. A local resident wrote to the newspaper praising the new library but added "kill the pig."

- Jess Rose, a customs officer in Ranier, was pitted against his childhood friend Bob Williams, the area's leading bootlegger.
- Rainy Lake, a character in itself, which still claims lives, especially of those who venture out on ice that looks perfectly safe when it is not.

My heart is full of gratitude to those who have generously taken time to read and comment on this story in its various stages of creation, including: Mary Dahlin, Erin Falligant, Gail Nord, Sheryl and Dick Peterson, Margi Preus, Steve Rutkowsky, Susan Swanson, and Karen Warren-Severson. In addition, a heartfelt thanks to my friend and editor extraordinaire, Erik Anderson; production editor, Rachel Moeller; agent, Fiona Kenshole at Transatlantic Agency, who believed in this story from the start; author and historian Hiram Drache, whose books capture the history of Koochiching County; the staff at the International Falls Public Library; Ed Oerinbacher at the Koochiching Historical Museum; Jim Hanson, for sharing lore from Atsokan Island (the inspiration for Baird's Island); the Oberholtzer Foundation and time spent on Mallard Island; and of course to my local writers' group and annual island writers' group. Thank you.

My deepest thanks goes to my family: Kate Casanova and Chris Koza, Eric Casanova and HaeWon Yang. Finally, thank you, Charlie, for being there with me, every valley and mountaintop along the way.

FOR FURTHER READING

Drache, Hiram. *Koochiching*. Danville, Ill.: Interstate Publishers, 1983.

——. *Taming the Wilderness: The Northern Border Country, 1910–1939*. Danville, Ill.: Interstate Publishers, 1992.

Paddock, Joe. *Keeper of the Wild: The Life of Ernest Oberholtzer*. St. Paul: Minnesota Historical Society Press, 2001.

Replinger, Jean, Charlene Erickson, and Barbara Garner, eds. *Ober and His Rainy Lake World: Scans from the Rainy Lake Chronicle, 1973–1982*. N.p.: Oberholtzer Foundation, 2010.

Searle, R. Newell. *Saving Quetico–Superior: A Land Set Apart*. St. Paul: Minnesota Historical Society Press, 1977.

Steinke, Gord. *Mobsters and Rumrunners of Canada: Crossing the Line*. Edmonton, Alberta: Folklore Publishing, 2003.

Vigoren, Peggy Ann. *The Adoption of Charlie Keenan*. International Falls, Minn.: North Star Publishing, 2013.

Williams, Mike. *Life at Kettle Falls*. International Falls, Minn.: North Star Publishing, 2014.

Mary Casanova is the author of more than thirty books for young readers, ranging from picture books, such as *Utterly Otterly Night* and *Wake Up, Island* (Minnesota, 2016), to novels, such as *Frozen* (Minnesota, 2012). Her books are on many state reading lists and have received the American Library Association Notable Award, Aesop Accolades from the American Folklore Society, Parents' Choice Gold Award, and *Booklist* Editors' Choice, as well as two Minnesota Book Awards. She lives with her husband in Ranier, Minnesota, a short paddle from the Canadian border.